THE
TRUMPET
LESSON

THE
TRUMPET
LESSON

A NOVEL

DIANNE ROMAIN

SHE WRITES PRESS

Published 2019
Printed in the United States of America
ISBN: 978-1-63152-598-8
ISBN: 978-1-63152-599-5

Library of Congress Control Number: 2018965117

For information, address:
She Writes Press
1569 Solano Ave #546
Berkeley, CA 94707

She Writes Press is a division of SparkPoint Studio, LLC.

Book design by Stacey Aaronson

For Sterling Bennett

One

AT THE BLAST, CALLIE QUINN STARTLED AND looked up from her rooftop terrace to see a puff of smoke high above her head. She turned, still shaken, toward the houses that stair-stepped up the opposite side of the ravine and focused in on the lime green one. Had Armando seen her?

She steadied herself. Soon another celebratory firework rocket would take off from the chapel, streak over her rooftop terrace, and explode above Guanajuato's historic center. She imagined that rocket catching the sheet she was hanging, lifting it and her along with it. How she would soar through the sky! Exhilarating. She looked down to the floor of the canyon, where pedestrian plazas nestled among soft-hued colonial buildings. Exhilarating, yes. But a long way to fall.

NO answer. Armando Torres flipped his cell shut, paced back and forth across his studio, and then sat on the stone ledge of a tall, deep-set window. He patted a salsa rhythm on his conga. Quick, quick, slow. Quick, quick, slow. No response. None at all. He thumped the conga. He hadn't been able to reach his love Claude in Paris, and now he couldn't reach Callie. But at least he knew where *she* was. He tapped a drum roll. Doing her laundry. Which she should be leaving to Doña Petra. Why have a cleaning woman, if she wouldn't let her clean?

He gave the conga a final pat and turned to peer across the ravine's patchwork of houses. There she was on her rooftop stretching toward a billowing sheet. It looked like she had a scarf tied around her curls. He leaned out the window. Could it be the silk one Claude had helped him pick out the summer before in Paris? Green to match her eyes, the scarf was perfect for her. He had told her that. Not that it made a difference. She never wore it when they went out. He had even suggested that gentlemen might show her attention if she wore it. Not that they hadn't checked her out before. Not surprising. She was nice to look at. And young looking. He turned to look at himself in the mirror. Well, not as young looking as he was. He leaned toward the mirror, patted his curls, and then stood back to look again. Of course, he looked young. He pulled himself up to his full six feet. He was only thirty. Same as Claude. And she was . . . goodness . . . maybe fifty! Anyway, he wouldn't mind if she went out. Once in a while. Still, he hadn't said anything about men paying her attention until he had given her the scarf. The next time she'd met him for dinner, she had covered herself in beige, including a muffler wrapped around her throat and curls, as if she were a mummy. He shrugged. *Ni modo.* Never mind. So she wore his gift to do the laundry. At least there on her rooftop she wasn't afraid to live.

A rocket shot up from the chapel below Callie's property. He watched her jump when it blasted. Then he turned to take in the poster over the foot of his daybed, the one of Claude bowing his cello. "Claude," he whispered, "where *are* you?" He looked for help from his statue of the Virgin de Guadalupe. Recalling the nuns saying that rocket blasts open the skies for prayer, he crossed himself and made a wish.

When the next rocket took off, he turned to watch Callie startle again at the blast. He shook his head. Five years in Guanajuato, and she still had not learned to listen for the telltale swoosh of an ascending rocket.

He dialed her number again and called across the canyon: "*Contesta el teléfono, Calabacita.*" Answer the phone, Little Squash.

WHEN she heard the phone, Callie, determined to finally answer in time, left a towel hanging from one clothespin in her rush to get across her rooftop terrace, down the spiral stairs to the entry terrace, and then through the French doors into her dining area. Still, she paused before answering, her heart racing.

When she picked up the phone, it was Armando, complaining that his *maldita* answering machine had garbled the message his Parisian love had left the night before and, on top of that, he hadn't been able to reach him all morning. Then he scolded her for hanging her laundry. She would be late meeting him in Plaza Mexiamora to search for Tavelé.

Claude would call back, she told him, and she would get to Mexiamora on time. That is, she said to herself when climbing back up the stairs, if she didn't have to go looking for a towel that had blown away.

She hurried to finish attaching the towel, knowing the phone would ring again. Armando never seemed to complete a conversation in one session or even in two. Three was the charm of Armando. She'd first experienced that habit of his when he appeared at her terrace door wanting French grammar lessons. Caught in the middle of her Saturday chores, her hair full of dust and her books in a pile, she had been reluctant to take on a French student, even one with an endearing Parisian accent. She had more than enough work as a translator. And, besides, she felt uncomfortable around strangers. After she'd turned him away as politely as possible, he'd knocked again, saying he'd forgotten to add that he was an emissary from her aunt Ida. Still, she had resisted. And so he went away, only to knock again a moment later. "But I haven't told you why I must study French grammar." He slipped a couple of sticks from his shoulder bag, tapped a drum roll on her door, and said, "*Pour l'amour, Madame la Professeure. Pour l'amour.*" A young man who wanted to learn grammar because of love. Well, what could she have done but invite him in? And so she had taught him grammar, and he had carried out her aunt's mission of getting her out of the house, often to search for Tavelé, that rascal street dog he had adopted, and who had, for the umpteenth time, run off, as usual on a Saturday afternoon, giving them an excuse for a Sunday walk. Not that she needed an excuse to spend time with Armando, whom she held dear, as much, she knew, because of his irritating fits as for his charm.

SHE had just finished pinning the towel when the phone rang again. This time she answered right away, still out of breath from her rush to the phone.

Armando began by teasing her about jumping at rocket blasts. "How about," he said, "learning to listen for the take-offs by the twenty-first century? That would give you two more years." That's why he had called, he said, and then, trying to make it sound like an afterthought, he asked her, not for the first time, to call Paris hospitals. "Claude must have slipped into the Seine. Or tumbled from *la Tour Eiffel*. Some awful accident. Like the ones that killed your husbands."

She tried to calm him down. "But, remember, my husbands and their accidents are *fictional.*"

He continued as if he hadn't been listening. "And all of

them dead before giving you a child. *Quel dommage.* What a pity. No children. No grandchildren to play with."

Her heart began to race. No child. No grandchildren. He had never come up with that before. "Armando, you're getting carried away. Perhaps I should stop telling the stories." Her voice sounded shaky. Would he notice?

"*Non, non, non, non, non. J'adore tes maris.*" He loved her husbands, he said, switching into French, as he did when he wanted to impress something on her. "Don't I pray for their souls? And, besides, your stories aren't giving me ideas. Accidents happen all the time in real life, as you must know, given your warnings about what could happen to Tavelé if I don't start keeping him on a leash. And Claude? What has happened to him? Is he *dead*—or something worse? I'd rather not know." So Armando said and hung up.

Callie stood looking into the receiver. Something worse than death? She shook her head. Funny. She replaced the receiver. And yet not so funny. Armando once again imagining Claude with another man.

She had just opened the terrace door when Armando called again, this time wanting to know how she had gotten to the phone so quickly the time before. "You have no business rushing down a spiral stairway. You might fall, and there you would be, alone, crumpled on your terrace. How could you do that me?"

CHURCH bells rang while she put the laundry basket away and wiped the washer. The bells had started at dawn. As had the drum and bugle bands. And the rocket blasts. In celebration of some saint's day. She didn't know which one. The only festival day she knew for sure was December 12, Guadalupe Day. On that day, she would take time off to watch the children—the boys dressed in white and the girls in colorful skirts and embroidered blouses—walking hand in hand with their parents up the hill to the temple of Guadalupe, carrying baskets of fruit for the Mexican Virgin.

She went to the railing and looked again toward the house where Armando lived. When he had described her crumpled on the terrace, she had heard him tapping, not as erratically as at his most anxious, but still worrisome. She had tried to reassure him. She would not fall, they would find Tavelé, and Claude would call. She also suggested that he talk to the Virgin, which she had learned helped calm him down, especially, it seemed, when he talked to the Virgin de Guadalupe. She thought again of the children hand in hand with their parents climbing the hill to the temple. As a little boy Armando must have celebrated Guadalupe Day, too. Someone at the orphanage would have dressed him in white, drawn a mustache on his face, and given him a basket of fruit for the Virgin. Even so, it was sad. Who would have held his hand? Still, like her aunt Ida said, there was no point in dwelling on the past.

Two

CALLIE STEPPED INTO THE PASSAGE BY HER HOUSE. Then she paused and cocked her head to one side, listening. Was that the phone? Surely not Armando again. Nor her aunt. Or her mother, who preferred letters and sent them in fragile envelopes with red and blue trim. She hadn't heard from her mother for a while. Still it *could* be someone else. It could be *her*, she told herself, even after all these years. She pictured the young woman, as she had so many times before, a rolled yoga mat over her shoulder, looking serene. Allowing herself a breath of hope, she stepped back inside. But by the time she had crossed the entry terrace and unlocked the dining area doors, the phone had stopped ringing. Shaking off disappointment—it was, she assured herself, better this way—she returned to the entry terrace and stepped back outside.

The cobblestone path sloped alongside her house, then became a stairway, then a slope with a few stairs, and so on down the canyon side to the center of town. Guanajuato. A maze of pedestrian inclines and stairways so narrow in places she could reach out her arms and touch the buildings lining both sides. Not a city of frogs, as the name Guanajuato implied. But a city of *callejones*. That's the term everyone used, even English-speaking transplants, because there was no single suitable English word for *callejón*. Alley, the usual translation, would not do. Pedestrians shared *callejones* with dogs and donkeys, and even, on occasion, with a motorcycle delivering pizza, but never with cars. Cars were confined to the Panorámica, a ribbon of road cut into the hills surrounding the canyon; to the tunnels through the ridges; to the few narrow streets up the sides of the canyon and along the bottom of it; and to the mysterious *Subterránea*, a deeper-level street that wound through the center, sometimes between historic foundations, sometimes under them, and that hid a river even deeper below.

Most people lived on a *callejón* where negotiating stairs became a way of life. They weren't that easy to manage either, given the cobblestones—and the dog poop. Some of it left by that rascal Tavelé, no doubt. She had to be careful not to slip or trip on the stairs. And there were lots of them. She looked down the *callejón*. One hundred from her place to Plaza Mexiamora alone. She'd already walked down and up them that morning, to and from the Sunday market. Still, she was ready for more, given that Armando had canceled their walk the week before. He had been sick. Something he ate. She stood a little straighter. *She* had not fallen ill from food once since moving to Mexico.

She pulled her entry door shut. When she turned the key, the lock felt funny, like a part was loose. She should ask Armando to have someone check it for her. But not now, there was something more important she needed to say to him.

She bowed her head to watch her feet while descending the stairs. Something more important. Yes. Something to help Armando calm down. That was more important. And she could do it. Calm him down. Something she never could do with her father. Oh, well. He had had her mother for that. And why was she thinking of her father, anyway? His sulks at some imagined slight would cloud their house for days, even with her mother's care. And his grudges. He never let go of them. She shuddered. Not at all like Armando, who never stayed angry for long. A walk with her would bring him out of his darkest mood. She was the only one who could brighten his day. At least with respect to Claude. No one else in town knew about Claude. But it was time they did. And time she got up her courage to tell Armando so. She'd thought about it often enough. How Armando would calm down for good, if he could just be open about Claude. As she walked along, she rehearsed what to say to Armando. Don't just meet Claude in Paris or even Veracruz. Invite him to Guanajuato. Stroll through the central plaza. Come out. She stopped. She would look him in the eyes when she said that. She gazed again at her feet and went on. Some people will make awkward jokes. You can handle that. Some will pray for you. It wouldn't be the first time. Some will feel hurt you were not open before. Don't let that stop you. Straighten up. Get a life. Oh, dear, she was getting carried away. She should stay calm. But what had Claude told Armando last week? *À cœur vaillant rien d'impossible.* To a brave heart, nothing is impossible. A message that Claude had waited long enough? Well, he had. It was over five years since Armando had left Paris to stay with Guanajuato's elderly symphony conductor, Maestro Chávez, after his wife died. And though he regularly returned to Paris, he had not once invited Claude to visit Guanajuato. "Too far," wasn't that what Armando had told her he'd made out from Claude's message the night before? Well, Paris and Guanajuato were too far apart for frequent visits. What young man wouldn't become impatient? It was time Armando spoke up. He might regret it if he didn't. And she? Quiet Callie. Did she regret not speaking up? No. Her case was different.

　　She paused a moment and looked up. Why not another

husband story? Armando loved the husbands, after all. And her stories about them had worked before to teach a lesson with a light touch. The husbands. So they called them, "husbands" being short for "husbands-to-be." Twenty-six of them, one for every letter of the alphabet. She had first named them after mathematicians. Then for sailors across the globe. Then Armando had suggested Biblical names. When they got to N and Armando suggested "Noah," she had blurted out, "No, Noah wasn't one of them." Then she had caught herself and said, "Oh, yes, of course. Noah. Noah's Ark." She had rambled on about the animals, two by two. It was a good name, wasn't it? Noah. Yes, indeed. Armando hadn't seemed to notice anything odd in her response. Still she had not suggested they rename the husbands again after that. But she had continued with the stories. It would have seemed strange if she hadn't.

So which husband would it be today? Perhaps the one who got locked in the wine closet the day they were to wed. She had never known for sure if he was hiding that day or just wanted a glass or two of his favorite Château Margaux. He often passed the time in the closet. No one but he and his wine steward knew of its whereabouts. Not even she, his intended, though he had said he had a surprise for her on their wedding night. Unfortunately, the wine steward was off in Bordeaux, and by the time they found the closet behind the bookshelves in her fiancé's study, it was too late. He had been pale, but smiling.

She glanced down the *callejón* and saw a pair of Jehovah's Witnesses talking with a neighbor at the foot of the stairs. If they cornered her, she would be late for sure meeting Armando. Luckily, from the looks of it, they hadn't seen her, and they wouldn't, if she was quick. She ran down a few more stairs and entered a passage she had avoided since she had encountered escaped geese there, flapping their wings, thrusting out their necks, and honking hysterically. She paused a moment to catch her breath, then went on. Better to risk the geese than be cornered by Jehovah's Witnesses.

What was it with them, anyway? No matter how many times she said she was not interested, they kept knocking at her door. Maybe she should put up a "We are Catholics" sign, as Armando had suggested. Her father would turn over in his grave, having given up Catholicism and the drink for her mother. But then he had not seen Catholicism as practiced in Mexico. The festivals with rockets, carnival rides, and Aztec dancers.

That gave her an idea. What if the Jehovah's Witnesses were to dance like Aztecs to her door, rattling seedpod ankle bracelets and shimmering peacock feather headdresses? Then she would invite them in. But not as they were. Smug ladies in nylons and pumps. Well-washed young men in shirts and ties. All of them seeking some vulnerability to exploit.

They never asked what she needed. Not that she needed anything. She could take care of herself. It was a simple question of keeping her house in order and meeting her translation deadlines. But what about Armando? If they really wanted to help, they could convince him to come out.

As she approached the property where the geese had lived, she slowed and held her breath, but the passage was clear. In fact, the whole place looked different. The yard, which had been bare, was alive with wild marigolds and cosmos. A new ornate iron fence ran along the *callejón*.

Odd, putting up an expensive fence. Most properties were walled in the colonial fashion. Only the very poor fenced their yards, and then it was with battered chicken wire or rusty bed springs. She leaned forward. The front door was open, but the house sat too far back for her to see inside.

A low, guttural sound came from within. She jumped. Could the geese be in there? She turned away and took a step down the *callejón*. Whatever it was sounded again, but more smoothly this time and in a different pitch. She tilted her head to one side. Not geese. But something familiar. And then it came to her. Someone was playing the trumpet. "Pedal tones" her father had called the low bass tones. To Callie and her mother, they were the sound of safety.

Three

ALREADY IN THE PLAZA WHEN CALLIE ENTERED, Armando ran over to kiss her on the cheek before blurting out, "Tavelé disappeared following a lady with a cake on her head!"

A lady with a cake on her head. Callie smiled thinking how odd that would have sounded to her before moving to Guanajuato where people balanced all manner of things on their heads, including, as was likely in this case, a frosted sheet cake resting on a piece of cardboard. She recalled, too, how risky those balancing acts once looked to her.

"*Un gateau,* Chou." Armando tapped the top of his head with one of his drumsticks. "*Sur la tête.*" He held the sticks two feet apart. "A cake this big on her head."

Her gaze lingered on the dark circles under his eyes. He looked more worried than usual when he couldn't reach Claude. He would feel better if Claude were here. But it didn't seem like the time to say so—or even to bring up a husband story, not with Armando looking so sad. He might end up feeling worse. Better to focus on Tavelé. If she couldn't bring Claude and Armando together, she could at least distract him from the anxiety of their separation. "Where was the woman with the cake?"

He directed a stick toward the south side of the plaza. "Over there."

She wanted to ask how in the world the woman got out of his sight, but her throat felt tight. She would sound accusatory. Still, he should keep Tavelé near, the way she did when Tavelé stayed with her. It was the height of the summer rains, after all. He would regret it if Tavelé were carried off in a flash flood. Oh, dear, she had once said that, and not with good results. But it bothered her, the risks Armando took. Now her entire chest felt tight. She needed to get off this line of thought. She sighed. This wasn't the first time Tavelé had spent a night on the town. Before Armando adopted him, he was a true *callejonero*, born and raised in the *callejones*. A rascal and a charmer. Someone would have taken him in. Maybe the woman with the cake herself. She felt her chest relax. But how did Tavelé get out of Armando's sight? She raised her hands to the sides of her head and wobbled them there, as if holding a jiggling sheet cake.

"Was the bakery woman jogging?"

"With a cake on her head?" He laughed and made a little check in the air with a stick.

She shrugged and held her hands out, palms up. "So . . . ?"

"A boy had fallen off the fountain rim, Chou. I stopped to see if he was all right."

Armando jumped on the fountain and started walking around, his arms and the sticks held out from his sides for balance.

She started walking beside him, feeling protective, but trying to look nonchalant. She had to think of a story. "Hmm. Did I ever tell you about the husband who used chopsticks for balancing after dining on Mandarin duck?"

"Like this," he said, scraping his sticks together as if cleaning them and then holding them straight out on both sides of his body.

"Well, yes, but it can be dangerous, you know, climbing with chopsticks. After that evening I never ate duck again. In fact, I became a vegetarian."

Armando continued walking around the fountain. "So what happened?"

"Well, it was such a lovely evening that he wanted to walk, and so he asked the limo driver to follow us."

"Limo driver?"

"Yes, that intended was wealthy. I didn't discriminate, you see. Gave my hand as freely to a banker as to a bohemian. You remember the one who lived on rice in a garret, don't you?"

"Didn't he fall, too?"

"Stretching out too far to see *la Tour Eiffel.* I was in the room below, putting on my gown. I heard him cry *'Je t'aime'* as he passed by."

"Men who love you seem unusually susceptible to falling."

"I suppose you're right." Her father had fallen, too, but that was a different kind of story.

"And the rich guy?"

"He was crooning 'Singing in the Rain,' conducting himself with his chopsticks."

"Didn't you say it was a lovely evening?"

"Well, if you like rain, as he did, and I didn't mind. It was a soft rain. No thunder or lightning."

He stopped a moment. "And so?"

She stopped walking, too. "He had on an ankle-length gabardine coat, and when he stepped up onto a retaining wall to continue his serenade from on high, he tripped on his coat and fell. His engraved chopsticks did him in."

"On your wedding day, I suppose."

"Not quite. The night before."

"Well, all right, I get the message." He jumped down from

the fountain, put his sticks in his shoulder bag, and took out a bottle of water, which he handed to Callie. "Have a drink on me."

She scanned the plaza while taking sips. On the near side, a vendor sat behind a card table stacked with wrapped candies and little plastic bags of freshly made potato chips. On the far side, beyond the fountain, children gathered around an English tutor and her portable blackboard.

She put the bottle in her backpack. "Was the candy stand here yesterday?"

"No. Neither was the English teacher."

"Well, someone must have seen Tavelé. Have you checked with the people in the copy shop or the grocery?"

"Everyone was watching the boy who had fallen. I tell you, Chou. He looked dead."

She gasped. "Dead!"

"He was fine, Chou. Jumped right up when his mother arrived. But until then all eyes were upon him."

"Then you don't know if Tavelé followed the woman carrying the cake or someone else?"

"I know Tavelé, Choucita. It was orange cake with cream cheese frosting. His favorite."

"And here all along I thought his favorite was vanilla."

He laughed and made another check in the air.

A gust of wind swirled through the plaza, lifting dust and candy wrappers. She hunched her shoulders and crossed her arms. "Should we call off the search?"

He put his hands on her shoulders and looked in her eyes. "I need your help."

Lightning split the sky above their heads.

The roar in her head matched the ensuing thunder. Yes, he needed her help. But he would not take her advice. If he used a leash, like she had suggested more than once, Tavelé would not

have run off. She felt her throat constrict again. She shook herself. Here she was again on the verge of chastising Armando,
when she just wanted him to be happy. What was *wrong* with her?

The first four notes of Beethoven's Fifth sounded from his
shoulder bag. He flung it open, and pawed around inside,
handing her the sticks, sheets of music, a half-eaten chocolate
bar, a compact umbrella, and *Du côté de chez Swann*, before
pulling out the cell. "*Bueno.*" He listened a while, laughing, and
then nodded his head. "*Oui, à Veracruz.*" He clicked off the
phone, did a pirouette, and said, "Claude's meeting me in Veracruz. I'll be there at least all of July and the first week of August. Claude, too. If I can get a ticket, I'll leave after Friday's
concert, so I'll have a few days there in June, too. That way I
can find the perfect hotel by the time Claude arrives."

She smiled. As usual on hearing Claude's voice, Armando
had made a spontaneous recovery from catastrophizing.

He took his things from Callie and stuffed them back into
his bag. "It'll be pouring soon. You need to get home."

"But . . . but what about Tavelé?"

He kissed her on both cheeks. "Don't worry, Chou." Then
he took off, calling back over his shoulder. "He always finds
shelter somewhere." He was in such a rush, he returned only
three times. First, to tell her again that Doña Petra should be
doing her laundry. Then, to say he needed to talk with her
about a personnel problem in the orchestra. And finally, to
insist she take his umbrella. No, he didn't need it. He would
outrun the rain.

She stood there, looking at the umbrella and pondering
Armando's sudden change of course, which even for him
seemed surprising. But was it so surprising? Hadn't it been
Claude, not Tavelé, who had triggered Armando's anxiety all
along? When she looked up, she noticed a line of teenage girls

wearing backpacks with rolled sleeping bags and carrying what looked like trumpet cases. They came into the plaza along one *callejón*, rounded the corner, and went out of sight up the *callejón* of the geese. At the end of the line and carrying only a bouquet of lilies was a tall, lithe woman who looked vaguely familiar, apart from her soft downy curls with corkscrew tips that glowed copper when a stream of sunlight broke through the clouds. The woman, happening to glance beyond Callie, froze. Callie followed her gaze and saw she was staring at Armando, who was exiting the plaza. When she turned back, she saw the woman disappear up the *callejón*.

Why did that young woman freeze on seeing Armando? He wouldn't hurt a fly. And, besides, the woman looked like she could handle anything. Her posture exuded confidence. And her hair. Daring. And elegant, as if styled for the Ebony Fashion Fair. Her boots, flowing black skirt, and fitted teal jacket were elegant, too. Armando would love her style. Callie shrugged. So the woman had rushed off after seeing him. She was probably just trying to keep up with the girls. Who were they? Not local students. That was for sure. Not with their quick-dry shorts and hiking boots. She heard her mother's voice. *Curiosity killed the cat.* Well, this cat was in no danger of getting close enough to be killed. Still, no harm in following them. She would get home just as quickly. And maybe she would find Tavelé. She hastened her pace. He had loved barking at the geese. He could be there now, looking for them.

This time at the house where the geese had lived, she heard several trumpets. Well, they got right down to it. Must still have their backpacks on. They hadn't taken the time to close the gate either. Was Tavelé inside? She crept through the gate. No need to talk to the young woman or the girls.

She had never felt comfortable meeting new people. One

summer during her college years, she had trained to sell vacuums door to door. She learned the spiel easily enough, but when the day came to begin sales, she'd retreated to a park across from the first house. She'd sat cross-legged under a tree all morning repeating "nothing ventured, nothing gained" and then quit at lunch.

That was a long time ago. But she could still feel the prickly grass and her legs unwilling to uncross. They would be stiffer now. She sighed. Well, she didn't need to knock here. The door was wide open. She could see the young woman and one of the girls seated at a music stand. Both with raised trumpets. The young woman would play a note, and then the girl would play it. When the girl's note sounded weak or wobbly, the young woman would point to her ear and play the note again. The girl's next note would sing out pure and clear. I could watch them all day, Callie thought, and then reminded herself she was there for Tavelé. All she had to do was whistle and if he was there, he would come running. She made a loop with her thumb and middle finger, the way her father had taught her, and raised it to her lips. Then she froze. The trumpet teacher would surely come out, too.

But she should try. For Armando. Besides, it was time she got over her nerves about strangers. She leaned toward the door, and then drew back when she felt her heart hammering against her ribs. What was wrong with her? She had nothing to be afraid of. No need to take flight. Even if she had seen the woman before somewhere, she had not let her down in any way. Not her. She knew that, though her breath caught, recalling the young woman's complexion, the color of caramel.

Scattered raindrops began falling again. She opened the umbrella and held it in front of her as she made her escape, backwards, through the gate.

Four

ALLIE HAD NO SOONER GOTTEN HOME THAN Armando had called. Luckily, given the sporadic sprinkles and her laundry still hanging, the conversation had been short. He only wanted to report, laughing, that Claude had said he was handsome—for a drummer. She had laughed, too, delighted with Armando's good mood and pleased that she would get her linens down before the deluge.

She lifted a pillowcase from the basket and shook it, looking around the rooftop laundry room while she did so. Everything on the storage shelves needed attention. The two-foot-tall stone angel, for instance. One of Juanito's recent sales. She eyed the wing tip that had chipped off. Secure it with Elmer's glue? No way it would hold. She held the pillowcase with one hand and reached out with the other toward a mirror in a hand-painted tin frame. She touched the crack along the top of the mirror. Juanito's first sale. She recalled that day when Juanito came knocking on her door. She had opened the high peep window in her terrace door and, at first, had thought no one was there. But then she looked down and saw the little neighbor boy who had led her to the philosopher's house, now her house. Then just seven years old and already a salesman, the boy offered the mirror as if it were a prize—granted, one that came with a price. "*No pasa nada,*" he had said, when she touched the crack. The crack wouldn't be a problem. She couldn't help but agree and gave him a fifty-peso bill, which he had kissed, and then he'd made the sign of the cross. He called out, "*Gracias, Señora, gracias,*" when he left.

She wiped her dusty fingers on her pants and then folded the sheet. If she were still living in Chicago, she would pile the angel, the mirror, and Juanito's other sales into her aunt's car and drive away to Goodwill. But here, on her *callejón,* someone would have to carry them off. Juanito would be sure to find out. And he had been so proud of his sales. Especially the stone angel, which he had managed to get to her house using Armando's dolly. Besides, if she did get rid of Juanito's sales, wouldn't she miss seeing them? Chipped, cracked, or paint-splattered, each, in its own way, touched her heart.

She folded the pillowcase and took out another. There were still boxes of the philosopher's books gathering dust. The philosopher had left everything when she moved out. Clothes hanging in the closets. Staples in the pantry. Books on the shelves. Slippers under the bed. Her toothbrush by the bathroom sink. Her things had been part of the deal. "If you take the house, you must take everything," the philosopher had said. She was moving to a mountain village in the neighboring state of Michoacán or, as she put it, "crossing the border to Buddhism."

She had not seen the philosopher since the day she left with only the clothes on her back, but she had received a postcard from her every summer inviting her to the yearly silent retreat. Callie snapped the pillowcase, folded it, and lined it up over the other one. If she ever fled across the border to Buddhism, she would not leave everything for someone else to take care of.

She shook out a sheet, folded it, and placed it on the pillowcases. Still, the philosopher's washer had come in handy, as had her furniture and dishes. She'd enjoyed leafing through the philosopher's books and had found herself lingering over love in Plato's *Symposium*. And though she would have been happy with no decorations other than the periodic table she had brought with her, she had kept the philosopher's collection of masks, and even her life-sized straw animals. She shuddered, remembering the look the jaguar had given her when she placed him and his coyote and baboon friends on the terrace for Juanito to sell. She had acquiesced and, for better or worse, they had kept her company since.

She took out another sheet. She had kept Juanito's grand-mother Doña Petra on, too, though she had balked at having someone else clean her house. Cleaning was personal. And, besides, it provided physical activity to balance hours at the computer. But Doña Petra had been part of the deal. "She needs the work," the philosopher said. "You have the income to do your part." The next year, when she got the idea to encourage Doña Petra, then sixty-six, to retire with full salary, Doña Petra had accused her of trying to run her off. So Doña Petra had stayed, and now, Callie knew if Doña Petra was to retire, she would miss her touch, too.

When she stretched out her arm to fold the sheet, she knocked something off the shelf. She gathered the sheet back and leaned over to look. There it was again. The package still wrapped in brown paper, tied with twine, and decorated with a sprig of lavender. What had Jacob been thinking, stopping by to give her the gift the morning she left Chicago for Mexico? Their relationship had been over for some months. Unequivocally over, in fact. She placed the package back on the shelf and sighed. She would never in her lifetime figure out what to do with it.

But she could finish the linens. After folding the sheet and arranging the stack as it should be, the sheets on the bottom and the pillowcases on top, she smoothed the top of the stack and leaned down to breathe in its fragrance of sunlight. Then she stood back and frowned. Doña Petra would be disappointed to find the laundry done. But with the rain so unpredictable, she really had to get it washed and dried while she could. Still, she had no excuse for folding it. One by one, she flipped the sheets open and crumpled them into the basket.

THE entry bell sounded a moment after her aunt Ida called. "I won't keep you," her aunt said. "I was just looking through some photos and found one of you in a smock. I thought you might like to have it."

She held her breath. A smock. She had worn one for months when staying with her aunt. Was that the one?

"You're about nine years old and straddling a branch in that old oak tree behind your folks' house," her aunt said. "You're wearing Mary Janes and reading a book. Your father's standing below laughing up at you."

She recalled the bark against her bare legs, her father's arms when she slid into them. She let out her breath. Just one of her aunt's reminders of good times with her father. Well, she hadn't been a threat to his ego at nine years old. She could give him that.

The bell rang again. She looked through the windows over her desk. Raindrops bounced off the patio tiles.

"The bell . . ."

"I'll let you go," her aunt said.

She pulled her sweater closer. "Is Mother okay? I haven't heard from her."

"I've never seen her so gay. Did I tell you she's been coming to our Wednesday morning coffee klatch? That makes five of us bald-faced Democrats in Farmtown."

"'Bald-faced,' you say. I suppose you'll have Armando using that expression next."

"You taught him French grammar, and I teach him Midwest talk."

She laughed. "And what do you mean five of you? Has mother come out as a Democrat?" She remembered her mother's nervous phone call after Aunt Ida had taken her to meet Farmtown's three other liberals in a popular café on the town square. "She would not keep her voice down," her mother had said. "A sixty-five-year-old. You would think she would know better." Still, Callie had thought she detected a hint of secret pleasure in her mother's description of local businessmen choking on their coffee at Aunt Ida's praise for the Canadian health care system.

"Say out loud she's a Democrat? Not your mother. But that doesn't stop her from attending our meetings. As a matter of fact . . ."

The bell sounded again. "Someone's at the door."

"Well, you go on now."

"But you were about to say?"

"It'll keep."

Callie opened the door from her bedroom to the patio and frowned at the water streaming down the stone stairway that connected the patio to the entry terrace above. The rain had begun in earnest and she had, as all too often, left her umbrella upstairs.

The ringing had stopped when she, curls pasted to her scalp, opened the peep window and saw the top of Juanito's head.

She tried to turn the key in the lock, but it stuck. "*Mo-*

mentito," she called through the window. She jiggled the key and tried again. It turned with ease. Maybe she wouldn't have to call Armando about changing the lock after all.

"Come in." She pulled the door open. "Come in."

"I have something to show you," he said, taking off his backpack on the way into the dining area. He unzipped it, his eyes sparkling with excitement.

She crossed her fingers and made a wish. Not another item for the storage shelves.

"Look, a trumpet." Juanito pulled the instrument from his pack.

She smiled. So it was.

"Do you like it?" Juanito said. "It's pretty. Isn't it?" He held it up in front of her, turning it from side to side. "Not a dent on it."

She laughed and reached out, then held back. If she touched it, she might buy it. "Beautiful."

"It works, too." He held the trumpet to his mouth, puffed out his cheeks, and produced a blast that rivaled the thunder.

"So it does." Could she learn to call Tavelé with it? She took the instrument.

"Do this," Juanito said. He closed his lips and stuck the tip of his tongue out and then quickly back in with a puff of breath, as if he were flicking something off it.

Someone pounded at the door. That had to be Armando. He never rang the bell. She put the trumpet under her arm and went to let him in.

Armando frowned at the trumpet. "What are you doing with *that piece of junk?*"

"You never know when a trumpet will come in handy," she said, and bought it.

Five

CALLIE WOKE IN THE DARK, HER MOUTH DRY, CHEST stiff, heart pounding, and she was panting as if she had been running a long time. The dream again. The starched white cap and heavy cross on a silver chain. The nurse looming over her. Whispering, "You little slut."

Her aunt's advice came to her again. No point in dwelling on the past. She focused on the driving rain. Thick arcs of water spilling from the rooftop gargoyles, splashing through the avocado tree to the patio. Streams of water rippling down the stairs to the garden. Flowing down the *callejones*. Finding its way to the vault-covered river that wound underneath the city center.

Everything would change by the morning. No dust coating the trees. No litter in the *callejones*. No pools of stagnant water in the stream beds. All would be fresh. She got out of bed, went to stand under the avocado tree, and lifted her face to the rain.

THE next morning, she woke to see the sky shining blue through glistening leaves. She stretched her arms over her head and yawned. Armando had been happy the night before. He even cut short his usual lecture about spoiling Juanito to tell her the good news: he had his ticket for Veracruz and had already called Claude to let him know. Claude had also complimented his French. So what if he now sounded like a character out of a nineteenth-century novel. Oh, not to worry. Claude said his grammar was *perfecto*, perfect, *parfait.* He whisked a CD of Ella Fitzgerald singing Cole Porter from his shoulder bag and gave it to her. *"Pour toi, mon chou."* Before he left, he pulled out a thick stack of flyers. "You wouldn't mind handing these out, would you?"

She showered, lathered her face in sunscreen, and dressed in her usual brown skirt, white top, wheat shirt, and Birkenstock sandals. In the kitchen making tea, she hummed along to Fitzgerald singing "It's All Right with Me." On the way out the door, she caught a glimpse of the trumpet reflecting the morning light. She lingered a moment. She could take it along. Blow it like the Pied Piper. Attract a following of stray dogs, barking and sniffing in her wake.

Partway down the *callejón*, a string of men carrying bags of cement across their shoulders overtook her.

"Chamba?" mumbled Nacho, the neighborhood carrier who organized delivery of construction materials and helped neighbors with other heavy items.

"No work today. Sorry." Maybe he could move the stone angel. But not right now. She needed to get to work on her translation, and first she must hand out the flyers about Tavelé.

As she continued down the *callejón*, she regretted not having told that lovely trumpet teacher about Tavelé the evening before. If he had shown up, she would have known to call. And if not, she could have been on the lookout. Best to go right in this morning. The teacher and the girls would be so busy with each other they wouldn't have time for conversation with her. Why hadn't she thought of that the day before? Oh, well. Now that she had the flyers, it would be easier to find something to say. All she had to do was show the flyer and translate it, if necessary. What had Armando written this time? She translated as she read.

> *Lost dog. Brown with black stripes. Short hair. His complete name is Tavelé Martin Torres Ruelle, but he answers to Tavelé (pronounced "Tav lay"). He's very social and doesn't bite. He likes orange cake, roast chicken, and the songs of Cole Porter. If you find him, please take care of him and call Maestro Armando Miguel Torres García. Cell: 044 473 100 3478. A reward of one hundred pesos.*

A reward of one hundred pesos. She paused and looked down the hill for Nacho. Gone. Too bad she hadn't thought of him earlier. She started walking and then paused again. What if the girls weren't there and she had to make conversation with the trumpet teacher? What would she say? She *could* tell her she just bought a trumpet. That her father had played, but she was thinking of using hers to round up stray dogs. She imagined the young woman laughing and then felt her face redden. Talking about herself would be silly. She was going there for Armando, not for herself. And why would that striking young teacher care about her anyway? She started walking again. She had to watch herself. Stick to her plan. Her breath started coming more quickly as she approached the iron gate. She stopped a few steps away. What had she decided to say? She took a flyer out of her backpack, her hands shaking. Oh, yes, just translate the words. That would be easy enough. She took another step toward the gate. Her knees felt a little weak. Think of how happy Armando will be when he sees Tavelé, she told herself and reached the gate without stopping again.

But when she got there, it was locked with a padlock on the outside. No one would be at home. Her hands still shaking, she rolled up the flyer and lodged it in an ornamental curl of iron. By the time she got down to Plaza Mexiamora she had stopped shaking, and only then, as she zigzagged between the clusters of children gathering for primary school, did it come to her that, instead of relief, she felt disappointment at missing the lovely teacher.

ON Truco, she veered left and dashed up the stairway to the Basilica, narrowly escaping the Jehovah's Witnesses. She planned to pass through and out the door to the next street. But when she entered, she noticed an elderly woman with a black lace shawl draped over her head coming from the confessional. She paused then, in the passage between the doors, and watched. The woman had swollen ankles and shuffled slowly, but her face looked soft and relaxed. Had confession brought her that tranquility? The nurse's voice came to her again. Could confession stop nightmares?

She glanced at the confessional and then back to the woman. She watched her kneel in a pew, take out her rosary, and hold it to her lips. Then the woman rose, aiding herself with a hand on the back of the bench in front of her. She paused and crossed herself again before sitting.

Callie cupped her hands over the back of the bench she stood behind and closed her eyes. She had once peed on a bench like this.

She should have used the restroom after Sunday school, like her mother had said. Instead, she had gone outside to look for grass to make her dolly a basket like the one Baby Moses had. Just before the service began, her mother found her sitting on the recently mowed lawn, crying. "We'll go to the lake later," she said. "We'll find some reeds for a basket."

She must have been around five years old. Old enough to know better. Old enough, too, not to talk in church. She had tried to hold the pee. She thought she could. She had before. And she did, until well beyond the end of the sermon. But when the pastor raised his hand for the final benediction, she felt something warm trickle through her clenched legs.

She wriggled back and forth on the bench, trying to soak the pee into her cotton A-line. If only she wore the many-layered petticoats and full skirts the girls across the street from her home wore. But she was not permitted such clothing. Modesty in all things. That had stayed with her. Modesty in all things.

Tears rolled down her cheeks, and her mother, who was by then gathering her gloves and Bible, gave her a concerned look and leaned down to whisper in her ear. She glanced over at her father, and then holding her finger to her lips, she looked down at Callie with tender eyes. When they stood to leave, her mother pulled her close to shield her damp dress from view and laid a bulletin over the puddle.

THE man on the bench before her stood to move to the confessional. Callie watched him lower to his knees and wondered what it would be like to feel the leather pad against her own knees, to bow her head, and to whisper not about a childhood mishap, but about the source of the nightmare. To seek solace.

She closed her eyes and recalled sitting before her father, her face burning with shame and frustration, and yet knowing that talking back would only provoke him further. And so, she had sat there silently, her hands on her lap, one on top of the other, trying to calm her racing heart. *He* could never forgive. No wonder it still came back to her in the night, that racing heart. That shame.

Her eyes moved again to the kneeling woman, and then she startled at a tap on her shoulder.

"Callie," Armando said, laying his hand on her shoulder. "What are you doing here?"

Six

CALLIE STOPPED AND CLOSED HER EYES A MOMENT against the sunlight that blinded her when she emerged from the church. What had Armando said, "You were right about the trumpet." Right? How so? She had not stayed to find out. Instead, confused and embarrassed, she had mumbled something about her deadline and left without even greeting Maestro Chávez who had been with Armando. But before going out the door, she had turned back to catch Armando's eye and wave goodbye. His quizzical look stayed with her.

She shivered. The church had been cool. The library would be cool, too, but she had a sweater in her backpack, and she longed to be sitting at a simple wooden table, working on her translation.

Walking along, warmed by the sun, she mused about her good luck in having work that suited her. It hadn't been the elegance of grammar, as she once thought, that led her from science to language and then to translation. She had had to admit, there was nothing more elegant than the periodic table. It was, instead, the near impossibility of the task that drew her. An English noun as straightforward as "potato" had no exact counterpart in French. *Pomme de terre,* literally *apple from the earth,* called a different image to mind. Even the same words spoken by natives with different histories had incommensurate meanings. Someone raised on McDonald's french fries understood "potato" differently from someone who had wiggled her fingers through the loose soil below a flowering plant and found oval tubers nestled like eggs under a sitting hen. Though she accepted that the fullness of another's meaning remained beyond her grasp, she found that, with effort and imagination, she could reach something close enough to understanding to feel connected.

This feeling came to her even when translating engineering documents. That's what kept her going, spending hours on those "dry documents," as Armando called them. Those flashes of understanding between languages worlds apart. The way she could bridge those worlds, despite the odds.

She had begun studying language in high school, first with two years of Latin. Then, to her parents' dismay, she had selected French over German. Odd for her, since she usually went along with their wishes. Life was easier that way.

But she took her parents on when it came to French. She had reasoned with them. It made more sense to continue with a Romance language after her two years of Latin than to switch to a Germanic one. But her actual motivation stemmed from a fascination that had been brewing since she first heard Edith Piaf sing "Milord" on *The Ed Sullivan Show*. She had been charmed by Piaf's accented English introduction to the song of a love that could not be, and then mesmerized by Piaf's delicious rolled *r*'s when she got underway in French. She had no idea if she could sound any more like France's Little Sparrow than she looked like her, but she would give anything to try. And, besides, it was her last chance to take a class with Steve, her best friend and confidant, who would be graduating at the end of the year. So, she said she wouldn't take another language at all if it wasn't to be French. She wouldn't leave her room either, and feigned illness to avoid going to school. Her mother, who couldn't stay home from the store indefinitely, convinced her father to let her have her way this once. She even bought her records for listening comprehension and pronunciation. The speakers, who were children, had nothing of Piaf's pizzazz, and Callie, to her chagrin and Steve's amusement, wound up, more often than not, speaking with a child's high squeak rather than with Piaf's throaty croon.

Though her father had conceded, he had done so with a "Mark my words, this will not turn out well." And he would yell to her mother, "They are at it again" when he heard her speaking French on the phone with Steve. But it wasn't Steve for whom she had yearned to sound like Piaf, though he was, in a way, responsible. Steve and Aunt Ida. For Steve, at her aunt's suggestion, had taken her to see *A Raisin in the Sun*. And so, when other girls her age developed crushes on a beloved teacher or older brother's best friend, she had dreamed of whispering *milord* to Sidney Poitier. At least until Noah came along.

Seven

WHEN CALLIE GOT HOME FROM THE LIBRARY, HER answering machine was flashing. She made herself a salad and then pressed the play button.

The first message was Armando reminding her to meet him at the Santa Fe for dinner. She sighed. She would prefer a dark corner anywhere, but Armando enjoyed the bustle of the plaza-side tables and, besides, had asked so sweetly if Chou would *dîner dehors* that, of course, she said she would.

The second message was from her aunt Ida. Had she spoken with her mother? That was all. She made a note to call her mom, but not then. Her mother would be at the store. She picked up her fork and started on her salad.

IT had been on the way to the store that she had gathered the courage to tell her mother. When she got there, she parked and sat watching the lights go off one by one, all but the series running down the center of the store. She saw Mr. Charles approach the door, then turn back toward her mother, lift his hand and say something, which she knew to be "Be good . . . and you'll be lonely." Usually she arrived a few minutes early, just to hear his nightly refrain and to watch the corners of her mother's lips curve into a quiet smile. But that night she had waited to enter until Mr. Charles left. She had paused at the door before tapping.

Her mother had been wearing her customary white cotton blouse, cardigan sweater, and a straight skirt that came just below her knees. She was thin. "Thin as a rail," Aunt Ida said. With narrow hips and a flat chest, she appeared drawn and even a little severe. Her dark hair was combed back from her forehead to the nape of her neck and twisted into a bun covered with an almost invisible circular hair net. She wore black pumps and nylons, whose seams never wavered.

She stood folding sweaters at one of the wide wooden chests that ran down the middle of the store. The sweaters had matching wool skirts with sewn-down pleats. All the popular girls wore them. Callie had asked to buy a set with money she was saving for college next year. "Absolutely not," her mother had said. "We've scrimped and saved for you to get an education. You are not going to waste money dolling yourself up."

Now she wondered if she would go to college after all.

"We can leave in a minute," her mother said when she let her in. "I just have to finish the sweaters. The Jensen girls came in an hour before closing, tried on all of them, and then pranced out without buying a thing."

Following her mother's lead, she picked up a moss-green cardigan, buttoned it, and laid it face down on the table. She smoothed out the sleeves, folded them across the back, doubled the bottom of the sweater to the top, and turned the sweater over.

"That would look lovely on you," her mother said. "I wish . . ."

"It's all right." She squared the edges of the folded sweater, held it to her cheek a moment, and then added it to the stack her mother had folded. "There's something . . ." The words did not want to come out. Maybe if they did not, everything would be all right. Maybe it was all her imagination. It had to be. Words would make it seem real.

Her mother looked up and searched Callie's face. "Callie, what's wrong? You look pale."

Her throat constricted at the tenderness in her mother's voice.

"Have you been sick again? Maybe you should sit down." Her mother straightened for a moment, rubbed her lower back, and sighed.

"No, Mother, no, not sick." She watched her mother push a loose strand of hair away from her face and tuck it into her bun, then lean toward the table again, and lift another sweater. How disappointed her mother would be. She felt tears slide down her face and watched them form circles on the sweater she was folding. "I'm sorry, Mother. I'm so sorry."

"It's all right, Dear," her mother said, taking the sweater from her. "You must be overly tired. You were up past midnight again last night. Sometimes I think you take school too seriously." She laid the sweater on the stack. "Your father wants you to do well, and so do I. But your health . . ."

She told her mother then of her periods, that she had missed two months of them, and of her swelling breasts.

"Oh, Callie." The words fell as softly and finally as the last leaf before winter. Her mother pulled opened a deep drawer and returned the stacks of sweaters, placing them side by side. Then she pushed the drawer shut and smoothed the top of the chest with her hand. When she had everything in its place, she shuddered and looked like she might collapse. Callie moved toward her. But before she could reach her, her mother gripped the side of the chest, steadied herself, and turned toward Callie. "Have you told Steve?"

Steve . . . ? And then it came to her. Of course, her mother would assume Steve was the father. She had not told her parents about Noah. And now she would not have to. "No one knows."

"Well, that's good. Maybe we can keep this in the family." She sighed and closed her eyes a moment. Then, she looked at Callie. "I have to tell your father."

Her stomach tightened. Tell her father. She had not thought that far into the future.

"It will be all right," her mother said. "We will find a way . . ."

Later, when she was upstairs sitting on the floor in the hallway outside her room, she heard her father yelling. "I'll teach him a thing or two. You'll not stop me."

But her mother prevailed. "Believe you me," she had said, "your daughter is the one who will be blamed. And we'll be blamed, too. Is that what you want?"

"We?" her father said. "You are the one who let her go around with that boy. I told her if she wanted someone to study with, she could study with the girl across the street. But no, she stuck up her nose. And you had to go and side with her, just like you always do." He was sobbing by then, angry choking sobs. "If anyone is to blame, you are. You dropped the ball. You. You and her."

"She can go away," her mother had said so quietly Callie had barely been able to make out the words. "Ida will take her in. No one here will ever know."

"They had better not know." He sounded weary. "They had better not."

In the end, there was no choice. She had to go away. She had to keep it quiet. No one there could ever know. No one.

* * *

SHE pushed her unfinished salad away. There she was, dwelling on the past again. She covered her plate and put it in the refrigerator. Her translation. That's what she needed. She felt better just thinking about it. Then she would treat herself by washing the small panes of the terrace doors.

SHE had finished the allotted portion of her translation sooner than she expected, leaving her plenty of time for the windows. She placed a stack of newspapers and a bucket of water with vinegar on a chair and a wastebasket beside it. She tore a section of newspaper and dipped it in the bucket. Then she stood on another chair to start with the top windows. Before reaching for the first small pane, she noticed the trumpet standing upright on its bell by the doors. She had not touched it since Juanito put it there.

She reached upward to the corner small pane. She would rub each pane nine times, as usual. She started rubbing and counting. One. Two. Three. Armando had said she was right about the trumpet coming in handy. She rubbed slowly, from top to bottom, taking special care with the corners, and then rubbed from top to bottom again. Odd, after having called the trumpet "a piece of junk."

She tossed the used newspaper in the basket and stooped to prepare another section of paper. Then started on the next pane. One. Two. Three. What could he have in mind?

She recalled leaning against the basement door, listening to the long, low pedal tones her father warmed up with before the birds began to sing. In the evenings, when he played songs, she would close her eyes and see soldiers marching through clouds of confetti, sad-eyed clowns dropping the pins they jug-gled, mothers cradling their babies. Scenes, she realized years later, that her father could not describe verbally without scorn or self-pity. It seemed that, by picking up his horn, he entered another world, one where he was free from the chip soldered to his shoulder. And so, if he stormed into the house after work, railing over some slight, her mother would suggest he go to the basement. If she caught him before he got really wound up, he would come up later with a little circular dent from the mouthpiece on his lips and a twinkle in his eye. He would take Callie's hands and swing her around in a circle. "Oh, your mum, she's a bonnie lassie," he would say.

She prepared another sheet of newspaper and started on another window.

She had thought her father's trumpet was magic, like the fairy godmother's wand. And so she loved going to the base-ment when her mother went for canned corn or string beans for supper. She would stand transfixed by the shining trumpet, hanging from a hook on the wall by the shelves. She longed to hold it and look inside the bell. But it, along with the saws on hooks beside it, was out of her reach, "for a reason," her father said. They were not toys. Neither was the basement, where black widows lurked, a playroom. And so the door remained latched with a hook and eye.

Still, it was easy enough for a curious child to scoot a chair over, lift the hook, and lean through the door to turn on the light. She wasn't such a little girl any more. She knew to hold onto the stair railing. She would not touch her father's saws. She only wanted to hold the trumpet, to find a clue to its magic.

She never found out. Her mother circled an arm around her waist as she leaned to turn on the light. "Oh, no you don't, young lady," she said. "You can't handle those stairs on your own." That very night her father had installed a lock and hid the key.

SHE looked at the newly shined pane in front of her and smiled. Imagine that. Thinking that a trumpet could work magic. She shook her head. What funny ideas children have. Still, when she finished the windows, she found herself picking up the trumpet and looking inside the bell.

Eight

W HEN CALLIE STARTED DOWN THE CALLEJÓN, SHE caught herself humming "Oh, What a Beautiful Morning." She felt her face grow red. What if someone heard her? She looked up to the window opposite her entry door. Shut. Good. She laughed. It wasn't morning, but it was beautiful. The sky was blue, the air fresh and with a slight breeze. Her translation was going well. With luck she would enlist Nacho in the search for Tavelé. And then she would have dinner with Armando, who would tell her all about his plans for seeing Claude in Veracruz.

Everything *did* seem to be going her way, but there was something on her mind, as she turned onto the dead-end *callejón* where Nacho lived. Her aunt's message asking if she had heard from her mother. She had not sounded worried, just bursting to tell Callie something. Well, she had news of her own. The lovely trumpet teacher. Her new friend. Well, not really. Not yet anyway. Probably never. But she could at least meet her. That would make her aunt happy. Her getting out of the house. Meeting someone new. But how would she meet the young woman? She could hardly just go up to her and introduce herself. And if she did, what would she say? Nothing. She paused a moment before knocking at Nacho's door to figure it out. Tavelé. He would surely turn up at the young woman's house looking for the geese. She would call Armando with the good news. And then the young woman and he would become great friends. He would take her along sometime to meet the young woman. The two of them would talk. All she would have to do was listen.

The shack where Nacho lived with his mother was made of tin pieced together with rough strips of wood. The door rattled when she knocked.

Nacho's mother opened the door. "*Buenos días, güerita.*"

She took in a breath. After years of being called "*güera*" and its diminutive "*güerita*" by various neighbors, shopkeepers, and peddlers, she still felt odd about the label given her on account of her fair skin and hair. But she preferred it to "*gringa,*" since "*güera*" was, at least, one of the descriptive nicknames Mexicans used for each other, apparently without intending offense. And it embarrassed her less than "*gordita,*" that is "fatty," which would, she feared, be equally fitting.

She held up a flyer and explained that Armando was offering a reward for Tavelé.

Nacho's mother took the flyer. "*Que le vaya bien,*" she called after Callie as she left.

Approaching the *callejón* to the young woman's house, it came to her. What if someone called the young woman "*morena*"? She paused. Would it bring up experiences of racial name-calling in the States, where no brown person was exempt from derisive labels? She shuddered, recalling the patronizing tone of the nurse with the cross necklace. "Time to feed your little darky." She continued straight down the hill. No need to stop by the trumpet teacher's house. She had already left the flyer in the morning. And, besides, Armando would walk her home later and could stop by to see the young woman on his way back down. He would be charming, the way he was with everyone.

She smiled, thinking of how Armando had hit it off with Aunt Ida. Thanks to the mummies, Aunt Ida's passion. She had shared that passion with Callie from the time she was tall enough to peep over the side of a sarcophagus. Mummies had, in a sense, led them to Guanajuato, for when Aunt Ida heard about Guanajuato's mummies, she had started packing. Because Callie had a break between translations, she had come along, though the only true appeal of mummies, as far as she was concerned, was that she need not speak with them. She had been relieved, then, when the day after their arrival in Guanajuato, her aunt returned from her morning coffee saying she met a nice young man named Armando who loved mummies, too, and had insisted on becoming her personal tour guide.

The next day the young man had taken her aunt to the mummy museum, where she learned that bodies buried in Guanajuato's soil mummify naturally, and so, she told Callie, she had decided then and there that, when the time came, she was to be buried in Guanajuato. On other days, Armando took her aunt to places where mummies, as he put it, "began their transformation": the bottom of a mine shaft, an inquisition torture chamber, a curve on a mountain road marked by a wreath of plastic flowers.

While her aunt was "off gallivanting," as she put it, Callie had wandered through the web of *callejones* that spread up the canyon sides. She got lost, sometimes for hours, and could only find her way again by asking a passerby for help, but that didn't stop her outings. She had become fascinated by the occasional property with vines creeping over the top of stone or stuccoed walls, suggesting a hidden garden.

One day, an older woman walking with a little boy saw her gazing at one such treetop. She introduced herself as Petra Rodríguez Gómez and the boy as her grandson Juanito. She said she knew of a house with a garden for sale. It belonged to a philosopher, a foreigner, like you, she had said. Callie followed the woman up the hill and alongside a stone wall to the house, but the philosopher was not at home. It had been a relief at the time. What would she say to her, after all? But, still, she could not stop thinking about the limb that stretched over the patio wall as if beckoning her. Their last day in Guanajuato, she took her aunt up the slopes and stairways to the philosopher's house, where she herself knocked on the door and asked if they could see it.

She loved everything about the stone house stacked on the hillside. She loved the upstairs kitchen with its beamed ceiling and tall French doors to the entry terrace. The small guest room with a balcony overlooking the patio below. The bedroom off the patio, with an alcove for a desk under waist-high windows. The bath tiled from floor to ceiling with soaring blue birds. Most of all, she loved the hidden garden.

Still she had balked at her aunt's suggestion that she buy the house.

"What more would you want?" her aunt said. "A lovely house, gracious people, live music everywhere, year-round spring, and mummies. And don't worry about money. It's not much in any case, and I'll have plenty to loan you after selling my house in Chicago. The house I'm moving to in Farmtown is half the price. So, what do you say?"

"No, thank you." She preferred to stay in Chicago. But her aunt insisted. "You can't spend your whole life there waiting."

She could, she knew, wait a lifetime, if that's what it took. Not, as her aunt thought, for Jacob. She had no illusions about getting back together with him. If anything, it would be easier being in Guanajuato than in Chicago, avoiding the places they had once entered hand in hand. And so she bought the philosopher's house.

In the end, her life in Guanajuato was not so different

from how it had been in Chicago. Though she knew no one was likely to call but Aunt Ida or Armando, her heart still skipped a beat each time the phone rang.

WHEN Callie got to the restaurant, Armando was sitting half-turned away from his table, talking with a couple behind him. He must have been recounting the story of losing Tavelé because at one point he held his hands up in a way that suggested the width of a sheet cake.

When the woman smiled over his shoulder at her, Armando turned to introduce her. "These people are from Seattle. Rick and Susie Gardner. Callie Quinn."

She nodded and tried to smile back. He would not invite the Gardners to join them, would he?

He pointed to the Yorkshire terrier asleep on Susie's lap. "Skippy took off a moment ago when a boy passed beating a drum." Armando moved his index fingers to show how quickly the dog's little legs moved.

"And look at him now." Susie looked down at the sleeping dog. Then she smiled at Armando. "Your Tavelé will come back, too."

A waiter approached with the couple's meal.

"*Buen provecho*," Armando said and turned his chair back.

She let out the breath she had been holding.

He rose to pull out her chair and then gestured to her glass. "Your mineral water, Madam." He returned to his chair and raised his margarita. "*Salud.*"

She clinked her glass against his.

"What a pretty shawl, Chou," he said, "but not as pretty as the purple one I gave you."

She had draped his present over her shoulders before leaving home. But she had felt conspicuous. The color was magnificent. Too much so.

"What were you doing at confession, by the way?"

She felt her face turning red. Would Armando notice? She took a sip of water.

"I thought you were agnostic. Is everything okay? Your mother?"

"Mother? She wasn't home when I called. But I'm sure she's fine. Maybe my aunt got her to go out to dinner."

"So you're okay. Everything hunky-dory?"

She laughed. "'Hunky-dory.' Did you pick that up from Aunt Ida? Or from that bass player you told me about?"

"Neither. A TV rerun. Anyway, you are okay. Right?"

"Right. I just ducked into the church because some Jehovah's Witnesses came between me and the library." She drew her shawl closer.

"So you fled to Catholicism?" He lifted his margarita to her. "Welcome."

She looked around the table. "Do we have menus?"

"I ordered your usual. I'm having chicken mole. It's perfect here. *Perfecto. Parfait.*"

His mentioning confession had distracted her. What had she wanted to tell him? Oh, yes, about the trumpet teacher and Tavelé. "Remember the *callejón* with the geese?"

A new, young waiter approached holding a large tray at shoulder height. As he passed, a basket of chips slid toward the rim. Armando ducked and the youth righted the tray.

Armando gave him a reassuring look, then turned back to Callie. "Did they get out again?"

"What?"

"The geese. Were they menacing you?"

"No, not that." She paused while a waiter moved her bread

plate to one side to make room for her soup. He laid a soup spoon by the bowl. Then he served Armando's chicken with mole sauce and replaced Armando's empty margarita goblet with a full one. "They're gone and the family, too."

"Good, Chou, now you can pass by there safely." He lifted a forkful of chicken dripping in savory sauce. "*Provecho.*" He paused, stared over Callie's left shoulder, and then whispered, "Don't look."

She had not gotten to the best part. About the lovely trumpet teacher. It was silly, she knew, her idea of getting to know her. But still Armando would want to know her. "There's more . . ." She started to turn.

"I said, 'Don't look.'"

"Don't look at what?"

He leaned forward again and lifted his head in the direction past her shoulder. "At *her.*"

Callie's shoulders felt tight from the effort not to turn. "Her? Who?"

"The one who's been causing all the trouble. That busybody. *Metiche. Fouineuse.*" He put the forkful of chicken in his mouth and chewed with conviction.

"Trouble?" She tried a spoonful of the soup. Lukewarm. Should she send it back?

He rolled a corn tortilla and dabbed it in his beans. "Remember I told you I wanted to talk with you about a personnel problem?"

She nodded and then glanced at the waiter who had just passed by.

"You need something?" Armando said. "Allow me." He turned to signal the waiter.

"No. No. It's nothing." She put her spoon down. "What problem?"

He turned back toward her. "At the orchestra. Pamela Fischer, the new trumpeter, is causing trouble there, but never mind about that now. It also looks like she's got Tavelé. The bakery lady told me he followed her to Pamela's house, and that's the last she saw of him."

A new colleague keeping Tavelé? Surely not. She turned her head slightly to catch a glimpse of the person.

He clicked his glass with his fork and whispered with emphasis, "Pamela will *see* you."

She turned back. "So?"

He put his palms on the table and leaned toward her. "She can't, or my plan won't work."

Oh, no. She had only recently gotten him to stop asking her to call Paris morgues whenever he couldn't reach Claude. And now he had come up with another crazy scheme. She moved her chair back. "The answer is no."

He laughed and switched to French. "*Je ne t'ai même pas dit ce que je veux.*"

"Agreed. You haven't told me what you want." She smoothed the napkin on her lap and smiled. "But, no, anyway." She jumped. Something was tickling her ankle. "What's that?" She looked down. The Yorkie. She laughed, gave him a pat, and then turned back to Armando.

"Like I said, good thing you bought the trumpet."

"You called it 'a piece of junk.' And you were right." She felt her chest tighten. He wasn't right. Still, there was no point. She would never play it. Not even try. "I'm going to give it away."

"Good idea, but not yet. First, you're going to take a lesson. That would be perfect."

She wanted to say, "That would not be perfect, it would be absurd," but a drop of soup caught in her windpipe.

He handed her a glass of water and paused until she

stopped coughing. "Don't worry, Chou. You'll just take one lesson. Then I'll find a home for the trumpet." His lips continued moving, but she could not hear him. Mariachis had surrounded the tourists' table, with the trumpets aimed in her direction.

She palmed her ears as discreetly as possible.

He took a little plastic bottle out of his pocket and showed her the label. FAST: Valve, Slide, and Key Oil. He mimicked squeezing drops of oil.

She caught Armando saying "oil for your trumpet" at a pause in the music. But the mariachis soon started up again. This time they played "*El Niño Perdido*" ("The Lost Child"). She lowered her hands from her ears to take in the melancholy duet and then turned toward the plaza. Where was the second trumpet? The one off somewhere, usually behind the trees, calling out like a child seeking a way home.

She had heard the song many times, but had never heard a trumpet's call choke with sobs. She moved from side to side to look through the trees.

He tapped her on the shoulder. "It's *her*. Pamela."

The trumpeter? Pamela? A lonely phrase drifted through the trees, evoking the image of a small, frightened child. She shifted again and glimpsed a flash of silver.

He tried to get her to face him, but she remained mesmerized by the trumpet. It evoked such longing that she rose to her feet and stood in silence until the song came to an end.

Callie leaned forward, fully expecting to see a frightened child emerge from behind the tree. But no. It was *she*. The woman with the downy curls. The lovely trumpet teacher.

Dressed in black tights and an emerald tunic, Pamela walked across the plaza with the grace of Judith Jamison. She paused by a mariachi seated under the tree canopy. When he tipped his hat to her, she bowed until her head touched her knees. She hung there a moment, then stood, removed the mouthpiece, and handed the trumpet to him. On returning to her table, she lifted a leather shoulder bag from her chair and tucked the mouthpiece in an outside pocket.

Callie stood transfixed. How could someone with her poise portray such vulnerability? Then she found herself taking a step toward Pamela, who was lifting her glass in response to a toast.

She took another step and then froze. What would she say?

A table to her right paid their check and began pushing back their chairs, the women collecting their purses, and the men leaning to rub out cigars.

She held her breath. Only a few more steps to go.

The young waiter passed by with a tray of margaritas.

She could toast Pamela. Nothing to it, really. Armando toasted musicians all the time. Aunt Ida was right. She should take a page from his book.

She drew her shoulders back, pulled in her stomach, and whisked past the waiter, scooping a margarita from the tray. Open your throat, she told herself. One word. That's all you need to say. One word. *Felicidades.* You can say that. *Felicidades.*

Behind her, a tray of dishes crashed to the floor, and Skippy, who had been following along, shot between her feet. She lurched to avoid him, but could not contain the margarita, which swished out of the goblet and splashed against Pamela's back.

She heard herself call, *"Felicidades!"* and then she froze. What had she done?

Pamela turned in surprise and then glared—not at Callie— but at Armando, who sighed in disgust and clamped his mouth shut.

"Oh, no . . ." Callie said, "I mean . . . I'm sorry. Skippy. I should have been more careful . . . The new waiter . . . I should have known . . ."

Pamela's hand went to her wet shoulder.

"Oh, that must be sticky. Let me help." She took off her shawl and started to offer it to Pamela, but her hands were shaking so much she dropped it. She looked down at the shawl. She must get a hold of herself or she would be lying there, too. Pick it up, she told herself. Fold it end to end, and then again. She squatted by the shawl and began to fold. Carefully. Perfectly. Still, it wasn't working. Her heart was beating so fast and hard she felt dizzy. She looked around desperately.

Then she noticed the bulge of the mouthpiece in the pocket of Pamela's shoulder bag. She pursed her lips. Breathe. Hadn't her father said that was the trick? She looked up and saw Pamela smiling at her. It came to her again that she looked familiar, though still not like anyone she knew. Armando's arm tightened around her and pulled her to her feet. She glanced at his solemn face and then back to Pamela's eyes, which twinkled with a mixture of curiosity and delight. She began to smooth the folded shawl over Pamela's shoulder. Pamela, still smiling, reached up to help and patted her hand. It felt warm and reassuring. Still, she was surprised to hear herself say, "I understand you give trumpet lessons."

Nine

RMANDO GUIDED CALLIE OUT OF THE RESTAURANT, handing the maître d' a handful of bills on the way, and then led her through the packed central plaza. He took her elbow when the crowd thinned at the narrow end of the plaza and escorted her to the quieter Plaza Baratillo, where he found a free bench facing the central fountain. "You're trembling," he said, and draped his jacket around her shoulders. After she sat down, he flopped down beside her and hunched over, looking down. "Why did you do that, Calecita? Why?"

She pulled his coat closer and then sat up straight with her hands on her knees, one on top of the other. Asking for a lesson and agreeing then and there on Thursday—only three days away. She shuddered. "I . . . I am not sure . . ." There was something about Pamela, the poignancy of her playing, the way she had metamorphosed from the lost child, the warmth of her hand, the familiarity she could not put her finger on. Was that it? Had curiosity overcome her shyness? Her voice had not even wavered when she asked about the lesson. But still it didn't make any sense. Asking for a trumpet lesson, of all things, and especially from someone she didn't know. And feeling so calm at that moment, though now she was shivering, as if she had been the one doused with a cold drink.

He turned to her. "Once she saw you with me, there was no point in asking for a lesson. She wasn't to know you knew me. Remember?"

Her hands felt clammy. He was right. He had said that. But

she hadn't agreed, had she? Not that she would have gone up to the young woman at all, if she had been in her right mind. And then why hadn't she just stopped with the toast? Or at least thought of another way to see the young woman again—which would not be difficult, in any case, given that they lived within blocks of one another.

He turned and looked at her. "Callie, are you listening?" He adjusted the jacket on her shoulders.

"It's hard to explain." Not wanting to get to know such a woman. Who wouldn't want to? Still, it was crazy, wasn't it, asking for a lesson?

"I had anticipated your protests. Your garden, your translations, your calls to your mother and Aunt Ida, your obsessive cleaning. You pack your schedule so tight I can barely get you out for a walk, and here you are planning a lesson on an instrument you don't even like. Don't deny it. I see you covering your ears when the trumpets start up. You might enjoy strumming a harp, but blasting a trumpet? Never. You have to breathe to play the trumpet, Callie. Breathe. And, besides, you don't know Pamela from Adam. That's what really gets me. How could you go up to a perfect stranger like that? And *her* of all people." He shook a finger at her. "Well, you'll find out what that *metiche's* like soon enough. Trouble." He leaned forward and put his head in his hands.

"I saw her the other day. With some girls. With trumpets. I thought you would like her."

"You would have known better, if you had been to the symphony recently."

"You know I've had deadlines . . ."

"I can't even remember when you were there last. Anyway, if you had seen what a spectacle she makes of herself, you would understand. That engraved silver trumpet she's so proud of. That hair glowing like the burning bush. No wonder Maestro Chávez gets distracted."

He went on, but her mind was elsewhere. She could remember the last time she had been to the symphony. Not the date or the program. It was the newborn that stayed with her.

She had waited outside, as usual, until the lights dimmed, and then she went to the section generally occupied by her neighbors, the Ramirez family. She took the seat by Paulita, the oldest of the three younger daughters, sitting side by side in full-skirted white dresses. Paulita held her tiny nephew bundled in a blue blanket. The young mother, sitting behind them with the older siblings, leaned forward from time to time to peek under the flap over the baby's face and then put her finger to her lips to quiet her whispering sisters.

Callie had not held a baby since releasing her own years before, but she did not need to hold her neighbor's baby to feel his weight against her arms or to breathe in his milky fragrance. She recalled her newborn lying asleep on her breastbone, then worming her way across her chest to rest her head on her breast, as she lay in drowsy wakefulness. She pictured her baby's face forming one emotion after another, eyebrows crinkled together, a flaccid jaw, a curled upper lip, a smile, pursed lips, raised eyebrows, lips turned under as if to begin a wail, a pout, another smile, all in one effortless flow. On the last morning, when her baby was taken from her arms, a questioning look had crossed her face. Had she sensed she was being taken away for good? Had she wondered, why?

"Callie, are you listening?"

What had he been talking about? The maestro getting lost. Well, he had been getting lost for a long time.

"Brash. Culturally insensitive. Arrogant. That's her."

"Pamela?" She did seem confident. But arrogant?

"She's only been here a month. She can barely speak a word of Spanish, and she's collaring musicians, saying it's time for the maestro to retire."

Oh, so that's what this was all about. Maestro Chávez. The maestro and his wife had met Armando when he came with the orphanage choir to sing with the symphony. They took him in when he attended the university music school. Then they sent him to Paris for additional study in tympani and composition. When the maestro's wife died, leaving the maestro alone and depressed, Armando had come back to stay.

"Was that the personnel problem you wanted to talk about? The maestro?"

"Not the maestro. *Her.* Pamela." He jumped up to intercept an errant soccer ball flying toward Callie's head. He kicked it in a high arc back to the boys playing across the plaza. Then he stood, looking down at her. "Look. Forget the lesson. She won't let you near Tavelé now that she knows you're my friend. And, besides, look at you. You're a wreck. But don't worry." He tapped out a drum roll with his fingers. "*Aux grands maux, les grands remèdes.* I'll take the police to her house. She'll have to give Tavelé to them, and, besides, once I have proof she stole Tavelé, I can get her fired, and with no job, she'll lose her visa. She'll have to go then."

Callie was too flustered at Armando's hysteria to think up an appropriate husband. The only one that came to her was the timid one who had dropped his car key and, finding himself on his knees in front of her, had blurted out his proposal, and then, apparently in shock, keeled over from a massive heart attack. She felt a little lightheaded herself. She had to calm down. She pictured herself putting her spices in alphabetical order. Allspice. Basil. She was crazy to have asked for a lesson. Cardamom. She wasn't just shaking, she was hyperventilating. Dill. But Armando was right about one thing: desperate situations called for desperate measures. E . . . Did she have a spice that started with E? Ah, epazote. She used it when cooking beans. Better to take a lesson than see Pamela arrested. If she did have Tavelé, she would give him to her. She was sure of that. But she couldn't contradict Armando when he was in a mood. Fenugreek. Greeks. The gods. Zeus. Hera, Aphrodite. Oh, the Virgin. "Why don't you talk it over with the Virgin? Then decide." She stood up. "I can walk home alone."

He began to protest, but then stopped to listen to a trumpet coming from the jazz club on the other side of the plaza.

The trumpet was playing "Birds Do It," one of the songs on the Cole Porter album Armando had given her.

"That's her." He leaned forward to kiss Callie's cheeks and then looked toward the jazz club again. "Okay, I'm out of here."

He started across the plaza and then came back. "Are you sure you'll be all right?"

She smiled. "Yes." She had stopped shaking.

He left, and then came back. "There really is no need for you to take the lesson, Calecita."

"Perhaps not."

"Then you agree, Chou?"

"Let's think about it."

"I have thought about it." He caught himself moving his shoulders to the rhythm of Pamela's improvisation, and drew them back into rigid attention. "I have to get out of here."

"Go. We'll talk later."

He gave her another kiss on the cheek, and then started walking toward the Church of Guadalupe. She stood watching him go. He walked slowly, turning several times to wave at her. When he began moving his shoulders to the music again, he stopped and shook them, and then he took off running.

Ten

ILTING HER HEAD TO ONE SIDE, CALLIE LOOKED at the trumpet standing on her center island. Armando could not see her blasting it. She crossed her arms in front of her chest. Well, neither could she. Keeping her gaze on the trumpet, she circled the island. She wouldn't have to blast it though. She settled on a stool. She could play quietly, like her father had when she had had a bad dream. "I'll whisper you to sleep," he would say and then go for his trumpet. Pamela could teach her whisper notes. Pedal tones would be okay, too. She had no reason to blow hard and high. She wasn't planning to don a studded suit and join the mariachis. She leaned toward the trumpet.

When her father went to the basement in one of his moods, his trumpet began by shouting accusations or whining resentments. And then it switched to singing lullabies sometimes ending with a song so sad that she, leaning against the wall opposite the basement door, held her baby doll close and cried. On those evenings, when her father found her there, he would give her a pat on the head and ask if she would read one of her books until her mother called her for supper.

Once when she went to the kitchen before being called, she saw her father sitting across from her mother at the table, his arms stretched out, his hands holding hers. He spoke of losing his mother when he was four years old. Of his older sister saying she was sleeping and would wake in heaven with the angels. He told of lying awake furious with the angels. Of being angry at his mother, too, for leaving him for them. Of his anger blotting out everything about her. And of wishing later that he had lain awake recalling the sound of her voice.

Callie laid the trumpet down, patted it as if hushing a child, and then knelt to open the safe under her kitchen counter. The philosopher had left it empty, and the only thing she had put in it was a manila folder, one she allowed herself to open only once a year.

INVESTIGATOR Joyce Lai's office had been in downtown Chicago on the floor above the Yang Café. "A good place for lunch," the investigator's secretary had said when Callie called for an appointment. But though she had had nothing but tea for breakfast and had arrived an hour before her two p.m. appointment, she passed the restaurant and climbed the stairs to the waiting area. The fragrance of ginger and garlic normally would have whetted her appetite, but that day it made her nauseous, and so she sat there enumerating the elements of the periodic table and trying not to breathe.

A few minutes before her scheduled appointment, she heard footsteps on the stairs. Her heartbeat picked up, and she adjusted herself in her chair, hoping to look calm. A woman appeared wearing a lavender dress with a jade necklace. "I'm Joyce Lai. Are you Ms. Quinn?"

Her mouth was so dry, all she could do was nod.

Joyce opened the door to her suite and motioned for her to enter.

The outer office looked cozy. Lace curtains, an oval braided rug, and two rocking chairs with needlepoint pillows. She felt her shoulders relax.

Joyce gestured toward the decor. "My secretary," she said,

as if to explain. "She's at her knitting circle." She nodded to a closed door and said, "I'm in here." She opened the door to an office furnished in Scandinavian design, offered Callie a chair, and sat down at her desk. "Now, how can I help you?" She looked more closely at Callie, and then asked, "Oh, excuse me, would you like a cup of tea or coffee?" She stood up as if to move to the outer office.

Callie shook her head.

"Some water then." Joyce leaned forward to pour a glass of water for each of them from the crystal pitcher on her desk.

Callie was thirsty, but she dared not reach for the glass. She could not trust her hand to stay steady. She managed a quiet "thank you."

Joyce sat back down and folded her hands on the desk. "Well, then?"

"I understand you help women . . ." Callie choked and then coughed until tears rolled down her cheeks.

"It's all right," Joyce said. She moved the glass closer to Callie, and then she turned a photo in a silver frame on her desk toward her. It was a photo of Joyce and a young man. He wore a black and white flowered Hawaiian shirt, his arm resting across her shoulders, both of them smiling broadly. "I know how you feel. Someone helped me find my son."

Callie handed Joyce a sheet of paper with the date and time of birth, the names, addresses, and telephone numbers of the hospital and adoption agency, and her own telephone number and address.

Joyce smiled. "You've done your homework."

"When do you think . . . ?"

"It shouldn't take long. A week, maybe less."

She drew in her breath. "So soon." She had waited almost thirty years.

Joyce leaned across the table to touch her hand. "How do you want to handle the information?" She looked down at the sheet again. "You live in Lincoln Square, right? Shall I mail it to you?"

"I can come down here."

"That will be fine."

"How much do I owe?"

"There will be no charge, unless I run into something un-expected."

"But . . ."

"Please allow me. It's my way of expressing gratitude for finding my son."

She looked again at the photo of Joyce and her son, their faces filled with joy.

Descending the stairway to the exit, Callie took in a long, slow breath. The ginger and garlic smelled like hope.

JOYCE had called before the week was out. She had sounded reassuring, saying, "Oh, yes, Dear. She's fine," when Callie had asked first thing: "Is she all right?" But, Callie thought as she sat anxious on the L to downtown, hadn't Joyce's voice sounded a little strained? Maybe she had meant she's fine now. It was before, sometime before, years before, that something terrible happened.

The first thing she noticed when entering Joyce's office was the file on her desk. She read the words across the top: Gwendolyn Annabel Brown. She nodded toward the file. "Her name?"

"Yes." Joyce gestured to the chair, but Callie just stood there. Her baby had a name.

"Gwendolyn." She liked the feel of it in her mouth. She

studied the words. Gwendolyn Annabel Brown. With such a beautiful name, her daughter must be safe. "Gwendolyn Annabel Brown."

Joyce opened the file.

Callie sat down and leaned forward. "Is she here? In Chicago?"

"No. Her family moved to Boston, while she was still in high school, and she went to college back East."

She leaned back in her chair. For many years, none of the dark young women who had taken her breath away in Chicago had been her daughter. "She graduated from college?"

"And completed an MA in Education. Your daughter is a sixth-grade teacher."

A teacher. She was all right then. She must be all right.

"Her husband, Earl Brown, runs a restaurant."

A husband. Callie felt a lump form in her throat.

"They have two children, a girl and a boy, ages seven and five."

Children. Tears came to Callie's eyes. Children. Was it possible? "Then she is all right? She's safe? She's well?"

"In perfect health." Joyce smiled and pushed the file toward Callie. "There's more information. Her address. Her telephone number."

"Oh . . ." Not her telephone number. Was that legal?

"I can make the call, if you like. Sometimes it's easier that way."

"Oh, no. I don't want to bother her. I . . . I just wanted to know that she was all right. That's all." She meant those words, she told herself. It *was* enough to know her daughter was all right. More than all right. Safe and happy. "She didn't see you, did she?"

"I wasn't there."

"Oh . . . You mean someone else?"

"We do this for each other. It saves travel."

"Of course."

"My colleague is very discreet. I asked him to drop by the neighborhood to take a photo. It's in the file."

"A photo, too." She would see her baby.

"Would you like to look through the file? You could use my secretary's office."

"Thank you, no." Callie clicked open her handbag and reached for her checkbook. "You said you might run into additional costs."

"We didn't do anything out of the ordinary."

She shut her handbag, picked up the file, and cradled it in the crook of her elbow. A manila folder with a few papers and a photo. Nothing out of the ordinary. Then why did her heart feel like it would burst with joy?

SHE put the photo of Gwendolyn back in the folder and smoothed her hand over the top. It had been over five years since she first saw the photo of the young woman with a yoga mat slung over her shoulder. Then she so wanted to show everyone the photo, the way other mothers showed off their babies, counting off every resemblance. She could hear herself saying the words, "Look how lithe she is, just like her father. And she's short, like me. She has his lips. That dimple in her left cheek is mine. And her skin's a blend of dark chocolate and peaches and cream. Imagine that? She has my father's hands and my mother's widow's peak . . ." Oh, how she could have gone on that day. On that day, too, the day she first held the photo of her grown daughter, she longed to see her face to face, to hear the timbre of her voice, to hold her close.

It was all she could do not to tell. Not just her aunt, but the clerk at the corner grocery, the librarian, the postman, complete strangers on the L. She wanted to tell them she had a daughter. A beautiful daughter. A smart daughter. A married daughter. A daughter with children. A safe daughter. In perfect health. With all her fingers and toes. Hard. It had been hard. So very hard not to show the photo. Of Gwendolyn Annabel Brown.

But she had promised not to tell. Promised her father. Promised herself, for her daughter's sake. It was her daughter's choice. She would not take that away from her. It was one thing for her to find her daughter, to know that she was safe, to see her face in a photo. It would be another to tell others, especially those who may not be so discreet as she.

It was best that way. Best that she not disturb her daughter. Best that she not talk. Best that she protect herself from longing. She looked from the folder to the trumpet. It looked just like the one that released her father's anger, uncovered his sorrow. Armando was right. She had no business playing it. She had her garden and her cleaning. She had a full schedule of work. She lowered her head slowly to one side and then the other, releasing tension in her neck. She had her calls to her mother and her aunt. Her walks with Armando. Juanito coming to her door with his treasures. The trumpet, no matter how softly played, would disrupt her life. She let out her breath with a sigh. She had grown accustomed to the sound of silence.

She opened the folder one more time and leaned over the photo of Gwendolyn. "Happy Birthday," she whispered. Then she put the folder back into the safe and locked it.

Eleven

ALLIE DROPPED HER KEY TWICE TRYING TO LOCK her entry door. It wasn't the lock this time, which turned easily when she finally got the key in. The problem was her hand, which was shaking.

Was she nervous about seeing the young woman again? She would have been, before finding Gwendolyn. Before, whenever she had seen a caramel-colored girl of the right age, she wondered if she could be her daughter. The child in the stroller. The girl tossing a basketball into a hoop. The teen in the march for freedom. The lead in the school play. Each time she would give her heart to the child as if she were her own. Often from a distance. Across a park. The last row of the bleachers. The back of an auditorium. To get closer to the children, she had become a volunteer tutor, changing grades every year, to the grade her daughter would have been in. And then, when she went to a school event, she could say, if anyone asked, that one of the children she tutored had invited her.

She started down the *callejón*. Armando had come by the night before, discouraged that the neighborhood cop refused to do anything. But *Chou* could help out, couldn't she? Pamela would never give Tavelé to *him*, but with Chou's sweet, motherly voice, Pamela would surely hand over Tavelé, in spite of her being his friend. He took a leash she had given him from his shoulder bag and asked her in French, of course, to please take the lesson after all.

She had never seen him so anxious. Not about Tavelé. About Claude. He had begun catastrophizing again and was sure there was another man. Perhaps the new violist Claude had spoken so highly of in his string quartet. That's why Claude wanted to meet him in Veracruz. To tell him in person.

Callie had taken a risk and told him about John-James, the husband with the two heads, both jealous because she could kiss only one set of lips at a time. She mimed the awful looks each made when she kissed the other. Armando had laughed and even thought of some things for John-James to say. But she could tell, by the way his shoulders dropped when he turned to leave, that he still feared the worst.

Her own shoulders sank at the thought. The least she could do was help find Tavelé. Take the blooming lesson. Not that she had nothing else to do. The translation service had called that morning wanting to move up her deadline, and then her aunt called when she was packing to leave. What had Aunt Ida said? Something about her mother's girlish laughter. Odd. She must not have heard right. Been too occupied trying to stuff the trumpet in her backpack. She had almost dropped it. But it was safe now, the bell bumping against the small of her back as she walked down the *callejón*.

Nacho passed her with a gunnysack of sand across his shoulders.

"*Chamba?*" he mumbled when he went by.

"*Ahorita, no.*" Not at the moment. She didn't need anything carried. Then she remembered and called after him. "But are you going to look for Tavelé?"

He turned and called back, "*Si, señora. No se preocupe.*"

She watched him continue down the stairs, his shoulders bent from the weight of the sand. Don't worry, he had said. How could she not? With Tavelé lost. And Armando as upset

as he was, and soon leaving. She'd done all she could think of
to help, even agreeing to take the trumpet lesson, though she
knew Tavelé wouldn't be there. There had to be some other
way she could help.

She looked up as if she could find the answer in the sky,
and her foot caught on a cobblestone. She reached out to a wall
to steady herself. Focus, Callie. And slow down. Better to get
there late than to break your neck. Actually, maybe she should
sit down. Scoot down the stairs. Oh, that was silly. She was not
disabled, just a little nervous. About Armando. But also about
the lesson. She did not know Pamela. And she had no good
reason for taking a lesson. What if Pamela asked her why she
wanted one?

"*El Niño Perdido*" floated through her mind. Oh, criminy.
Of course, Pamela would ask. Why hadn't she thought of that
before?

She turned to head back up the hill. She would call Pamela.
Explain that she'd been out of her mind. She had been, hadn't
she? A woman her age taking up the trumpet, of all things.
Pamela would understand. But Armando. What would she say
to him? She willed herself to turn and take another step down
the *callejón*. And then another. And another. She could do it.
Slow and steady. Almost to the corner. She wouldn't be late,
would she? She glanced at her watch, and so didn't notice the
loose cobblestone on the stair below. It tilted down when her
foot struck it, and she lurched forward. She began stumbling
and couldn't stop. Her father's voice came to her, "Roll." She
lowered her shoulder and closed her eyes. Her feet lifted off
the ground, and then her shoulder bumped into something soft
and strong. She opened her eyes and looked up into Nacho's
surprised face.

She pulled away, "*Perdón.*" She coughed. "*Perdón.*"

Nacho laughed and said that she had hit him, her head lowered like a bull.

"*Como un toro,*" he said, putting his index fingers up to his head to make horns. "*Un toro.*"

She watched him walk up the *callejón* with the empty gunnysack, turning several times to laugh at her.

She looked down the *callejón* of the geese and then down to the corner where she'd seen the Jehovah's Witnesses before. Where were they when you needed them? She shrugged and continued on to the lesson. Might as well get it over with.

"LET'S see your ax," Pamela said, motioning Callie to a folding chair opposite hers.

"What?"

Pamela laughed. "Your instrument."

"Oh." Callie unzipped her backpack and pulled out the trumpet. The leash was looped around its bell. Why in the world had she brought that thing! She glanced up.

Pamela was smiling. "Were you afraid it would run off?"

She felt her face redden. "Ah, no." She shook the trumpet, and the leash slid back into the backpack. She held out the trumpet, her hand shaking so much she almost dropped it.

"Hold on there, partner," Pamela said, taking the trumpet. "Is this your first lesson?"

She nodded.

"Well relax. Badgering students is old school." She turned the trumpet from side to side, checking it out. "Looks like a genuine Chinese knock-off." She took the mouthpiece out, put her own in, and played a scale. "It will do." She took out her mouthpiece and handed the trumpet to Callie. "You can put it away."

Put it away? Did Pamela suspect something? She wouldn't have called her "partner" if she had, would she? She unzipped her backpack, put the trumpet in, and then wiped her sweaty palms on her shirt.

"You won't need this either," Pamela said, holding up Callie's mouthpiece. "Some teachers start with buzzing, but not me."

She reached for the mouthpiece. What would Pamela start with?

"Just a minute."

She sat on the edge of her chair, holding her breath, waiting.

Pamela poked around in her bag and then drew out a little leather pouch. "This will protect it." She put the mouthpiece inside. "You'll need a case for your trumpet, too, if you want to avoid dents." She smiled. "I've got an extra one around here I can loan you."

Callie nodded and tried to smile back. So Pamela must be planning to give her a lesson, after all.

"Well then, let's get started." Pamela leaned forward. "When I was studying in Paris, my teacher told me 'Sound is a gift of the breath.'" She made a gentle swooping motion with her hand outward as if she were trailing the sound coming from her breath. "I like to think of playing that way, as offering gifts of the breath."

Callie smiled, pictured ribboned packages floating from the bell of her trumpet.

"The musician receives the gift, too. That's the best part. Once we learn to breathe, the sound comes along as effortlessly as if it were a gift. But like other gifts, the gift of sound is not always welcome. You may not like all the sounds you make."

If she could make a sound on a trumpet at all.

"But don't let that bother you." Pamela waved her index finger from side to side. "Pleasing is not the point. Focus, instead, on playing with integrity, expressing your own vision, speaking with your authentic voice. Especially when playing jazz."

Well, she didn't think she would be playing jazz . . .

"It's also useful to focus on being true to yourself, to your own musical expression, when playing classical music—though conductors may not agree." Pamela laughed. "And to do that, to speak from your heart, or your gut, you've got to relax, open up, and breathe fully and deeply. If you hold your breath, as if expecting something terrible to happen . . ." Pamela held in a breath and opened her eyes wide as if terrified, ". . . it probably will, at least when playing the trumpet."

Callie noticed that she, too, was holding her breath. Was she expecting something terrible to happen? She took in a deep breath. Pamela had seen the leash, but she had made a joke. She needn't worry about being found out.

"Watch how I am sitting, back straight and relaxed, feet against the floor. Now close your eyes. Feel how the chair supports the weight of your body."

Callie adjusted her weight. She felt heavy.

"Lift your heart when taking in a breath, and then relax your shoulders, letting your shoulder blades fall together."

Her back felt stiff from ramming into Nacho, but her spine felt protected when she drew her shoulder blades together.

"On the next in-breath, feel the length of your spine, from your tailbone to the base of your skull."

She found herself sitting taller.

"Rest your hands palms down on your knees. Feel the warmth of your knees against your palms."

She noticed the nubby texture of her linen pants.

"Feel the support of the floor under your feet. Let your toes expand and relax."

She wiggled her toes.

"Feel the surface of your feet. Feel how the soles and straps of your sandals feel against your feet."

She noticed several sore places on the underside of her toes. They must be from careening down the *callejón*.

"Feel the air against your feet and the freedom of your feet."

Too free—given her fall.

"Let out a slow breath. Tap your toe, one, two, three, four, as your breath goes out. When your breath is all the way out, let another breath enter slowly."

She tapped to four. Was her breath all the way out? She could not tell.

"Tap your toe, one, two, three, four, as the breath goes in."

This toe tapping was distracting.

"Let out the breath slowly. Let it out all the way. Then let it out more. Now let it out more. Push the last bit of air out with the muscles of your abdomen."

Her throat constricted from the effort.

"Now relax, all at once. Notice how your lungs fill effortlessly."

Her throat still felt a little tight, but air did flow into her lungs.

"Let the air out slowly."

Was she supposed to tap her toe again?

"Now breathe naturally."

She no longer knew what that was. At least she could stop tapping her toe.

"And feel the breath as it goes in and out of your nostrils."

That she could do. It tickled.

"Feel your tongue relax. Feel your throat open."

Oh, that did feel better.

"Now imagine a beautiful pitcher."

She recalled the crystal pitcher on Joyce's desk.

"Imagine that it's a warm day, and you are sitting in the dappled light of an oak tree by a small rapid in a brook. You are relaxed and happy."

She heard the water rippling. Happy? Yes. She imaged Gwendolyn there beside her, wearing her yoga clothes.

"You are holding the pitcher, and it feels light in your hand."

Crystal can be heavy . . . But Gwendolyn reached over to hold it with her, and then the pitcher felt weightless.

"When you tip the pitcher to the right, the waterfall fills it—effortlessly."

She watched the water splash into the bottom of the pitcher.

"When you tip the pitcher to the left, the water spills effortlessly back into the stream."

Yes, it did, and looked lovely, too, reflecting the dappled sunlight. She smiled, and so did Gwendolyn.

"Let out your breath completely. Imagine the pitcher tipped all the way, and the last drip of water falling into the stream."

She and Gwendolyn tipped the pitcher together. She let out her breath fully. It felt easier that time.

"Now take in your next breath. Feel how your breath goes to the bottom of your lungs, the way the water goes to the bottom of the pitcher."

Her breath *had* come in on its own. She and Gwendolyn looked at each other, breathing out and then in together, freely and naturally.

"You can open your eyes now."

Open her eyes? Then what would happen to Gwendolyn? She squeezed her eyes more tightly shut, but Gwendolyn disappeared anyway.

"Callie?"

She opened her eyes and saw Pamela leaning toward her.

"Oh, sorry . . . Is the breathing over?"

"The exercise, yes, but do keep breathing."

Callie laughed. "We . . . I liked pouring from the pitcher. That made it easier to let out the air, and then air just flowed back in all on its own."

"You have to learn to let go. That's the secret."

PAMELA'S cell rang. "Excuse me. I've got to take this. I have a feeling it's my house guests."

Left on her own, Callie took in the furnishings of the living room. Built along the opposite end was a wooden bench, lined with rolled sleeping bags. Above it were small-paned windows to the side garden. On the wall to the left hung a row of framed photos. One drew her attention. It had a building in the background that looked familiar. Her heartbeat picked up. Was it possible? She looked back toward Pamela, who was still giving directions complete with hand motions indicating steps and corners.

Pamela put her hand over the phone. "This may take a while. Stretch your legs."

Callie rose and walked as casually as she could to the photo. She took in a breath. A girl, dressed in a graduation robe, stood with an older couple in front of a tall blue sign: Wendell Phillips Academy High School. Written on a banner: "Congratulations Class of '81." She gasped, and then looked to see if Pamela noticed. No problem. She was concentrating on her directions. She turned back to the photo. Gwendolyn's high school. A predominantly African-American high school where Callie had volunteered. She had never seen her daughter there. She was sure of that when she saw her daughter's photo. She would have remembered that face. But perhaps she had seen Pamela. Maybe that's why *she* looked familiar. She leaned closer to the photo. But the girl in the photo didn't look like Pamela. Or did she? She studied the photo again and then looked back over to Pamela. Same eyes, same mouth and nose. Just different hair. She looked back toward the photo. The girl there had a short, trim afro. But, yes, she was Pamela. And the couple with her must be her parents.

The man, who resembled Nelson Mandela, wore a gray suit, and the woman a tailored black dress and a wide-brimmed hat with a white band. The man had his arm around Pamela, and the woman stood slightly apart. They were both turned toward Pamela, looking at her with warmth and love. Pamela, however, looked straight ahead and appeared uncomfortable. To the right of the graduation photo was another photo of Pamela, this time smiling broadly, and with her present hairstyle. She wore a tux and stood arm and arm with a woman dressed in a pearly-white kimono and wearing a headpiece that reminded Callie of the starched caps nurses once wore.

To the left of the graduation photo was a photo of Dizzy Gillespie wearing a fez and looking pensively at his trumpet with the tipped-up bell.

Callie glanced at Pamela, still on the phone, and then she looked again at the middle photo. Too bad it wasn't a group photo. There wasn't even anyone in the background. But someone had to take the photo. Who was that? She leaned closer, checking out the school windows to see if there was a reflection, but she couldn't make out anything. Well, the photographer could be Gwendolyn. And if so, she and Pamela had been friends, best friends even. Maybe they'd been friends from the time they were children. She imagined them sitting on the sidewalk, skinny legs splayed, playing jacks.

Wouldn't that be wonderful, taking a trumpet lesson from Gwendolyn's life-long friend? She took in the size of the school. Maybe she was going too far. Gwendolyn would have been a year ahead, and they would have only overlapped a year, since Gwendolyn had moved after her first two years. Still, it would be wonderful if she were in the living room of someone who knew her daughter. If only moments before she was learning to breathe from someone who knew her daughter. If sometime soon, her next lesson maybe—why not take another?—she would learn more about her daughter.

WELL, that wasn't so bad, Callie thought as she shut Pamela's gate behind her. She felt lighter as she walked along the *callejón*, the trumpet now in a case bumping against her leg like an old friend. She had wanted to ask Pamela if she knew Gwendolyn, but she could not think of a discreet way to mention her. She had not wanted to sound too much like the mother of a lost child. But it wouldn't have to be obvious. After all, she had volunteered at Wendell Phillips. That cover had worked before. No reason to think it would not work now. She could ask about students Pamela knew to see if they knew any in common. She would practice saying the words to make them sound natural. She would remember to breathe first. She wouldn't mention Gwendolyn's name, though. Still, if Pamela was Gwendolyn's friend, she would be sure to bring her up.

She stopped to savor the fragrance of orange blossoms hanging over a wall and took in a slow breath, tapping her toe. She would have another chance to ask, and soon. Pamela had asked her to take a walk on Sunday. Only a few days away, but time enough to think. Even with her weekend chores. Armando would be away. Oh, Armando. She slumped a little.

How would he feel if he knew about the walk? Betrayed, that's how. She squared her shoulders and started again. He *was* like that husband with the two heads. Jealous when there was no reason to be. That must be why he had said Pamela was dangerous. He resented the attention Maestro Chávez gave her.

When she rounded the corner, she noticed the loosened cobblestone and placed it to the side. She shook her head. What had gotten into her? Nervous about taking a trumpet lesson. She didn't even have to blow into it. All she had to do was breathe. Nothing to it. She continued up the *callejón*. She would practice every day, imagining the brook and the pitcher. Perhaps Gwendolyn would be there, too.

The sun felt good on her shoulders. She was happy. Gay. Wasn't that how her aunt had described her mother? Gay. Not a word she would have expected. Her mother's voice always gentle, always kind, had carried a hint of sadness since her father died. But, now that she thought of it, there had been a lightness in her mother's voice these last few months. She recalled how happy her mother had once been. How she would protest, "with my apron on and the dinner getting cold," when Callie's father beckoned her to dance, something they were expressly not to do, given their religion. How her father would respond, "Oh, don't bother about dinner. Callie doesn't mind, do you girl?" And, of course, she had not minded. Her parents would waltz around the kitchen table with her father whistling to the tune of "The Blue Danube." She had loved her mother's smile when she danced. It reminded her of a photo of her mother as a girl wearing the first dress she made herself. A shy, sweet smile. That smile of her mother waltzing in the kitchen. The same shy, sweet smile of the girl with the braids across her head wearing her newly made polka-dot dress.

Callie unlocked her door and entered her terrace. She

leaned over. Ah, a postcard. A reminder from the philosopher of the yearly silent retreat. She flipped it over and studied the view of the lake surrounded by high, forested hills. Maybe she would go this year—a thought she had had the previous five years but never acted on. On the other hand, she had never had a trumpet around before. Some quiet time might come in handy.

She looked at the lake again and then slipped the postcard into her pocket. Had the postman slid any other mail under her door? A letter from her mother, perhaps? She looked around the terrace floor, but didn't see anything. She tried to remember when the last letter from her mother had come. At least a couple of weeks ago.

But, now that she thought of it, her mother seemed to be tending less to her usual occupations. She had commented recently that she couldn't find the beans in her garden through all the weeds. When Callie asked if she had been ill, she laughed. "Oh, no. Just busy . . ." She hadn't specified further. What *was* she doing? Surely nothing to worry about. Not with that lilt in her mother's voice. Maybe her mother had taken out her father's trumpet. Found a teacher. Learned how to breathe.

Twelve

$\mathcal{S}$MILING AT THE IMAGE OF HER MOTHER PUFFING
out her cheeks, Callie picked up the phone to call her.
When it started ringing, she placed it between her ear and
shoulder and opened the trumpet case. She lifted the trumpet
and placed it on the dining table, its bell down. Would it fall?
She turned it on its side and looked closer. It was covered with
fingerprints. Her mother's phone continued ringing. Strange.
She was usually at home at that hour. Perhaps she was at Aunt
Ida's. Well, no need to interrupt their visit. She should call
Armando anyway. And get busy wiping off those fingerprints.

"DIGA," Armando answered, as was his custom. Still it threw
her off. "Speak" sounded so abrupt. She paused, and before she
could say anything, Armando said, "What took you so long,
Chou? You should have been back from Pamela's hours ago.
Are you all right?"

"I'm fine." She cradled the phone between her ear and
shoulder, lifted the trumpet, and began rubbing its bell with a
fold of flannel.

"She wouldn't give him to you?"

"She didn't have him. Anyway, I didn't see him."

"Well, no wonder," he said. "She had plenty of time to hide
him. You should have arranged the lesson earlier in the week,
Chou. Oh, well. I'll think of something else. At least you don't

have to bother with the trumpet. I'll get rid of it for you when I come back."

She cradled the trumpet against her chest.

"Can't think about it right now. I'm trying to figure out what to pack. How many *guayaberas* do you think I'll need? I was thinking of the linen ones with the narrow pleats, but maybe I should take some embroidered ones, too."

He sounded anxious, but no more anxious than on any other trip.

"Should I just use my black shoes or take my white ones, also? The men there usually wear white, but I'll be wearing black pants on the plane. By the way, I'm thinking of buying Claude and me matching Panama hats. Or would we look too much like the American couple? The one who dressed like they were after big game."

Callie smiled, recalling a middle-aged tourist couple they once saw wandering Guanajuato's plazas in matching safari shirts, pants, and hats. "I don't think you need to worry about that . . ."

"Right. I should save my worrying for Pamela. I overheard her badmouthing Maestro Chávez again today. What if she tries to get him fired?"

It would be better for everyone if the maestro would retire, sweet as he was. But she couldn't say so. He would think she was siding with Pamela.

"Maybe I should stay."

And stand up Claude? She cleared her throat, but paused before saying anything. He would never do that. "And waste all the time you've spent packing *guayaberas?*"

He laughed.

"Have you called your driver Jorge about taking you to the airport?"

"I'd better do that now. How was the lesson, by the way?"

She looked into the bell of the trumpet. What was she to say? He would not want to hear anything good about Pamela, and she could not mention Gwendolyn.

"Did she teach you anything or just talk about herself?"

If only she *had* talked more about herself—and her friends.

"I suppose she took most of the time showing you her house, the way Americans typically do."

"Well, not really." She exhaled on the valve casings and began wiping them.

"You mean you didn't ask for a tour? You didn't search, Chou?"

She thought of the graduation photo. "Sort of . . ."

"Are you sure you're okay, Chou? Pamela's such a pain. She didn't accuse you of anything, did she?"

"Accuse me?"

"Was she suspicious? Did she ask why you asked for a lesson?"

She gazed at the trumpet bell and thought of the leash dangling from it. Her chest tightened.

"I mean, it *is* a little odd, a woman your age—not that I think you're old, Choucita."

"She didn't seem suspicious." She shined the trumpet's lead pipe.

"No, I suppose she wouldn't be. She didn't question you at all, did she? Why would she? Wouldn't everyone want to study with the great Pamela? Like those groupies that followed her around. They were ridiculous the way they sat, eyes peeled on her at rehearsals. At the break one day, I told them to scram. One of them must have tattled. You should have seen how Pamela glared at me after the break. What a witch."

He was going too far. "Armando." She said his name softly hoping he would listen then.

"Okay, okay, Chou. Pamela plays well. I'll give her that. Very well, actually. Okay, great. But that doesn't give her the right to hide Tavelé." He paused a moment and then continued. "I've got an idea. Ask to see her house. I know. I know. It will be a pain. But you can do it, can't you? *Pour* Tavelé, Chou. For Tavelé."

She thought of Pamela talking about breathing from the core, about expressing your truest self. "She's really not so bad, Armando."

"Oh, you're just trying to make me feel better. You're too sweet, Chou."

"No. Actually . . ."

"Look, I've got to go. Anyway, thanks. Oh, and be sure to go to the symphony tomorrow. It's the last of the season, you know. Congratulate Pamela afterward. Then she's sure to ask you around."

"Actually . . . I'll see her soon anyway. Sunday."

"Why didn't you say so before? That's great."

"But . . ." She wanted to say there was no way Pamela would steal Tavelé. She might even help find him.

Armando interrupted. "Got to go. Bye, Chou."

She had no sooner hung up than he called again.

"I'm leaving right after the concert, but I'll call you from Veracruz. Got to go."

He hung up and then called again, this time to remind her to meet him before the concert for a complimentary ticket.

She held up the trumpet and turned it from side to side. Not a fingerprint anywhere. Might as well call Aunt Ida. She and her mother would have had time enough to catch up by now.

"Your mom? No, she's not here. If it weren't for the group and Sunday service, I'd never see her these days."

"The group?"

"The Democrat coffee klatch. Remember?"

"Oh, yeah." Strange her mother being seen on a regular basis with outspoken Democrats. Or had Aunt Ida quieted down?

"So you haven't heard from her?" Aunt Ida asked.

"Oh . . . Well, she said she's been busy. Crocheting, I imagine. But she wasn't at home when I called."

Ida laughed. "Then she hasn't mentioned any news to you?"

"News?"

"I think she has some, all right, but she's being tight-lipped about it," Ida said, laughing.

Callie relaxed. Can't be bad news, not with Aunt Ida chuckling like that. "Well, I have news, too. I have a new friend. I think. Anyway, I took a trumpet lesson from her." She took in a breath. She shouldn't have mentioned the trumpet.

"You've decided to play the trumpet?"

"Well . . ." She hesitated. She had an answer, but not one she wanted to say. Still, there was always Armando. "It was one of Armando's schemes. He thinks she has Tavelé."

"He's run away again? This time to the call of the trumpet?"

She laughed. "So Armando thinks."

"So you're posing as a trumpet student? And how did you come by a trumpet? I suppose Armando provided you with one."

"No, I had one."

"Oh, Juanito."

"How did you know?"

"That boy could sell you anything. Can you play a tune?"

"No, but I can breathe."

"That's handy."

Callie laughed. "And Pamela, my teacher, invited me to go for a walk."

"Oh. How's Armando taking that?"

Looks like he'd been complaining to Aunt Ida again. "It was *his* idea. He wanted me to get to know her, in case she does have Tavelé."

"And if she doesn't? Then what. You'll drop her?"

"Uh. No."

"Joking aside, Callie, there's something fishy going on here."

Her aunt was right about that. Still she wasn't about to say so. "You're always telling me to get out more. Meet new people."

"Under the pretext of looking for a dog?"

"Not just that . . . I like Pamela. She reminds me of you."

And she did, she realized saying it. They looked nothing alike. Her aunt, like Callie, was short and plump. But Pamela spoke her mind, like her aunt.

"And the trumpet?"

"I like that, too."

"Since when? Your father wanted you to play. Remember?"

She did remember. But only because he had learned that band class met at the same period as French. "That was different."

"Well, it's your life."

Yes, it was her life. And any friend of Gwendolyn's would be a friend of hers. She checked the trumpet again, and then put it back in the case.

If her mother was not crocheting, what was she doing? She rested her hand on the top of the case, tapping it while she thought. Her mother wouldn't be up to anything adventuresome. Not like Aunt Ida traipsing about the world, chasing mummies.

So, what could her mother's news be? She had been talking more about birds recently. Had she joined that birding group Aunt Ida mentioned? Or the choir? She'd said the new director had been trying to recruit her. And hadn't she mentioned a reading group? Could it be all three? Her mother suddenly social?

Whatever her mother's news, it would have nothing to do with babies. That Callie knew with certainty. After she had left home, her mother, who formerly reveled in such news, never again mentioned pregnancies, baby showers, or births. And so, after her father's death, when she went home for the first time in years, she had been surprised to see the church pews sprinkled with another generation of children.

Thirteen

HE WAITED FOR ARMANDO, AS USUAL, AROUND the corner from the concert hall. "I'm glad now you don't meet me in front," he said. "Pamela would be butting in, trying to give you her ticket."

Not likely, with her house full of visitors. Could she say that?

He gave her the ticket and started off. Then he turned back. "Don't forget to talk with her after the concert." He turned to look behind him, then back to her. "Don't worry. I'll stay clear." He kissed her cheeks, turned to go, and then turned back. "I'll call you."

She lingered, the way she always did, her face pressed into a newspaper, until the smokers put out their cigarettes and went in. At the balcony entrance, she paused to listen for the applause indicating the concertmaster had come onstage, and then, when she heard the oboe sound concert A, she opened the velvet curtains. A muffled baby's cry came from the area where she usually sat. The family, who had been watching for her, pointed to a seat in their row. She held up her thumb and forefinger to signal "in a minute."

When the maestro entered to warm applause, she looked toward the stage where she focused not on him bowing briefly to the audience, nor on Armando, but on Pamela whose broad shoulders rose from a shimmering narrow-strapped black dress and whose hair glowed under the stage lighting.

Armando's eyes, too, were on Pamela, as were the maestro's from the looks of it, since, after climbing to the podium and welcoming the orchestra with his arms held out widely, he stood with his head turned to the right toward the trumpet section. Callie found herself holding her breath until Armando coughed twice, and the maestro lowered his arms, smoothed the score flat against the music stand, and then raised his baton to begin.

She looked back at Pamela. And then at Maestro Chávez. Why? And then it came to her. The photo she once saw on the maestro's mantel of a tall young woman with shoulder-length auburn hair, wearing a low-cut velvet gown and singing with her arms held out on either side as if ready to embrace her audience. Armando had said the photo was of the maestro's wife, Patricia, taken shortly after they met.

Maestro Chávez and his wife would have made an unusual couple, she thought. The slight, bald conductor, forever diffident, from his gentle smile and tone of voice to the way he looked down at his feet when he shuffled across the stage. Even when conducting, he appeared to be inviting the orchestra to play rather than directing them.

The tall, broad-shouldered woman in the photo, on the other hand, had the bearing of that Minoan goddess who held a dangling snake in each of her outstretched hands. There was something of her in Pamela, too, that daring to grasp a snake. No wonder the maestro was transfixed. It was not Pamela he saw, but his beloved Patricia.

Fourteen

WHEN CALLIE WOKE TO THE ALARM AT FIVE A.M., it was still dark and chilly. Normally she would have lingered in bed on a Saturday, but today she leapt up. There was so much to do to be ready for her walk with Pamela the next day. She smiled as she stood in the shower, remembering waking several times in the night, already as excited as a child on Christmas morning. Silly, she knew, but it felt a little like that—hoping Pamela would talk about Gwendolyn. It wasn't too much to wish for. Had she not been a good enough girl? Oh, that *was* silly. Pamela knew her daughter or she did not. It had nothing to do with her. Still, while drying herself off, she couldn't help but think that she had better not cry, better not pout.

She dressed quickly, went upstairs to set up her breakfast tray, and then went back to her bedroom. All the while images came to her of Pamela and Gwendolyn, the two of them shoulder to shoulder in the cafeteria, passing notes in class, whispering secrets over the phone.

This is silly, she thought again when putting her tray down on her desk. She mustn't get her hopes up. She lifted and dropped her shoulders, as if that would help clear her mind. She took a sip of tea. Given the lesson, polishing the trumpet, and reassuring Armando about clothes, she hadn't made as much progress on her new translation as she would like. She would go straight to the library after her chores. Then she would finish up at home in the evening. By working efficiently, she would have everything done in time to see Pamela. Her daughter's friend. She imagined the two of them laughing over some private joke. Oh, my, she thought, there I go again. What would Aunt Ida say? She couldn't imagine her aunt getting lost in wishful thinking. And neither should she. She had to get on with her chores. But not all the usual ones. Perhaps there was something she could move to another day. She looked at the periodic table on the wall over her bed for inspiration. Everything there so nicely in order. She flipped through her rotary card file to the card with her list of chores for the first Saturday of the month. She moved her index finger down the items.

Weed and remove dry leaves from patio plants
Dust bedroom beams and bedroom furniture

She looked up. The beams didn't look too bad. She could get up early tomorrow to do them. She took a bite of yogurt and then made a sticky note, moving the beams to the Sunday list.

Check clothes in armoire for wear
Check socks for holes

She glanced at the hand-painted box where she kept her socks and then continued down the list.

Check items in medicine cabinet
Make muffins for Armando

Armando had left, so there was no reason to prepare things for him. But she needed to make something for the walk. Why not muffins? Was there anything she needed to add to the list? She looked up. She took out a sticky note, sharpened her pencil, and added *Pack the picnic backpack.*

Then she pulled out the card with the list *Things to take on picnics.*

*Sunscreen
*Water
*Cloth napkins
*Snacks: veggie sticks, fruit slices, deviled eggs or muffins

Ah, muffins were on the list, and she had just enough eggs for them. Well that settled it.

*First aid kit

She went to her bureau, took out the bag of first aid items, and put it on top of the bureau to check it. The latex gloves and the gauze pads were each in their own bag, and the tweezers and scissors shared a bag. These bags and the rest of the items fit perfectly in the larger bag, because she had made the bags herself. Everything was as it should be. All items present, everything in date, and the bags still in good shape.

She put the kit in the backpack, along with a bottle of water and the sunscreen. She would add the snacks the next morning. Was there anything else she needed?

She looked up. Oh, there was something. The cell Armando had given her for Three Kings Day. "Now I can reach you anytime," he had said. She started to put it in her backpack and then stopped. She hadn't called her mother. It was early. But still. At least she would be at home. No time like the present. But not on the cell. She put it away and then dialed her mother's number on the extension by her bed. She sat on the bed listening to the ring. She should give the cell number to her mother, just in case. Not that she was likely to call. Aunt Ida might, though, and she hadn't given her the number either. She had forgotten. And her mother? Was she getting forgetful? Was that why she hadn't written? She wasn't answering her phone either. She hung up the phone. Where was her mother now?

Perhaps she should get her mother a cell, though she couldn't see her mother accepting. She hadn't even given up her rotary for a digital phone. Callie hadn't wanted to accept a cell either, but she had, for Armando's sake. He worried less when he could reach her. Not that he would be worrying in Veracruz. He would settle down, as usual, once he was with Claude. She pictured the two young men walking through the plazas wearing their *guayaberas* and Panama hats, humming lines of music to each other, stopping at a café for coffee and sweet rolls. Armando might not call at all for a few days. Still, just in case he did, she would put a message on her machine to call her cell. She paused. Was that just announcing to potential burglars that she was not at home? Or would they imagine their target, listening, deciding whether to answer or not?

BACK in her bedroom after washing her dishes, she noticed the trumpet case by the armoire. She frowned. She had forgotten all about breathing. What would her daughter think? Where did that thought come from? She sat down on the end of the bed. Pamela. She might tell her friend Gwendolyn about the student who forgot to breathe. Of course, her daughter would not know that the student Pamela spoke of was she, her mother.

What *else* would Pamela have said? "She's a new student, an older woman who's taking trumpet lessons for the first time. She's at least fifty. Imagine that." What would her daughter think about that? A woman in her fifties taking up the trumpet. It sounded, now that she thought of it, adventurous. But she was not adventurous. Goodness knows how much effort it took Aunt Ida to get her to go away. So, Pamela would be giving her daughter a false impression. She should be clear with Pamela that she's not adventurous, though she's taken a trumpet lesson. And moved to Mexico. After all, she hardly left her house other than to go to the library. She could be living anywhere, really. She could slip in that information when walking with Pamela.

But then she might sound like a recluse. And that was not so either, regardless of what Aunt Ida thought. After all, she did agree to take the walk with Pamela, whom she barely knew, and she went out with Armando, and she went to the symphony. Her daughter shouldn't think her anti-social.

She noticed she was hyperventilating. She had gotten carried away. Here she was sitting on the bed, imagining all kinds of things, when she should be checking the armoire. Pamela may never have met Gwendolyn. She looked at her watch. Still, she would do her breathing, just in case. She could spare twenty minutes.

But where? She looked around her bedroom, then through the windows to the patio. Under the avocado tree, of course. There would be the most oxygen there. If she were lucky, Gwendolyn would come back, too. She moved a chair to the patio, set a timer for twenty minutes, and sat the way she had at Pamela's. She tried to remember what Pamela had said. About the stream of water. The way it filled the crystal pitcher. She imagined her lungs as the pitcher, filling and emptying.

Her body felt grounded and yet light, as if it were floating. She sat there breathing to the image of the pitcher receiving and pouring pure, sparkling water.

When the timer went off, her eyes popped open. Someone

had come to the stream and helped her hold the crystal pitcher, but it hadn't been her daughter. It was Jacob. She stood up quickly. She couldn't linger there. She had things to do.

She moved the chair back to her bedroom, opened her armoire, and looked at the clothes. They suddenly looked so, well, dowdy. Jacob came to her again, teasing her about the "uniforms" in her closet in Chicago: baggy flood pants in browns and beiges, loose-fitting, cream-colored tops. Here it was years later and her closet looked the same. Could all her tops really be the same style and color? She looked through them. So they were.

She took out an armful of clothes and laid them carefully on the bed so they would not slide. She shrugged. She didn't have Pamela's sense of style. That was for sure. Did her daughter? Or did she favor yoga attire, like she had on in the photo?

She took out the rest of her clothes, wiped the inside of the armoire with a damp sponge, and then, after checking each piece carefully, put them back one by one. Then she glanced through the clothes once more, looking for something she could put in the give-away basket she kept for Doña Petra and Juanito. She took out a sweater she had bought from an elderly woman sitting on a *callejón*. She had never worn it. That would do. She did not wear her parka or lined wool slacks much either, but she needed them now that she visited her mother every Christmas.

The week after she had returned to Chicago from her father's funeral, she received a letter from her mother saying, "I would like you to come home for Christmas this year. I can buy your ticket." She had worried that her mother thought she would not otherwise go home. But with her father's death, she no longer had a reason to stay away. And, besides, she knew Christmas that year would be painful for her mother. She had chastised herself on reading the letter. She should have been the first to bring up going home. She called her mother immediately and said of course she would come, and she would be happy to buy her own ticket. And so she did, arriving on Christmas Eve and attending service with her mother on Christmas morning, choking up during the first hymn, recalling her father's warm baritone.

Still, when her mother had tried to give her his trumpet—"He would have wanted you to have it, Dear"—she would not take it. "You must be kidding," she had said, recalling how her father had tried to distract her from French, and then softened at the hurt look in her mother's eyes. "I would like the photo of Dad on the basketball court."

She swiped the dust cloth across the framed photo on her bureau. There he was at eighteen, his curly red hair, freckled nose, and stocky frame. He was short for a basketball player, but agile and effective. "The Glove," they had called him.

She looked at her watch. Where had the time gone? She must get the muffins made.

She ran upstairs to light the oven. Nothing happened. Had she run out of gas? She went outside to switch to the second tank. But she still could not get the stove to light. Had there been a leak? She hadn't smelled it. She must have forgotten to have it refilled when it ran empty. Strange.

She poked her head out the door. There was no one on the *callejón*. It was, after all, only 8:30 a.m. and a Saturday, but the gas man came by every morning and should be there soon. She went back to the kitchen to get everything ready, each ingredient in its separate bowl.

When "*gas . . . gas butano*" drifted up from the *callejón* below, she went to the door and yelled *gas* herself until the man arrived to change the tank.

A couple of Jehovah's Witnesses looked at her hopefully when she let him out.

The doorbell rang repeatedly while she stirred the muffins. Must be them again. She frowned and stood her ground. Surely she had a right to her privacy on a Saturday morning. She imagined herself explaining that to them. Then she caught herself over-stirring the muffins—thanks to those meddling Witnesses. Her muffins would not rise as high as she liked. Oh, well. She shrugged, put the pan in the oven, and then went downstairs to finish the armoire.

When she opened the armoire, Jacob came to mind again. She recalled seeing him for the first time at one of the schools in African-American neighborhoods where she went to watch the children. Various men, when looking about the auditorium, had lingered a moment over her, in spite of her being in the back, her hair covered with a black scarf. But none of them drew her attention until she noticed the tall, lanky man whose looks and comfortable air of confidence reminded her of Noah.

He seemed to be working the crowd, going up to everyone there. "Jacob," he said, when introducing himself to her, "but everyone calls me Jake." Everyone but her. She called him Jacob. He said she sounded like a schoolmarm, but he seemed to like that about her. She sensed that she could be her shy, reticent self with him. He didn't take it personally as some had, including her own father, who should have known better, calling her "standoffish" or "stuck-up."

"I've got a nephew in this performance." He had no children of his own, he had told her, and then added, "Yet." He was, he said, "waiting for the right broad-hipped woman." He had looked at her, as if she might be the one. Impertinent, she thought.

"Are you, like me, a family member?" He laughed. "Not that you look like one."

So, she told Jacob of her tutoring, not the full story, of course, and he accepted it without question. Though he had been surprised to learn she lived so far away when he offered her a ride. "Oh, don't worry," she had said, "I can take the L."

From then on, he often sat next to her at events, but in spite of that passing glance at her hips, he didn't ask her out. For that she was relieved, she thought. Though she was curious. Was he gay? Or did he have a deranged wife in his attic?

She really didn't care. It was easy to be around him, as there was always something else to focus on, which he did well, passing along scuttlebutt about the new cheerleader uniforms or the real reason the understudy was taking over for the lead in the school play. He had a low, warm laugh she liked, and though it was Noah she thought of when Jacob first ambled toward her, she gradually found herself drawn to him for himself.

She was comfortable, too, because, when the play or game or concert came to an end, he politely took his leave to mingle with the crowd, allowing her to slip out on her own.

It turned out he, too, attended school events with an agenda, one he shared readily enough with her. He was a social worker doing community building, and he sought connections with parents through their children. And so, she learned, he went to events even when he had no nephew or niece involved, as she occasionally went to one when no student had invited her, and more so as her comfort with him grew. Eventually she was attending events all weekend long at one school or another, and, often as not, he would show up, too, and make his way through the crowd, nodding and shaking hands until he was by her side.

One night he got it out of her that she, like he, had no reason to be at that particular event other than to be together.

Only then did he invite her out. "How about sitting beside each other somewhere else, a place for adults?" he asked, and when he described the jazz club he had in mind, she liked the idea. It would be dark, and they could sit in a corner. She wouldn't be expected to talk to anyone but him. "I don't drink," she had said. But neither, it turned out, did he, and so it seemed easy enough for her to say okay. And that's how she had slipped down the slope into his arms.

THE timer rang the moment she finished the armoire. When the muffins were out of the oven and cooling, she changed from her sweats into one of her "uniforms." Then she packed her other backpack for working in the library. At the terrace door, she lifted her hand to open the lock and then remembered the silk scarf Armando had brought her from Paris. Just like the ones Claude's aunts wore to cover their hair when dusting, he had said. Too lovely for dusting, she thought, but just right for sun protection. She went back downstairs, found the scarf, and tied it around her throat. She caught a glimpse of herself in a window on the way down the *callejón*. The scarf was lovely. Too bad Armando wasn't there to see it.

Fifteen

ALLIE HAD BEEN SO EXCITED THE NIGHT BEFORE that she couldn't go to sleep, and then she had over-slept that morning and so had not been able to dust the beams as planned. Nor did she have time to breathe. She had showered, dressed, added the muffins to the backpack, and was halfway up the *callejón* to the Panorámica, where she would meet Pamela, before she remembered the leash. Armando had called the night before to remind her to take it along. Then he went on for some time complaining about Pamela insisting on seeing Callie on Sunday, which was *his* day with her, as Pamela had weaseled out of him before he had known better than to tell *her* anything.

Callie had wanted to respond that Pamela could hardly be faulted for selecting "their day" for a walk while he was not in town. And she had hoped to tell him about her insight that Pamela reminded the maestro of his wife in her youth. But she didn't have a chance to do either. When Armando finished his rant, he said he had to get back into the club—Claude was waiting—and hung up before she could say anything.

SHE paused on the *callejón* and looked at her watch. There was time to go back for the leash, though she would have to move more quickly than she liked.

When she opened her door after retrieving the leash,

Juanito was standing there. "I rang your bell yesterday, and you didn't answer."

"Sorry, Juanito, I thought you were . . . ah . . . well, I was busy."

"Look what I have for you."

A letter from her mother, delivered to his grandmother's by mistake. Not the first time. She should have guessed.

"Just a minute," she said, as Juanito was turning away to leave. She would walk up the hill with him. She went back in to lay the letter on the dining table. When she turned to leave again, the jaguar by the door looked at her with reproach.

She went to the kitchen and wrapped up some muffins for Juanito, his younger sister, and his grandmother, Doña Petra.

After Juanito bid her "*Que te vaya bien*" at his doorway, she noticed a couple of Jehovah's Witnesses gaining entry to a house further up the hill. Better them than me, she thought. Then it came to her that she hadn't reviewed her answers to personal questions that might come up with Pamela.

When Armando had asked her about men in her life, she had distracted him with the potential husbands, all of whom, for one reason or another, died before the wedding. He had loved her stories and started making up ones of his own. His husbands, however, never died. They were always still out there somewhere, hoping. Several of them, wearing scarfs and berets, in Paris.

They had enjoyed playing that little game together, when walking along looking for Tavelé. But then there had been that time when he named one of them "Noah." She stopped for a moment to catch her breath. Diverting the question with fictional husbands wouldn't be the way to go with Pamela, in any case. If the topic came up, she would give her standard reply. She liked living on her own.

And if Pamela asked about children? Well, she had had plenty of practice with that question, since every child in the barrio and almost every other Mexican, including taxi drivers, asked first thing, "Do you have children?" That was something she could not joke about. She had told them the truth. She would love to have a child. "It's not too late," a taxi driver once said to her. "I hope not," she had dared reply.

She looked at her watch and realized she needed to hurry up. She did not want to be late. Nor did she want to trip herself up this time.

She trudged up a few more stairs. The backpack did not make it any easier, not that she had stuffed it full. No trumpet bumping against her back. Just the picnic items. And the leash. Would it help if she stuck her tongue out and panted like a dog?

And to think that just yesterday under the tree her breath was slow and relaxed. If she practiced regularly would she breathe that way wherever she was? It could pay off with deadlines, since she typically ended up hyperventilating as they drew close. She had almost passed out once.

A baby's breath speeds up, too. She had watched her baby's chest rise and fall, slowly and then more quickly. Had listened to the little sounds she made. Had noticed, cradling her in her arms, how time disappeared. And then the nurse came, and the social worker. And the baby was gone.

Now her baby was a grown woman with children of her own. A grown woman who knew nothing about her. She stopped. A grown woman who had made no effort to find her. A grown woman who didn't want to know her. Isn't that what she would learn from Pamela? That Gwendolyn had no desire to know the woman who let her be taken away.

She felt her heart racing. What had come over her, agreeing

to take a walk? A lesson was one thing. Conversation focused on the techniques of breathing and, eventually, she assumed, the details of playing the mouthpiece and trumpet. That was fine. But this. This meandering across the hills. That was another. Anything could come up. And it was not what Armando had in mind when he asked her to see Pamela again. She was to go to Pamela's house. Not to the mountains. Tavelé never ran off there. She really should stay home. She had those beams to dust.

She continued up the hill. She would explain it all to Pamela. She would understand.

SHE startled when she saw the Mustang convertible. Pamela had said, "I'll be in a red car." Then she added, "Don't worry. You can't miss me."

She did not know much about car makes, unlike Armando, who knew all of them, though he did not drive. But she knew a Mustang when she saw one. There had been a couple in her high school, the tight end on the football team and the head cheerleader. His father had given him a red Mustang when he graduated. They died in it.

Pamela got out of the car when she saw her, and called, as she walked toward her. "Ready?"

She hesitated. No. She had no business going off into the hills and certainly not in a convertible. She would not be asking Pamela any questions about her friends. That's for sure.

Pamela came closer. "Are you all right? You look pale."

She paused. She should be at home. The beams. A new translation. She had some more lists to make, too. And there was Tavelé to look for. "Well, I am feeling a little . . . off." Her head ached, didn't it? Was it a migraine coming on? She had never had one, but there was always a first time.

"Here, let me help you." Pamela reached for her backpack. "A walk in the country is just what you need."

A walk where anything could come up? She didn't think so. She stepped away from Pamela's reach. She really should get home. So why didn't she just say so? Nothing was stopping her. Pamela had even given her an opening, saying she looked pale. But Pamela looked so hopeful. How could she let her down? She took in the lines of the car. Imagined them crumpled.

Pamela noticed her gaze and walked back toward the Mustang. She patted the hood. "I bet you don't see many of *these babies* around here."

"No. Not around here." But she had seen them plenty of times. Never without thinking of the young couple who had died.

"Well, come on. We can put your backpack here."

She approached the car following Pamela's gesture. There in the back seat was a leash. A leash? Had Armando been right after all? She sighed and slipped out of the backpack straps.

Pamela took it from her and tossed it in the back seat. "Nothing breakable I hope." She shut Callie's door behind her and then got in herself. "Tighten up your seat belt."

She leaned back in her seat, resigning herself to death.

Sixteen

I'M GLAD YOU COULD COME TODAY," PAMELA said. "I've had some company, but I haven't made any friends here. Oh, I played a few times with some of the mariachi guys. But I don't know enough Spanish to strike up a conversation with them." She stopped and signaled for a woman holding the hand of one child while carrying another to cross the road. Then she drove on. "I thought Armando and I would become friends. He plays in a Latin band—he's good, you know, and he invited me to jam a couple of times. But when I asked him about gay clubs in town, he gave me the cold shoulder, and it's only gotten worse since. What is it with him, anyway?"

Had Pamela suspected Armando was gay? "Well . . ."

"Oh, don't worry, I don't expect you to explain for him. Anyway, I've wanted to get to know you even before you tossed that margarita down my back."

She felt her face begin to glow again.

Pamela laughed, but then, noticing Callie's discomfort, she reached over and put a hand on her arm. "Oh, don't feel bad. I was feeling sorry for myself that night, and the splash brought me out of it. That, and you, looking so distraught." She put her hand back on the steering wheel. "Anyway, before Armando stopped talking to me, he mentioned this friend of his who taught him French grammar and who was also a wiz at Spanish. That's you, right?"

"A wiz. Well, I am not sure."

"Well, he insisted you were. But tell me, did you really have twenty-six husbands? I've been dying to ask you, but I didn't want to ask at your lesson. I hope it's not too personal."

Too personal. The husbands. No. Though she was surprised Armando had mentioned them. "Well, no." She smiled. "I've never been married."

"Well, I am married. Not in the eyes of the law, mind you. But in the eyes of those who matter. And happily."

If only Armando could come to see himself that way. Happily married to Claude. But how could he, when he wouldn't even tell anyone in Guanajuato other than Callie of his love?

"She would be here now, but she's at an artist's retreat, making a new dance. She's talented, as well as beautiful. But then you've already seen that for yourself."

"I have?"

"My photo gallery. Didn't you notice her?"

"In the kimono."

"Yes, Ami Mai. I won't get to see her when I am in the States, alas, but I will see an old friend from high school."

She took in a breath. What if it were Gwendolyn? Those images that kept coming to her of Pamela and Gwendolyn as friends. Could they be true?

Pamela turned off the panoramic road along the hills above Guanajuato and headed up a gravel road on the edge of a ridge that dropped down to a mountain stream. A battered truck loaded with chunks of bluish-green stone lumbered down the road toward them.

"We went to school together. Graduated a year apart." Pamela looked toward her. "She was my best friend." She laughed. "We would stay up all night on weekends. Shared all our secrets. You know, the way high school girls do."

Best friends. Then Gwendolyn would surely come visit.

She imagined waiting with Pamela at the airport, seeing her daughter emerge from customs, hearing her voice, shaking her hand. And then she caught her breath. How would she contain herself? What if she blurted out something her daughter did not want to know? She peered over the side of the road to the stream below. A long way down.

Wouldn't it be better if Pamela had known Gwendolyn casually? That one day, maybe today, Pamela would mention her in passing. Perhaps some forgotten memory of a girl from her high school. She hadn't known her long. They had only overlapped a year. But she suddenly found herself thinking of her. Maybe something about her, herself, reminded Pamela of that classmate. Like the way she paused before she spoke. Now, what was her name? Pamela would say. Oh, she thought it started with a G. Gina. No. Not Gina. And then Callie would give a hint. Gwen? Could it be Gwen? Ah, yes. Pamela would say, "Gwendolyn. Like in *The Importance of Being Earnest.*" Wouldn't that be lovely? Gwendolyn, Pamela's acquaintance. Remembered, because of Callie. Lovely. And safe. She crossed the fingers on both hands and turned toward Pamela.

"She went to college the year before me."

As had Gwendolyn.

"She took her finals early, so she could be there for my graduation."

She held her breath and looked at the road just in time to see Pamela swerve out of the way of the truck. The dust kicked up by the passing truck made her cough until tears began to form.

Pamela pulled over. "Sorry about that." She waved at the cloud of dust. "There are some drawbacks to convertibles." She offered Callie a bottle of water and noticed her crossed fingers. "You can uncross them now," she said. "We're safe."

Safe? She tried to laugh, but she could not stop coughing, and the tears were getting worse. Her face felt hot and her arms sweaty. What a sight she must be.

"Try taking a breath," Pamela said. "Slow and steady. Notice the feeling of the air going in your nostrils. Follow it down into your lungs."

Once the dust settled, the air felt fresh and clean. Her throat started to relax.

"Breathe out. Notice how the air feels warm now."

"Thank you." She had never stopped coughing so quickly. But it could start up again. She might as well ask, while she had a chance. "Who, ah, who is she?" She started coughing again.

"Be patient. Follow another breath."

If she waited, she might not ask. She managed to get the question out between coughs. "Your high school friend?" She put her hand over her mouth to muffle the coughing.

"Oh, sorry. Her name is Jenny. Jenny Thompson. She's a dancer. I have her to thank for Ami Mai. She introduced us."

She sighed. "Oh." She was safe. But her sigh felt more like one of disappointment than of relief. She untied her scarf and wiped the tears from her eyes.

"I'm sorry I didn't know you before. I could have introduced you when she was here."

"Jenny?"

"Oh, sorry. No. Ami Mai. She managed a weekend here before going off to the artists' retreat. She would have stayed longer, but my move took her by surprise. Well, took both of us by surprise. But it threw her more than me. I jump into things, but she likes everything planned in advance. She was a good sport about it, though. And she has a sabbatical coming up soon. She'll figure out some way to stay here."

Once Pamela got started talking about Ami Mai, her words

of love flowed like the mountain stream, sparkling with energy, thundering in places, quiet and deep in others, and always fresh and clear. Awash in Pamela's words, Callie felt at the same time calm and exhilarated. She couldn't wait to speak to Armando, to tell him what she felt had to be true. That if he would let his words of love for Claude flow freely, then nothing could stand in their way.

Seventeen

*P*AMELA GESTURED TO THE HILL THAT ROSE BEYOND a small community of one-story houses, all made of the blue-green stone they had seen in the truck. "I can't wait to see the mine shafts."

Mine shafts. Callie shuddered recalling the time she had been invited to descend. "Do it," Armando had said. "You'll get a view of mining those documents you translate can't provide." The cables that lowered the cage had looked strong, and after the initial jolt, the ride was smooth enough, but, even so, she had broken out in a sweat approaching the darkness below and had blacked out before they reached bottom. Still, she knew plenty about mines, not just from documents, but also from reading up on Guanajuato's mining history. She could tell Pamela about the precious metals hidden deep in bedrock so hard in places that it took hours of labor to break through inches of it, the work so dangerous in colonial times that the miners, adolescents most of them, survived only a few years.

Pamela pulled up by a small building with a rusty Coca-Cola sign over a waist-high window. She nodded toward the window. "They'll know where the ruins are." She got out of the car and waved to a boy who had come to the door of the house. Then she walked over to him and started gesticulating with her hands.

The boy seemed to understand and pointed to a road through the village.

Callie, meanwhile, had gotten out of the car and approached the two.

"You see," Pamela said when she noticed Callie. "I told you they would know."

"So you understand what he said?"

"Not really, beyond starting at the village," Pamela said. "But you will. How about asking him to make a map."

Callie laughed, remembering Juanito once making a map for her.

"What's so funny?"

"If his map is anything like the one my neighbor boy made for me, it will look like spilled spaghetti."

Pamela laughed. "Better than nothing."

The boy told Callie he could take them to the mine shaft, if they liked. But if they preferred to use a map, he would make one. Then he could stay and watch the car.

Pamela chose having him watch the car. "It will be fun following a map. And, besides, did you see how big his eyes got when he saw this baby?" She made circles using her thumbs and forefingers to show the size.

The boy pored over his map for some time and then walked them through the village, all the way peppering Callie with questions for Pamela about the car. At the other side of the village, he stopped by a nopal cactus, its pads edged with fruit, like lines of tiny barrels, and pointed toward the path they were to take. A path that, as far as Callie could see, crisscrossed with numerous other paths through the landscape of rocky soil, occasional vines with tiny flowers, and scattered cactus. She considered asking the boy to guide them after all, but he had been so enthusiastic about the car that she didn't want to disappoint him, and, besides, she told herself, they could survive on nopal fruit, if need be. Pamela concurred, and so off they went.

Callie cleared her throat several times, preparing to begin her discourse on mining when Pamela said, "Now it's my turn for questions."

She took in a breath.

"So what brought you to Mexico?"

A safe enough topic. She let her breath out. "Mummies."

"Mummies?"

"Well, they brought my aunt Ida, and I came along to keep her company."

"And you liked the museum so much that you stayed?"

She laughed. "I haven't been to it."

"No? It's grisly, but fascinating. You're a translator, Armando said. Is that why you moved?"

"Oh, not really, I could translate almost anywhere."

Pamela turned to her and asked, "But you're not thinking of moving are you?"

She sounded worried, which surprised Callie. "Oh, no. No."

"That's nice," Pamela said. "But then, if it wasn't for the mummies, why *did* you move here?"

"I was walking along the *callejón* where I now live and saw the limb of a tree reaching out over a stone wall. Actually, that's why I moved here, I think. That limb. It looked as if it were beckoning me."

Odd, she thought, her openness. She had not even described the limb that way to her aunt. Was it Pamela? Armando, it seemed, had been open with her. He had, after all, mentioned the husbands. Had he let anything else slip?

"I know what you mean," Pamela said. "Something beckoned me, too."

"Not an avocado tree."

"No," Pamela laughed. "Though I love guacamole. I tried out for the job because I was tired of gigging, but what drew me, once I got here, was the people. They're kind." She raised her eyebrows. "Well, with a certain exception."

By Pamela's look, she knew she meant Armando, but she chose not to comment. Instead she translated something Juanito once said when enthusing over Guanajuato: "Even the drunks are nice."

"And everyone's some shade of brown. Well, most people, anyway. I have to admit, I like that. But how do you feel. Being so white?"

Callie coughed. What a question.

"Oh, I hope that didn't offend you. Ami Mai says my directness can be off-putting. But I like to get right down to things."

"I see. Well, I did feel like I stuck out like a sore thumb, at first. I suppose I still do." She thought about being called *güera* and coughed again.

Pamela stopped and offered Callie her water bottle again.

"Oh, that's okay, I have some." She reached in her backpack.

They stood for a moment, sipping water.

Then Pamela said, "There's something about you. You listen. Has anyone ever told you that? How you listen?"

Jacob had said he had never seen anyone listen the way she did. "It's as if nothing in the world draws your attention more than my words." He had laughed then. "*When* you listen. Other times you seem miles away."

"I noticed at your lesson. You don't interrupt. You don't wait for a pause and then go on about your own experiences. You just, well, listen. I feel like I could tell you my whole life story."

Pamela's whole life story. That *could* include Gwendolyn. Couldn't it? If only there were a way to ask.

"But I won't, don't worry. Ami Mai taught me that. I should show interest in others, not just talk about myself—and the trumpet."

The trumpet. Another safe topic. Maybe she needn't have worried so.

"And I *am* interested. I just got into the habit of being the center of attention. Raised as an only child, you know. And you, do you have a host of siblings?"

"No." But then she hadn't needed siblings to avoid being the center of attention. Not with her father.

"Well, welcome to the club. Did you ever want siblings?"

"Not really. I liked playing alone." Even as a little child she had felt cozy alone in her room reading a picture book. "Did you miss siblings?"

"No way. I preferred the attention of a parent. Ideally, both of them. Mother says that before I went to school—when she had me on her hands all day long—she would arrange play dates with neighbor kids, hoping to have some breathing time. She would set us up with toys and then sneak off to bake a pie in peace. But it wouldn't be long before I would pull on her apron, wanting her to come play." She laughed. "Then when Dad came home, I'd go to his study and insist *he* join in." She laughed again. "Now let's get back to you, where did you come from?"

Another safe question. She smiled. "Well, I was born in a small town in Missouri, but I lived in Chicago many years."

"Chicago? You know I'm from Chicago?"

"I recognized your high school. Actually, I tutored there for a while." What had come over her? She hadn't needed to say that much.

"You weren't that woman who sat in the back at band concerts?" Pamela asked. "The one with the black scarf."

She felt her face burning. She had hoped to disguise her difference, covering her light hair with the dark scarf.

"We were all curious about her."

They had talked about her? She fanned her face with her hand. Would Gwendolyn have joined in? Her hands felt sweaty.

"But then a friend told me she had invited a white woman, her tutor, she said."

"That must have been me." She wiped her hands on her shirt.

"Mystery solved." She laughed.

She felt her shoulders relax and smiled.

"But I didn't recognize you here. Or you me, I imagine." She took off her hat and shook her curls loose. "Not with this hair." She laughed again.

She smiled.

"So you were that woman. Small world." She spread her arms out and spun around.

She looked around. "Small world. Yes. But big enough to get lost in. Which is where I think we might be now. Lost."

Pamela handed her the map. "How about trying to decipher this?"

She took her time. Time enough, she hoped, to get off the topic of her in the back of the auditorium. It was safe enough, thanks to her cover story. But still it made her think of Jacob, which she didn't want to do. How even after they had parted, he would come sit next to her. How his shoulder brushing against hers had filled her with desire.

She supposed the delay worked, since, after they figured out the route, Pamela switched to a different topic. "Have you ever thought about what type of grandmother you'd like to be?"

Where did *that* question come from? And how could she

answer it without giving herself away? She couldn't say one who's privileged to know her grandchildren. Best to deflect. "I didn't realize grandmothers came in types."

"According to Ami Mai's research they do. Sporty. Adventuresome. Conventional. Arty. Hippie. Distant."

Distant. She didn't want to go there. Research. That was better. "Is Ami Mai doing research for a dance about grandmothers?" She could be helpful with that. "She could use the Purépecha dance of the *viejitos*. Instead of children portraying little old men, they could become little old ladies bent over their canes, clacking their wooden sandals."

Pamela laughed. "Not a bad idea. But she wasn't researching a dance." She paused, as if trying to decide how to go on and then continued, "They didn't have a category 'Aproned,' but that would have been my grandmother. My mother's mother. I didn't know my father's. I never saw Granny without an apron. Well, hardly ever. She took it off for Sunday morning service. But otherwise she always had one on, the pinafore type, like the aprons kindergarten children wear here. She loved to cook, Granny. Just picturing her turning pieces of chicken in a sizzling skillet makes my mouth water. I'd like to be a grandmother like her. Cooking up delicious foods. That and playing the trumpet, of course. But here I am going on about me again. What about your grandmothers? Would you like to be like them?"

Callie told Pamela she had not known either of them, since her father's mother had died when he was small and her mother's shortly after her own birth. "Sometimes," Callie said, "I pretended our next-door neighbor was my grandmother. I used to climb the tree in our backyard and watch her weed her garden. She wore a cloth sunbonnet."

"Oh, a bonneted granny."

She laughed. "When she saw me, she would ask my mother if I could come help her. When we finished, she would offer me snickerdoodles from a tin."

"Silent as a mouse," she recalled Mrs. Wilson saying to her mother when she walked her back home from her first visit. "Silent as a mouse, your Callie." Mrs. Wilson's grandchildren had been there that day. But the next time, when she was the only guest, she had talked nonstop. She didn't remember anything she had said, but did recall Mrs. Wilson saying, "Oh, Callie, you are droll," and how she had rushed home afterward to look up the word.

"So," Pamela said, "Would you like to teach your grandchildren to garden and then offer them snickerdoodles?"

Callie nodded. She would be happy to offer her grandchildren anything. Gardening, cookies, new words. Anything. If only she could.

They stopped to check the map again. Callie looked around and then tapped on the "R" for "ruin" marked on the map. She pointed off to the right. "It's that way to the ruin. Looks like the mine shaft is not far beyond it." They started walking.

Now that they were near the mine shaft, it seemed appropriate to fill Pamela in on some mining history, Callie thought. But she had barely started when Pamela interrupted with a question. At first, she thought she hadn't heard right. "What was that?" she asked.

"I said 'What do you think about babies?'"

An image of her baby curled by her chest came to her mind. She stopped to catch her breath. "Babies?"

Pamela stopped, too. "Sorry, I just can't focus on minerals at the moment. You see, Ami Mai and I are planning to have one. A baby."

"Oh, you and Ami Mai." So that was why Ami Mai was reading about grandmothers? Why hadn't Pamela just said so?

"Well, what do you think?"

"I think that's wonderful."

Pamela started walking again, waving her hands as she told of their plans. Not just one baby, but two. They would be close enough in age to play together and far enough apart to give the first one a good start before the second came along. Ami Mai had it all figured out. "Like I said, she plans everything—to the last detail." Ami Mai wanted to go first because she was "'not getting any younger'—can you believe she said that?" but she had some performances coming up that she didn't want to do pregnant. "Not that she's one of those choreographers whose dancers all look prepubescent. Actually, that's why she and my friend Jenny became fast friends. Jenny's a fantastic dancer but doesn't get many parts because she's plump. Pleasingly plump. Kind of like . . ." She glanced at Callie, then went on. "Anyway, Ami Mia created a dance starring Jenny. It was the hit of the camp." Ami Mai worked with disabled dancers, too, people whose movement was blocked in one way or another. "Kind of like me. I help students whose air is blocked. People who would sing, if only they could breathe."

Like her? Had she stopped breathing again? Well, she did not want a lesson on breathing now. She wanted to know how they planned to get pregnant.

Pamela returned to the subject without prompting. She explained, as they walked along the rocky path, that she and Ami Mai had thought of adopting, but they both wanted a baby genetically related to them. "An Ami Mai-Pamela baby." When they told Nori, Ami Mai's older brother, he offered to donate sperm. "We didn't even have to ask. I felt bad for having thought him a nerd," Pamela said. "But you would know what I mean, if you saw his studio." She rolled her eyes. "Sterile."

Sterile. Callie thought of the masks and straw animals the philosopher had left. Were they enough to save her house from a similar judgment?

Besides being a computer wizard, Nori was an amateur dancer. "Even Armando can't top his salsa steps." So, the baby would be a dancer.

She smiled, imagining a toddler wobbling to music.

They had done one insemination before Pamela came to Guanajuato. "It didn't take," she said.

Callie recalled the yearning Pamela expressed when playing "The Lost Child." "Oh, I'm sorry."

"I was upset for a few weeks," Pamela said. "But I'm okay now. And I have another insemination scheduled for Wednesday when I'm back in California."

When they reached the ruins, Pamela pointed to an area shaded by a stone wall. "How about stopping a while before going on to the mine shaft?" She took off her backpack and spread a blanket. When Callie had settled down, Pamela stretched out and put a forearm over her eyes. "Do you believe in love at first sight?"

She did, but saying so could open a door she didn't want to enter. She stalled, and instead asked Pamela, "Do you?"

"I do." Pamela said. "The moment I saw Ami Mai, I knew she was the one." She laughed. "It took her a little longer." She turned on her side, facing away from Callie.

Callie leaned toward her. Would she ask again? She waited. Then she heard Pamela's rhythmic breathing. Safe again, she leaned against the wall and closed her eyes, recalling her first love.

Eighteen

CALLIE HAD LOVED NOAH FROM THE MOMENT HE faced the congregation. His long legs, broad shoulders, and elegance reminded her of Sidney Poitier. And then, when he began to speak, she loved his words, their warmth and intelligence, and the way he spoke them with easy confidence. And finally, she loved the lips that formed those words. She could not take her eyes off them.

Afterward, when she saw him enter the church basement, everything else disappeared. Gone was the chatter of the other kids. The Melmac bowls of potato salad, sliced tomatoes, and sweet pickle relish. The platters of ham and turkey. The fragrance of warm sweet rolls. The Formica counter tops, the six-burner stove, the aluminum sink. The humming refrigerator, the buzz of florescent lights, the tick of the wall clock. Gone, the white cinderblock walls, the linoleum-tiled floor, the little circular holes of the acoustic ceiling.

There was only Noah, walking toward her carrying a stack of pink bakery boxes. Noah smiling and setting the boxes down on the counter beside the plate of deviled eggs she had just filled. Noah, smelling of cinnamon and cloves, saying with those lips that the pies came from his aunt's bakery. He pronounced "aunt" with a broad A, unlike her family who pronounced "aunt" with a short A like "ant," the insect. And for that reason, she knew Noah came from another world.

Years later, she read that painters feel with their eyes. She remembered then that, when she first saw Noah, she felt his lips. Weeks before they touched hers, she felt them.

SHE traced the outline of her lips and then caught herself. She turned to see if Pamela had noticed. Sound asleep. She folded her arm behind her head. Lips. That was not exactly what Callie's Pastor Walters had had in mind when he invited youth from a Kansas City congregation to his church. A "Negro congregation," Pastor Walters had called it, was celebrating its new church. There was to be a weekend devoted to youth as part of a month-long celebration. The pastor there, a friend of Pastor Walters, invited him and his youth group. Pastor had told her father he thought the parents would be more willing to let their teens go if they met some of the nice young people from the "Negro congregation." And so youth from the city came to Pastor Walter's Sunday service, and Noah, whose parents were both high school teachers and who was in his first year of pre-med, had been selected to offer the invitation at the end of service.

Those lips. She felt a sweet shiver in the pit of her stomach. She stretched out her toes and then let herself return to the past.

After service, she had thought of nothing but Noah's lips through the interminable Bible story game. And then when he sat down at her table for lunch, she stole glances of them forming words, which, through those lips, took on new meaning.

She and Noah had not talked much that day, as she had been too shy, but she crossed her fingers she would find some words by the weekend for youth at the new church. She couldn't wait to see Noah again. Nonetheless, so as not to draw suspicion, she resisted, as was her custom, when her father pressed her to join in on youth activities.

"At seventeen, young lady," he responded, "it's time you stop being so standoffish."

"But dear," her mother said, trying to be supportive of Callie, "Callie has a difficult French test the week after."

Her mother's kindness left her in a panic until her father put his foot down and said, "French or no French, my daughter is going to celebrate with those deserving Negroes." She ran from the room so quickly that her mother followed and knocked at her door, asking if she was all right. She had responded as calmly as she could, that yes, she was. She *would* see Noah again. She couldn't believe her luck.

She had never had trouble sleeping, and in the weeks after meeting Noah, she luxuriated in drifting off to sleep recalling his posture, his voice, his lips. But she barely slept a wink the night before the drive up to the city, and when, in the morning, the mirror showed her face pale with fatigue, she wished for the first time her parents let her wear makeup. She had to make do with pinching her cheeks and applying a thin layer of her mother's Ponds cold cream.

She would not, she feared, know what to say to Noah when she saw him again. But she needn't have worried. He welcomed her to the Saturday social with the broad smile of an old friend. Then, as if to make up for lost time, he told her all about his family between bites of fried chicken, sliced tomatoes, and corn bread. His mom taught remedial math and also trained the students who excelled for math contests, and his father taught social science and coached basketball. He told her about his little twin brothers who were just entering first grade and could already read, and his sixteen-year-old sister, who primped all the time, designed her own clothes, and would have been at the social, were it not for a serious cold. There were uncles and aunts, too, and cousins. While folding and stacking chairs after lunch, Noah talked about his plans. He would not get married any time soon, he said, as if he knew she was thinking about that. He wanted to get through college and med school and set up a practice. Then he would be ready. He would do community work, too. Now he helped his father with basketball workshops, but, once he set up his practice, he would organize workshops on health education. He planned to marry a woman who shared his goals.

She made her own plans while he spoke. His sister would be her maid of honor. His youngest cousins could be ring bearers. They would wait a few years after marriage to start their family, and then they would have a large one, so their children would not be shy. When the youngest went to kindergarten, she would go back to work, teaching high school, like his parents. And, yes, she would help with health education. Just like he wanted.

She planned all of this—and the kiss—before they finished stacking the chairs.

In the late afternoon when her youth group was piling into the van to be dropped off at family homes for the night, Noah asked her pastor if he could take Callie on a tour of the city and then give her a ride to the home where she would be staying. He knew the couple well because they had served with his father on the committee to select the minister for the new church.

Pastor gave his immediate approval. "Don't you kids stay out late," he said. "Our choir's singing in the eight a.m. service, and we count on Callie."

On the way to the car, she felt so buoyant she wanted to take Noah's hand to make sure she did not float away. But there was no way she could touch him. Not with Pastor's eyes following them. Instead she would hurry to the car where she would be safe.

She picked up her pace, getting ahead of Noah who called out, "Hey, hold on, the tour's not that exciting."

She stopped and looked back. Her face must have turned bright red by the flash of warmth she felt rising to her cheeks.

He laughed and then pointed to a station wagon with "Better than Momma's Sweet Potato Pies" painted on the side. "Race you there."

He got there first and held the passenger door open for her.

"What would you like to see?" he asked, when he settled into the driver's seat.

She was out of breath, but in any case speechless, since there was nothing she wanted to see but him. Not that she could look at him. She stared straight ahead.

He started the car, pulled out of the gravel lot, and drove down the road.

"Well?" he said, when they turned onto a wide boulevard.

She felt the blood drain from her face. Why couldn't she be chatty like other girls?

"How about the park?"

Aunt Ida had taken her there to see a starlight performance, and she had been to the zoo, too. "I love the park," she said. She imagined saying "I love you" and felt her face grow hot again. But for once she did not mind being embarrassed. Noah there beside her was all that mattered. She got up the courage to look at him and found him looking at her.

He looked back at the road just in time to swerve around a bicyclist, and she fell toward him on the bench seat. He reached out and drew her closer. "That's better."

She wanted to lean into his shoulder. But what if someone

saw them? She thought of the two little African-American boys who had been convicted of molestation after a little white girl had kissed them on their cheeks. That had been some years before and in another state, but even so, she had never seen a white girl alone in a car with a Negro boy in her small town. Was it different in the city?

PAMELA stirred, and Callie checked her again. She lay deeply asleep and with a soft smile on her lips. Callie relaxed and returned to her memories.

She had rubbed her hands on her skirt and taken a breath. "Is it all right?" she asked. "You and me . . . together?" She looked around. If only she had a scarf to cover her hair.

He stiffened, and she dared to touch his hand with hers. "I mean . . ."

"I know what you mean," he said. "I may join your church. I may make the winning hoop at the playoffs. I may graduate with honors. But I'm not someone you take home to meet the family."

She pulled her hand away. "That is not what I meant."

"Well, plenty of whites think that way, and, honestly, my family wouldn't exactly be delighted," he said and put both hands on the steering wheel. "I am to be a leader in our community, married to a 'respectable Negro woman.'"

She pulled herself up straight and smoothed her skirt against her legs. This was not going according to plan.

"To tell you the truth, hanging out with a bunch of do-gooders was the last thing I wanted to do on a Saturday, but my parents . . . Tolerance. They're always preaching tolerance." He slapped the steering wheel. "When I resisted going, they got heavy on me . . . 'As long as you are under our roof, young man . . .' So I went in spite of myself. And then I have to stomach those boys moving between me and the girls when I came in, as if they needed to protect them, and the girls with their fake smiles and artificial voices." He mimicked their greetings, and Callie flushed at how like them he sounded.

"So," she said so quietly she could almost not hear herself, ". . . a do-gooder. Is that what you think of me?"

He turned to look at her. "No, Callie. No. I knew you were different from the moment I saw you off by yourself hovering over your deviled eggs." He laughed. "That's why I made a beeline for you. But tell me, honestly, how comfortable is your congregation with blacks? I didn't see black people besides us there."

"Not at all comfortable, I suppose." What else could she say? The only other black people she had seen there were visiting missionaries from Africa and that had been on just one occasion. Local black people had never attended her church.

"So tell me, then, what would your parents think about our being together?"

She started coughing. She had, after all, known better than to tell her parents she liked Noah. And not just because her father would be jealous of any boy she showed interest in. He even resented Steve. But Noah. She could never take Noah home. Never. She wanted desperately to disappear. Too bad she hadn't floated off leaving the church. No chance of that now. She felt heavy as lead. And she could not stop coughing.

Noah's voice softened. "Are you all right?" He pulled onto a side street and parked the car.

She reached for the door handle.

"Wait, Callie. Look. I am sorry."

She sat still, looking down. "No, you are right. There's no way I could invite you home."

"But still I shouldn't have talked to you the way I did. I need to watch my tone. My parents are right about that. I shouldn't have let those kids get to me."

Were they right about his future wife, too? The "respectable Negro woman." Her chest went into spasm and tears ran down her cheeks. She turned her face away.

"They said the kids would be uncomfortable. And they were right. Those kids didn't know how to act."

He laid his hand on her shoulder. "And our parents. It's understandable how they think, but our generation will be different."

Would it? She hoped so. She looked up at him and tried to smile.

"So, are you are all right? Are we friends?"

She nodded.

"I have a cousin who has coughing fits. When she was called up to the podium to receive a prize at the science fair, she coughed all the way there and back. You kind of remind me of her."

Callie turned toward him. "Your cousin. . . ?"

"Look at you. White shirt and plaid skirt. You look like you just walked out of a library. All that's missing is a stack of books. Hold on a minute." He turned and gathered the books scattered across the back seat. After sorting them, putting the largest on the bottom, he set them on her lap. Then he leaned back and pretended to take a picture. "Perfect," he said. "I'm right, aren't I? You're a bookworm."

She smiled. Being called a bookworm had never sounded so good.

"Now take some slow breaths. Relax your throat. You'll be all right."

His voice, calm and warm, reassured her. He would be a

good doctor. She started looking through the books and stopped coughing long enough to ask, "Are these yours?"

"The chemistry and calculus texts."

She opened up a chemistry book and glanced through the pages.

"Hey, Bookworm," he said and started up the car. "There's a great science library at the university. Want to see it?"

SHE often sat across from her friend Steve in the high school library, but he had never looked at her the way Noah did that Saturday afternoon. And when Steve went in search of a book, her eyes had not followed him the way they followed Noah.

She had not been like other girls in her high school, giggling about boys in the library. The sign posting the library hours attracted her gaze more than the boy at the front desk, the one other girls flocked around, whether they had a book to check out or not. She would sometimes stand behind the magazine rack and wonder what drew them to that skinny boy with his crew cut and pock-marked face?

There in the science library with Noah, she saw differently. The shelves of books where she customarily would have centered her attention became the background for Noah. Noah walking along slowly, savoring science books. Noah's lips forming the words of their titles. Noah's eyes lighting up as if seeing old friends. She noticed, too, how Noah's polo shirt revealed the muscles of his shoulders. How he dipped one hip when he paused to read.

Noah selected a book, opened it, turned, his smile widening, and then sat down and spread it open. He looked up and saw her looking at him. "What?" He smiled another kind of smile and cocked his brow. "What are you looking at?"

She felt exposed, out of her element, her familiar world of numbers and formulas. Abstract and alienating to some, but to her concrete and comfortable.

And what was she looking at but a boy in a library reading a book? She stood up abruptly, "I want to look at the books." Standing by the shelves, her hand slipping along the books, she read the titles. They all attracted her. But she selected just one. Albert Einstein, *Relativity: The Special and General Theory.* When she turned to sit down again, she noticed Noah studying her. She felt her face flush and turned away, pretending to take an interest in another book. When she turned back, he was working out formulas on a yellow pad by an opened physics text. He mumbled while he wrote. She sat across from him and lay her book down. But before opening it, she leaned forward to see what he was reading about. The attraction between positive and negative charges.

Did that explain it? Her attraction to him. To some they may seem opposites. But seen from another point of view they were not opposites at all, she and Noah. When she looked at him, hunched over his book, didn't she recognize herself? Well, maybe she did not mumble or chew on her pencil, but she twirled her hair, and sucked her lip. And what if her lips were thin, not full like his? They formed the same words. And if he was tall, lithe, and dark, and she short, plump, and light— well, their bodies were both made of flesh and blood. They both loved science, and they sang the same hymns. And Noah spread mayonnaise on sliced tomatoes after peppering them first, just like she did. And if he was confident, well-spoken, and strong. Well, she wished to be, didn't she? So he was all she was and wanted to be. Not her opposite. Her other half. She smiled, opened her book, and began to read.

It seemed only a few minutes later when Noah waved his

hand in front of her face. "Hey, Bookworm, you've been reading over an hour. Wouldn't you like to take a break? Get something to eat?"

She looked up at him and then down at her book again. She sighed. She would have to leave it there in the library.

"Even a bookworm like you can't get much nutrition out of that. Trust me, I'm pre-med."

She laughed and closed the book.

He came around the table and pulled her chair back. "I've never seen anyone concentrate like you."

Wasn't that just what she had noticed about him? She stood, still looking at the book she had been reading, but she was thinking of his hand on the back of her chair. When she bent to pick up her purse, she dropped it.

"Are you okay?" He picked up her purse and handed it to her. "You're not going to start coughing again, are you?"

She laughed. "Let's go."

"I know a great barbecue place. You'll love it."

While they walked side by side across the campus, she kept up a steady report on Einstein's theory.

At one point, he stopped and looked at her as if appraising her anew. "You know, Bookworm, you got more out of Einstein in one sitting than I would have in five."

It wasn't true, she knew, but she liked his saying it. It meant she was safe with him.

They started walking again, this time occasionally bumping against each other. She stepped away each time and continued telling Noah about Einstein's theory, but all the while her mind relived those moments when Noah's shoulder touched hers.

Soon he stopped again. "I'm getting lost," he said. "What were you saying?"

She stopped talking and looked at him. What had she been saying? "I . . . I don't know."

He laughed. "So even *you* can lose your place." He took her hand. "We need to get that brain of yours fed. But would you mind if we make a stop on the way to dinner? I'm looking after a prof's cat. It'll only take a minute."

She looked down at his long, sure fingers wrapped around hers. His hand warm and familiar, as if it had held hers many times before. Her own hand began to warm, and her heart slowed down to a steady beat. A minute alone with Noah.

She looked up at him and smiled. "Did you know Einstein liked cats?"

He laughed again. "Let's go," he said, and they ran along the campus path, across the street, and down to the next street. Halfway down the block, they turned onto the sidewalk of a brick house with a wide porch, protected by a trellis covered with wisteria. The front door had a stained-glass window of a calla lily framed in amethyst. He took out the key and opened the door. Her heart rate had picked up again with the run, and she was gasping for air, but she had never felt so happy. The doorway looked like the opening to a new world.

Nineteen

"So do you?" CALLIE FELT SOMETHING BRUSH against her shoulder and took in the words as if in a dream. Believe in love at first sight, wasn't that what Pamela had been asking before falling asleep? Not a safe topic. She kept her own eyes closed.

Pamela began again. "I was wondering. Do you miss the people you've left behind?"

She roused and saw Pamela propped on one elbow, gazing at her, a questioning look on her face. That last, long look on her baby's face came to her again.

She sat up and brushed fallen leaves off her clothes. "What?" Her hands were shaking. Whom did she have in mind?

Pamela lifted a leaf from Callie's hair. "The ones you left back in the States."

An image came to her of Gwendolyn leaning across the cafeteria table, whispering to Pamela: "I never want to know my birth mother. Never." She cleared her throat. "I have left people. When I went to college, I left my father. In my twenties, I left any number of lovers. But there are those I have never left, no matter how far away I lived." She started packing her backpack, her fingers trembling. "I have not left my mother or my aunt." When she stood, she dropped her backpack. "We talk regularly, and I go back for visits." If only her hands would stop shaking.

"I'm sorry. I'm afraid I've been too direct again." Pamela reached down for her backpack. "Here let me help."

"I'm fine," she said. "It's just that we need to pack up. It looks like it could rain." She dropped her backpack again. Darn.

"Callie." Pamela put her hand on Callie's shoulder. "Are you sure you are all right?"

"I'm fine, really." Callie said. She leaned toward the backpack.

"Allow me," Pamela said, picking up the backpack. "They could follow you, you know," she said, holding the backpack for Callie to slip her arms through. "You know, like that song 'Whither Thou Goest?'"

She felt the backpack settle into place. All those months at her aunt's, waiting for her baby, she had dreamed of Noah following her. Imagined him patting her growing tummy, his warm smile, the fragrance of cinnamon. Would he have followed her, if he had known? If the world *had* been different then? She remembered sitting at her aunt's dining table, having a cup of tea, the newspaper spread open in front of her, her aunt reading over her shoulder, saying "Well, it's *about* time."

Callie recalled the date. June 13, 1967. The Supreme Court had ruled bans to interracial marriage unconstitutional the day before. About time, yes. Too late for her. By then her baby was almost four years old. And with a new mother. There was, by then, no point in Noah following her, even if her father would have accepted him. She cleared her throat and turned to Pamela. "A song. You mentioned a song?"

"'Whither Thou Goest.' My mother sang it for weddings," Pamela said. "She had a beautiful voice. Still does, though she rarely performs now. She sings her way through the dinner dishes. Spirituals, blues, Cole Porter."

The words to "Night and Day" came to Callie. He had been the one. In spite of it all. For a long time, the only one. Noah.

"My mom taught me what I know about phrasing, vibrato, and breath," Pamela said. "I still sink at my knees to reach a high note the way she does." She modeled the posture, bending her knees slightly and lifting her arms as if she were playing the trumpet.

Callie was adjusting the straps of her backpack and humming "Night and Day."

"Callie . . . Callie?" Pamela waved her hands in front of Callie's face. "Like this." She held her hands up again to hold the imaginary trumpet, bent her knees, and sung a high C.

It looked so easy. She bent to lift Pamela's blanket and then rose to fold it. Her hands felt steady now. "Were you saying something about your mother?"

"'Whither thou goest I will go.' That's what my mother said when I left home. And she has, too. Though she's terrified of flying, she flew to France twice when I was there. She regularly visited me in California. Took the train. She's been here already and will be back again later this summer."

And your high school friends? Callie wanted to say, Do *they* follow you? She put the blanket in Pamela's backpack.

"When I started playing jazz, she came to every one of my Chicago club dates, though she's not one to drink or smoke." She shifted the backpack on her shoulders. "She came early enough to get a table right in front. Had her Bible with her."

At a jazz club?

"She would take it out and put it on the table by her glass of mineral water." Pamela mimed the way her mother placed the Bible with the weight of conviction. She started down a donkey path. "Come on."

Callie patted Pamela's backpack. "Got a Bible in there?"

Pamela laughed.

Callie pointed to a place ahead where the path divided into two branches. "Which one should we take?"

"The one that goes to the mine shafts."

Callie laughed, then shivered. A cloud had drifted in front of the sun. "Even if we knew which that was, are you sure it's a good idea?" She pointed up to the darkening sky.

Pamela laughed. "Are you made of sugar?" She fished the map out of her pocket, turned it this way and that, and then tilted her head in the direction of the path leading to another ruin. "Come on. I think it's in this direction . . . Anyway, I'm not finished talking about the trumpet."

Twenty

CALLIE ZIPPED HER JACKET AND FOLLOWED PAMELA up the path. "You look so natural playing the trumpet, as if you were born blowing one."

"Well, not quite. My first instrument was the piano. Good for learning theory. Oh, and I played the flute for a week."

"A week?"

"Yeah. In seventh grade. When the band director handed out instruments, he offered trumpets, tubas, trombones, and drums to the boys and flutes, oboes, clarinets, and chimes to the girls. I picked flute. But no matter how I blew, I couldn't get it to sound like a trumpet."

Callie laughed.

"Mr. Ringle said I could try the French horn, if I liked, but the trumpet was out. When I told my father, he shouted to raise the dead. 'No one is going to prevent my daughter from playing the trumpet!'" Pamela laughed. "And he had been so pleased when I came home with the flute. He had played one, you see." She stopped walking and turned toward Callie.

"Your father must have been disappointed with your choice, and yet he supported it," Callie said. Her father had been able to do that. Sometimes.

"He sure did. Dad went out that weekend and bought me a trumpet. First thing Monday morning, he took me to school with the flute and marched into the principal's office." Pamela started walking again, illustrating her father's determined stride.

"He handed the flute to the principal and said, 'My daughter is playing the trumpet, and if she wants to play tight end on a football team, she'll do that too.'"

Pamela stopped again and looked at her. "It's hard to operate against societal expectations, but it's not always a good idea to operate within them either. In either case, there's stress—of holding yourself back or of standing up to those who expect you to 'stay in your place,' whether that's the back of the bus, the kitchen, or the flute section."

Or with a mate of the opposite sex. Pamela seemed comfortable challenging that expectation, too. Unlike Armando.

"Following your heart, pursuing your deepest desires, gives you courage to face the naysayers. But you need support, too, to be yourself in a hostile environment."

"Your passion and your dad's support allowed you to choose the trumpet. I understand that. But I am still puzzled. How do you have the courage to *play* the trumpet? I mean to play in public." She had once fainted when giving an oral presentation. "Just thinking of playing for other people, even kind ones, makes my hands sweat."

"You and a lot of other people," she said. "I once read that for many people public speaking is more frightening than death. Playing in public would be worse, I suppose. But, like anything else, it's not so hard, if you practice, taking it one baby step at a time. You may wobble a little with those first steps, but eventually you get it. I learned that from my Louisiana cousins."

As they walked along the path, she told Callie about her cousins. The girls were older, already married with babies of their own. Pamela and her mom spent long summer days with them and their mom shucking corn for canning. The babies took wobbly steps from chair to chair.

"Is that how you learned about taking baby steps?"

Pamela laughed. "No, my younger cousins, all boys around my age, taught me to take baby steps, though they never used those words."

Pamela took Callie's arm as they walked along. She related how as a preteen she had roamed the woods on hot, humid days with the boys, dressed like them in overalls and floppy loafers. They taught her to dive at a rocky outcropping by a pool in the river that wound through the woods. They never dared or teased her. They just invited her to dive along with them, each day going a little higher up. They made it look like so much fun, whooping before they dove and crowing when coming to the surface. She belly-flopped a number of times. But fear never crossed her mind, even that day when she dove from the highest place on the rock.

Pamela let go of Callie's arm and stopped to look at her. "I use the baby-step technique with my students." She laughed. "It works . . . most of the time."

Could it work with Armando?

Pamela sat on a flat rock by the path. "All this talking makes me hungry."

"I have muffins." Callie dredged around in her backpack. "Somewhere." Seeing the dog biscuits, she ducked her head closer. She pulled out the bag of muffins.

"I'll take that," Pamela said, reaching for it. She beckoned Callie to sit beside her. "There's something I've been meaning to ask you. "

What now?

"Do you hear that?"

Was that the question?

Pamela pointed to Callie's backpack. "Do you have a cell in there?"

Armando, of course.

"Why aren't you home dusting?" he asked when Callie answered his call.

Callie mouthed to Pamela: "Armando." She stood and walked up the path a ways.

"I am with Pamela. Remember."

"Oh, right. Poor you. Is Tavelé there, or has she hidden him? Just a second, Claude. I know she has him, Chou. A friend saw him with her groupies. It's 'ajo,' not 'ojo.'"

"What's that?"

"Not you, Callie, Claude. He just ordered pizza with an eye, instead of with garlic." He lowered his voice. "He's constantly talking to waiters. It's driving me crazy. They love it, of course."

Was he jealous or proud? It sounded like both. She heard music in the background and Armando tapping.

"The music is Cuban."

"What?"

"Claude was just telling the waiter how much he loved Mexican music."

"And?"

"They're playing *Cuban* music."

"But you love Cuban music."

"Yeah. But I don't congratulate Mexican waiters for it, Chou. Look, I've got to go. When will you be home?"

"I'm not sure."

Callie turned and saw Pamela coming. She backed up.

"Well, no need to stay after you find Tavelé. Just make your excuses and leave."

"I can't just leave. We're in the mountains."

"You walked all the way to the mountains?"

"Pamela has a car."

"You let her take you in that death trap? Well, you'll have

to find an excuse not to drive back with her. I don't want you and Tavelé risking your lives."

"Tavelé? He's not here."

"Then why are *you* there?" The tapping stopped. "You never go to the mountains with me."

What was going on? He never wanted to walk in the mountains. He must be feeling jealous because she was with Pamela.

She glanced up. Pamela was getting closer, and so she backed up again.

"And you are always buying useless things from Juanito."

And jealous of Juanito. "Are you okay?"

"Fine. I'm fine."

He sounded impatient. Perhaps if he talked to the Virgin. "Didn't you say there was a historic church near your hotel?"

"What's that got to do with Juanito? Anyway, don't worry. I'll get rid of that junk as soon as I get back. Oh, and I'll call Jorge. Now. He'll come pick you up. Hold on a second."

She heard him call out to Claude: "I'm coming."

"I don't like this, Chou. Claude's whispering to the waiter and looking over here."

"Callie, watch out!" Pamela grabbed her arm, and the phone flew up over her shoulder.

She turned. The mine shaft. Her phone bounced, landed, scattering some loose rocks at the edge of the shaft, and then fell in, landing with a plunk. She leaned toward the shaft, cupped her hands around her mouth and called out, "Armando. The Virgin. Talk to her."

Pamela whooped and nodded toward the mine shaft. "What a piece of work."

She shook her head. Pamela gleeful. And Armando, anxious, on the other end of the phone. She kneeled, peered into the pit, and broke out in a sweat. She closed her eyes and scooted back. She needed to get away. Clear her head. But what if Armando were calling out to her? She had to do something. She tightened her jaw and turned an ear to the shaft. Not a sound. She leaned to look inside. Just for a second. But long enough to notice woody-stemmed plants growing from cracks. Maybe the phone hadn't fallen to the bottom. The plunk could have been a loosened stone. She held her breath and inched closer.

Pamela squatted by her. "I suppose he doesn't like it that you're with me," she said and added, "I saw how he shuttled you off that night at the restaurant."

Of course, he had shuttled her off. He had been upset. And now when he was upset again, she had dropped the phone. And there she was feeling queasy when she should be trying to reach him. She forced herself to look into the shaft again. Had one of the plants caught the phone? She had to find out. Gripping the edge of the shaft with her left hand, she closed her eyes and felt down between the plant and the side of the shaft, moving her hand slowly to avoid accidently dislodging the phone, in case it was there.

She thought she felt something smooth with the tip of her fingers and leaned to reach a little further. Then her left hand slipped and her collarbone struck the edge of the shaft. Her right hand jammed into the woody base of the plant and grabbed hold.

"Whoa," Pamela said, putting an arm around the back of her waist.

She sensed the shaft swirling around her.

"You're okay. I've got you. Let go."

She wasn't okay, and she couldn't let go. She tightened her hold on the plant.

"Come on, Callie."

Bile seeped into her mouth.

"You're already safe. Just let go."

It was taking all her energy to avoid throwing up.

Pamela tightened her grip. "You're going to be okay, Callie. Let go of the air in your lungs. Remember? Slowly, fully." She put her face next to Callie's. "I am right here, breathing with you."

She felt Pamela exhaling and began exhaling with her.

"Now let the fresh air pour into the bottom of your belly."

Air swept into her.

"That's good. Keep it up. I'll count."

After ten breaths, the spinning stopped. After fifteen, she felt the weight of her knees on the ground. She opened one finger at a time and then drew her arms from the shaft.

"See," Pamela said. "I've got you. Now put your palms on the ground by your shoulders."

She did so, and Pamela pulled her back into a squat, and then helped her stand up. "You need to sit down, but not here. How about over there?" She gestured toward a high stone wall.

She nodded.

Pamela kept her arm around Callie as they moved toward the wall, then helped her off with her backpack, and settled her on a boulder.

"Thank you."

Pamela put an arm around her shoulders again and gave her a little squeeze. "You can count on me." She found Callie's water bottle. "Now. Drink."

Callie took a long drink.

"Better?"

She smiled. "Much better."

"Good." Pamela stood and started walking back and forth

as if orating on a stage. "No wonder you lost your balance. That Armando. As I was saying." She enunciated each word carefully: "A. Piece. Of. Work."

Her chest started to feel tight again. Armando. His sporadic tapping. His anxious voice.

"He thinks I stole his dog. Can you believe it?" She lifted her hands, palms up, and shrugged her shoulders. Gray clouds hanging in the sunlit sky beyond Pamela provided a backdrop to her performance.

Armando's insistence that Pamela had Tavelé *was* crazy, she thought, but not his anxiety about her budding friendship with Pamela. She felt a twinge of guilt. What if Pamela was making Armando's life difficult? Shouldn't she, as *his* friend, keep her distance?

"I have no idea where that scamp is. He *was* at my house, nosing around the garden as if he were looking for something."

The geese.

"*After* eating two pieces of cake." She smiled. "I recognized him immediately when he showed up."

Callie's eyes followed the clouds, which looked amorphous at first and then settled into huge resting hippos.

"I tried to call Armando. But there was some automated message I didn't understand, so I hung up. Not that I wanted to talk to him, given how he treats me."

She had a point there. Armando was being difficult. If only they would talk with each other. And listen. A hippo roused and began to lumber across the sky.

"I figured, if I left the gate open, Tavelé would head back down to the center." She stopped and motioned as if opening a gate and then started pacing again. "But he didn't. The next morning, he was still there. He'd dug up all my bulbs." She laughed. "I was mad, but not for long. He's such a flirt, the way he looks out of the corner of his eye." She mimed the look. She couldn't stay mad at Tavelé. That was a start.

"Anyway, by Monday morning he had left. I tried to tell Armando, but he lit into me about Maestro Chávez before I could open my mouth."

She should lay off the maestro. Let Armando take his time. Another hippo rose in the sky.

"I told him it was his own darn fault his dog was missing." The hippos stood head to head, mirroring each other.

Pamela sat down by Callie and leaned back against the wall. Her voice softened. "It's not easy being the new kid on the block."

Her tone reminded Callie of the night she played "The Lost Child," half-hidden behind the tree in the *Jardín.* Callie put her arm across Pamela's shoulder.

"I thought Armando would be a natural ally, but, like I told you, he cooled toward me right away. As if I had some contagious disease. And then when Maestro Chávez started getting lost, Armando blamed me." She pulled away and faced Callie, her eyes serious. "It's true, he stares at me and skips a beat or two. But it's not my fault." She put a finger to her temple. "He's losing it." She lowered her hand. "Armando refuses to see that." She sighed and looked out toward the sky.

Callie followed her gaze. The hippos slowly backed apart as if trying to find a way to gain an advantage.

"The strange thing is, as awful as he is to me offstage, he's fully there onstage, backing me up, you know."

"That's Armando. When it matters, he's there."

She turned to Callie. "Really?" Then she smiled. "Well, anyway, he is a fabulous musician." She looked back toward the sky. "Wow, look at that!" She pointed toward the hippos Callie saw. "They look like enormous corn fritters."

Twenty-One

HE MOMENT CALLIE ROUNDED THE CORNER by Doña Petra's house, the rain that had held off all morning began to pour. Her mother would say it was raining cats and dogs. Armando favored the French *comme vache qui pisse*, like a cow peeing. She recalled the clouds in the mountains. Hippos peeing? She smiled and ducked under the rectangle of tin sheltering the step at Doña Petra's entry. Good thing the pee had not started while they were driving back to Guanajuato.

A stream of rushing water swirled around the corner and lapped up against the step she stood on. It continued on down the *callejón* toward her house. Not a stream she wanted to splash home through, given the dog poop she'd seen on her way up the hill.

She huddled as close to Doña Petra's metal entry door as she could. Still, water splashed up and dampened her ankles. She pictured Tavelé shaking off water. Had he found shelter? She drew in her feet until her heels pressed against the base of the door. No point in knocking. Doña Petra, wearing her beatific smile, would be at church. Juanito and his sister would be there, too.

She hunched her shoulders against the wind. She could use a nice warm shower. If only the rain would stop.

She took in the flourishing basil plant by the front door.

Doña Petra had placed it there to ward off envy, she had said. Against the envy of people like Nacho and his family, Callie had thought. Compared with their dilapidated shack, Doña Petra's house, with its newly tiled floor and insulated roof, was warm and cozy. But when she commented on the size of the plant, Doña Petra told her the plant had been there for years, from the time her house had had a dirt floor and tin roof.

She wondered, then, about the need for basil, until she recalled first meeting Doña Petra. How sad she sounded when speaking of the poor philosopher, who had such a big house and lived there *solita*, all alone. When Juanito's mother Carla came home for the winter from working in the States, she told Callie she missed her mother and her children the long months away each year. But by working up North she could earn enough to finish her family's home. She would come back for good then. And meanwhile when away, she shared living spaces with other farm workers. She was never *solita*.

Callie looked again at the basil plant. And what about herself? She lived alone. Did Doña Petra and Carla pity her? She pulled her shoulders back. Well, *she* enjoyed living alone. Always had, since she moved from her aunt's flat crammed with souvenirs from mummy trips to the studio, where she enjoyed beautifully bare walls.

She would be happy to be all alone in the quiet comfort of her house right now. If only the rain would let up.

She looked through the downpour to the abandoned lot on the other side of the *callejón*. It looked beautiful at this time of year, overgrown with broad-leaved plants that hid the garbage underneath. She shuddered, recalling the rotten papaya she had once stepped on when retrieving a sheet that had blown off her line. Armando had laughed when she complained about the papaya. "You should be more worried about the rubble piled against your wall. Any kid could climb to the top and shimmy down your avocado tree."

Callie shivered and pulled her jacket closer. The rain had slowed, but the wind had picked up. The awning no longer protected her. She looked into the sky. Gray and thick with clouds. The rain would go on a while, and even if it stopped soon, the stream would continue. Should she wade? The water wouldn't be as dirty as when the rain first started. She looked down at her shoes. They would get soaked. Her feet would dry faster. But did she really want to put her feet in that water? Then she recalled Pamela's words about driving with the top down, "It will be more exciting this way." And it had been. Careening down the curves under a sky streaked with lightning. She raised an eyebrow. Terrifying, but exciting.

She rested her bottom against Doña Petra's door to take off her shoes and socks. Then she took in a deep breath, stepped into the *callejón*, and splashed down the stairs.

Twenty-Two

AFTER HER SHOWER, CALLIE DRESSED IN SWEATS, wrapped a towel turban-style around her hair, and climbed the stairs to the dining room. The sun had come out and was shining across the room onto the dining room table. She would take another walk. Look for Tavelé in town. But first she would read her mother's letter. She smiled. Usually she saved her letters until after her chores, but her routine was already off. She might as well treat herself to the letter now. She opened the envelope and took out the thin sheets written in her mother's even handwriting.

Dear Callie,

I have been in your room, remembering you there with your books and the cloth doll Ida made for you. You would hold her for hours in your little wooden rocker, telling her stories from one of your favorite books. You sang to her, too. Tell how she could have as much ice cream as she liked, play in the snow until her nose turned blue, and pick strawberries in the full sun.

She went everywhere with you. You probably don't remember, you were so little, but one day I found you teetering on a chair at the basement door. You were reaching for the light switch. She was by your feet, and you were looking down, telling her not to touch your daddy's saws. The chair tipped so that your doll slid off. I was terrified you would fall, too, but I managed to catch you.

That evening—do you remember?—your father found you a block away from home, with a bag of your clothes and your doll. You sang to her in your room for a long time afterward, promising never to yell at her or give her the silent treatment.

Callie leaned back in the chair and closed her eyes. She remembered telling Pamela she had liked playing alone in her room. But she hadn't been all alone, had she? She returned to the letter.

I found your doll this morning in the back of your closet, wearing her gingham dress and white apron. The nylon stuffing was poking through one of her mitten hands. The red ribbon that tied her hair was gone and so was one of her blue button eyes. But she still had her embroidered-on smile.

I sewed up the seam and tied a new ribbon for her hair. I'm pretty sure I can find a matching button. I thought, maybe now, you would like to have her.

She frowned. She had once planned to keep her doll safe for her own child and for that child's child and all who came thereafter. But then, when she left home for college, she left everything, including the suitcase her mother packed for her. None of her old clothes fit anyway. On that last morning the first thing she saw in the dawn light was her doll sitting pretti-ly in the little wooden rocker. The doll must have seemed a symbol of all that could not be, for she found herself twisting and pulling at the doll until she looked, she realized now, the way she herself had felt inside.

Going through these things takes me back to the past. I never told you, did I, that I feared—when you left for college—that I would never see you again. When you came home

*after your father died and stood beside me at the sink, a
towel in your hand, wiping the dishes as naturally as if you
had never left my side, I was so relieved tears came to my
eyes.*

A lump formed in Callie's throat. She remembered her
mother trying to hide her tears that first evening home. But
she thought her mother had been grieving her father's death.

*Still, I worried that one day you would leave again and that
even Ida would not know where you were. When you said
you were moving to Mexico, I was terrified that I would lose
you for good. But then you came to visit from so far. Then,
finally, I knew that wherever you went, I would not lose you
again.*

*Now when I remember things of the past, I cherish them all,
the joys and the sorrows.*

Callie read the last phrase again, "the joys and the sorrows."
Was there a message there? She turned the page over.

*Well, Dear, I have gone on some, but I wanted you to know
about your doll. Don't worry, I'll have her fixed in no time.*

Everything here is fine and dandy.

Love, Mother

Strange. Not a thing about what had been keeping her
mother away from home. Or the news Aunt Ida suspected.
Was mending the doll her mother's news? And that "fine and
dandy," a familiar enough phrase coming from Aunt Ida, but
odd from her mother. And what a strange jump from "the joys
and the sorrows" to "fine and dandy." In any case, on that

score, she had her doubts. Her father had died, but he had left his mark, and if it had faded from her mother's point of view, it had not from hers.

She had never wished her father dead, but still she returned for his funeral only because of her mother. She recalled her mother, sitting beside her on the front pew, one hand on top of the other, the way she always held them when her father had done something outrageous.

Well, he had done something outrageous that time. What had he thought while the ladder was falling backward? Did he see his life projected on the sky above him? Did he hear his last words to his daughter? Did he wish that once over the years that followed he had taken one second to say he was sorry he had thought only of himself? Sorry he had not offered her a word of comfort? Sorry he had chosen blame instead of compassion?

She saw herself that last night before leaving for college. On her knees begging him. He would not have repented, even within spitting distance of the pearly gates. If he looked back on his life at all, it would be to find others responsible. Never himself. He was probably still standing before the gates, his chin raised, blustering.

Twenty-Three

WHEN CALLIE STOOD UP, SHE FELT LIGHT-HEADED. She'd better eat something before dusting the beams. She started toward the kitchen and then noticed the answering machine message light blinking. Ten blinks. Ten messages. More than she had ever gotten before. Had something happened to her mother or Aunt Ida? And then she remembered the mine shaft. Armando. Of course. She should have called him first thing. She pressed the play button.

The first. "Great message, Chou-Chou. Now everyone knows you're not at home. I'll try you on your cell."

The second: "Callie, what happened? I was talking to you and then the phone went dead. Call me as soon as you get back." There was tapping in the background, but not too erratic.

The third: "I don't know what I was thinking before. There's no way you could have gotten back by now, even assuming you haven't fallen off a cliff. I'm sending Jorge to look for you." Poor Armando. If only she had noticed the answering machine before the letter. Reading it had only put her in a dark mood anyway. Not that that was her mother's fault. But then what had she thought when she first saw the condition of her doll?

The fourth: Drum roll. "Claude just left to look for souvenirs for his aunts." Cymbal crash. "I'm staying here at the hotel. Call anytime." Well, at least that message sounded less anxious.

The fifth: "I can't believe it. I just looked out the window and saw Claude around the corner with that waiter he had been whispering with." Oh, dear.

The sixth: "You know why I don't take you to the mountains: cliffs, loose bulls, rattlers, lightning strikes." She shivered. Mine shafts.

The seventh: "Lightning strikes. Oh, God. I just remembered overhearing Pamela say something about flying kites. First, she steals my dog and then she electrocutes my best friend. Isn't it enough for her, trying to get rid of the maestro? That reminds me, I'd better check on him." Vintage Armando. But someone did need to check on Maestro Chávez. She hoped to God *he* was okay.

The eighth: "He's at home. Safe. No word of you at the hospitals, the *Cruz Roja*, or the fire department. And Claude's not back." The dull, repeated thud of a funeral drum. "He's not coming back. I know it. God, Chou, I hope you're all right." How could she have let him get this hysterical? She should have borrowed Pamela's cell to call him right back! She felt her own heart beginning to race.

The ninth: "Guess what, Chou. Claude just came waltzing in." He laughed. "*Danzoning* in, I mean. With presents for *me*. A pitcher for coffee and another, a *lechero*, for hot milk. Just like the ones used at our favorite restaurant. A waiter holds them high, one in each hand, and then, in unison, pours streams of steaming coffee and milk into your cup. The waiter's giving us some tips on using them. Claude's the best." She smiled. He is. Now, if only Armando would stay on that track instead of getting constantly derailed by jealous thoughts.

The tenth: "We're going dancing." And then in a whisper. "The waiter, too, but don't worry. His wife will meet us at the plaza. Get it? They have five children. What luck." There were five taps and then, "If you're still alive when you play this message, call me ASAP."

That was her Armando, one minute expecting disaster, the next one dancing. She looked over at the jaguar. "Wipe that smirk off your face."

When she called Armando to reassure him that she was okay and only the cell fell into the mine shaft, he was so enjoying dancing that he only ranted a little about Pamela risking his dear Chou's life. Still, he would not hang up until she promised never to go to the mountains again. "At least," he added with a laugh, "not unless you are tethered to me." He hung up and then called back. "Be sure to get another cell." Then he called again, reminding her to look for Tavelé every day and to call him first thing when she found him. As if she could forget. She hung up the phone, shaking her head.

She waited a second in case he called again, and then dialed her mother. She pictured her, needle in hand, mending her doll. How kind her mother was. She wanted to tell her that, but thought it best not to broach the subject. Instead she would assure her mother that she would never run away again. As it turned out, she needn't have worried about what to say. The phone rang and rang. No answer.

WHEN her hair dried she set off in search of Tavelé. She would visit a different neighborhood each day, starting with the next neighborhood over and then continuing neighborhood by neighborhood around the canyon clockwise. She made other plans while walking along calling "Tavelé." She would remind Jorge, Armando's driver, to look for Tavelé and to spread the word to other drivers. She would visit all the butcher shops in town. And she would get word to the mail carriers.

She walked up and down *callejones* until her legs cramped. On the way back up the hill to her house she composed a mantra. *You have to be safe, Tavelé. You have to be safe.*

Twenty-Four

A S WAS HER CUSTOM, CALLIE COVERED THE BED and furniture with worn sheets, wrapped her hair with an old pillowcase, and then dusted the beams of her bedroom with a long-handled mop.

When she finished dusting, she hefted in an aluminum ladder that, when folded into an inverted V, reached ten feet high. Standing a few rungs down for safety, she began wiping a cloth sprayed with Pledge over the beams. It felt good to have nothing on her mind but caring for her beams. Making them shine.

Luxuriating in the sensation of cloth moving against wood, she laughed over stumbling at the mine shaft. Had she stumbled, as Pamela implied, because of Armando? She paused and reflected. Well, yes and no. Listening to him, she had become too anxious to be attentive. She began shining the beams again. But she hadn't had to absorb his anxiety, had she? And yet she had. And then, as was usual with Armando, there had been nothing to worry about. And it wasn't just Armando. She had also worried about how to stay on safe conversational ground with Pamela. But then that had gone as smoothly as her cloth moved across her lovely beams. She could credit herself, couldn't she, with having dared to lean back into the car before Pamela drove off to ask her what question she had wanted to ask up there in the mountains, the one interrupted by Armando's call.

Pamela had laughed. "Oh, I just wanted to know what kept you from playing the trumpet until now." Then she had added that as a child she thought everyone would play the trumpet if they could, and so there had to be a reason, like her seventh grade band director, why they didn't.

She climbed down, shoved the ladder a few feet, and then climbed back up. Lucky for her, Pamela had not asked why she took up the trumpet. And then, even better, after posing her question, Pamela drove off without waiting for an answer. She had called out after her: "You could write a self-help book: *Find Your Inner Trumpeter.*"

She moved to another section of beams. What if everyone had found their inner trumpeter? Flower vendors, baristas, delivery men, politicians, teachers, clerks, cooks, and cabbies. All would play the trumpet. She pictured trumpeters roaring from the rooftops, blaring across the balconies, crooning on the *callejones*, tooting through the tunnels.

Would playing shift their moods, the way it had shifted her father's? Though not always. Not when someone had "dropped the ball," as he put it. And, in his mind, someone was always dropping the ball. She rubbed hard against the beam. Paint store clerks. Waitresses. Other drivers. She rubbed harder, recalling him standing before her. "This time, young lady, you have dropped the ball, big time."

He had spoken as if he had never dropped a ball in his life. She spit on the cloth. Sure, his hands had been quick. He could make a coin disappear and juggle half-a-dozen apples. But he had dropped the ball when it came to her. He had never even asked her if she wanted her baby. If she wanted to get married. "A hasty wedding for Alexander Quinn's daughter. No. Not for my daughter."

The ball he carried and carried well was the ball of blame.

He blamed his temper on his mother's death. He blamed his not having gone to college on the war. He blamed her and her mother for her "disgrace." He had passed that big ball of blame on to her. She had tried to drop it, all right. Toss it. Kick it. Send it on its way. But it boomeranged back each time. Bouncing at her. You did it, you did it, you did it. And then when she lay down to sleep, it dribbled into her dreams.

Sometimes she felt relieved she had not kept her baby. She might have passed that blaming ball on. It would have been different if Noah had been with them. He would have tossed blame back to the rightful owner and taught his daughter to do the same. She sighed. But that could not be.

She climbed down from the ladder and lifted the dust cloth off her dresser, revealing the photo of her father dressed in his basketball uniform, his eyes shining with hope.

Aunt Ida had mentioned a photo of Callie and her father, the one when she was straddling the tree limb, her father smiling up at her. Her aunt said she was holding a book. Now she remembered something else. A ball. That was it. Her father had tossed a basketball, and she had caught it—without dropping the book—and then tossed it back. That's why he had been smiling.

She ran her fingers along the top of the picture's frame. Had she been unfair to him? She crossed her forearms on the bureau and stared into those shining eyes. He would have been around seventeen, her age when she met Noah. She lifted a hand to the picture and moved a finger across her father's cheek. Then she recalled how quickly that lopsided smile would become a curled lip of scorn. She lowered her hand and leaned in closer. "No. I am not unfair. When it came down to it, when it mattered most, you were not on my side. It was about your dishonor. Your broken dreams. Always, always,

Twenty-Five

CALLIE HAD JUST FINISHED BREAKFAST THE NEXT day when Pamela called. "Hey, I forgot to ask you something."

She coughed. What could that be?

"Would you like a lesson before I go? You know, like you said, to release the inner trumpeter."

She pictured herself in that line of triumphant trumpeters stretched across Guanajuato's rooftops and laughed.

"That is, unless you're too busy," Pamela said. "Ami Mai thought you might be. You are still working, after all. But I've got time now, if you do."

Another lesson so soon. What would Armando think? She looked over toward the jaguar. He wouldn't mind her going to Pamela's, if she were searching for Tavelé. The jaguar appeared to raise an eyebrow. But then she had no reason to think Tavelé *was* there. He had run away from Pamela, too. That's why she had bought a leash. In case he turned up again. "Armando really should keep him on a leash, you know," Pamela had said. Oh, boy, did she. And you think so, too, she thought, staring down the jaguar.

"Callie?"

She continued directing her thoughts to the jaguar. If they did find Tavelé, Pamela could be the one to take him to Armando. They would surely become friends then. So, really, there was no reason to stop seeing Pamela on Armando's account. The jaguar's expression was hard to read. She leaned toward him.

"Are you still there?" Pamela asked.

"Oh . . . yeah . . . ah."

"I'd like to get you playing, and not just on the mouthpiece, so if you would like a lesson, bring along your horn. What do you say?"

She looked over at the trumpet case. It seemed a pity not to take a lesson when she had a perfectly good trumpet. "Okay. Sure. I'll be right down."

"SO," Pamela said when they were seated together at a music stand, each with a trumpet on its bell by her side. "What are your goals?"

"Goals?" She caught herself glancing to the photograph of Pamela at her high school.

"For this baby," Pamela said, gesturing to Callie's trumpet.

"Oh, well." There was, wasn't there something about the trumpet? And then it came to her again, how her father would come up from the basement after playing. A changed man. And so she told Pamela about that. And about how she thought, as a child, that there was something magical about the trumpet.

"So that's your goal? To discover the magic in the trumpet?"

She laughed. "I guess so."

"Okay, I can work with that. Do you read music?"

"I know the notes."

"And you sing?"

"A little."

"Play any instruments?"

"None."

"Singing is good. Can you harmonize?"

"I sang alto in the church choir." Her father had said she had to join in on something at church, and, given the anonymity of singing in a group, the choir seemed an easy way to save herself some grief.

Pamela picked up her trumpet. She played a note and asked Callie to sing "ta" to the note she played.

"Okay, let's go up the scale."

Callie sang along.

"Okay." Pamela said, "Now I'll play C. Sing along, and then hold the C while I switch to E and G."

They started, and she tried to sing out, remembering how her father would say, "Sing up," like he would say, "speak up." Funny. "Sing up, Callie," he would say, "I can't hear you."

"All right," Pamela said when they finished. "You stayed right on the C. Brava."

She smiled. Her mother had a soprano voice, light and always in key. "That's where you got your ear," her father would tell her. "Not from me. Or I would be on *Ed Sullivan* instead of up a ladder."

She and Pamela did some breathing exercises, and then Pamela showed her how to buzz her lips. "There are various schools of thought about lip buzzing, as there are on every aspect of learning the trumpet," Pamela said. "I'm one who finds lip buzzing useful—even for a beginner, if you take it easy."

"Okay," she said when they finished buzzing a few notes. "And now for buzzing the mouthpiece." She showed Callie how to hold it with the thumb and first two fingers. "Let's go."

The mouthpiece felt cool against her lips, but not uncomfortable. She tried to vibrate her lips, but nothing happened.

"Just relax," Pamela said. "And try again."

Eventually she made a sound. A nice quiet sound. A friendly little buzz. She smiled.

Pamela buzzed several notes, and Callie tried to match her. Then Pamela took her mouthpiece away from her lips. She leaned over and picked up her trumpet and put the mouthpiece in. "Let's go!" She nodded toward Callie's trumpet. "It's easier than buzzing. You'll see."

Callie reached for her trumpet. Then she looked toward the open front door. It was one thing to sing or buzz with the door open, but play the trumpet? What if someone heard her? And, besides, her lips were tingling from the buzzing, so that's what she told Pamela.

Pamela laughed. "That happens at first. Okay then, this is as good a time as any for my little lecture."

Pamela leaned back in her chair. "My father came home late for dinner one fine fall day, and when we asked what happened, he said the car had 'wandered.'" She laughed. "But he found his way back—and with apples from a stand that he would not have passed, if his car hadn't 'wandered.'"

She leaned toward Callie and raised her hand, with her index finger up. "So, too, the trumpet may wander. You want to be aware when it veers off course. But treat each departure as an opportunity for exploration."

She lowered her hand. "Leave frustration by the wayside, if you can. And if you can't, take a break. Once you're relaxed again, pick up the trumpet. Your goal is to feel good about playing. *However* it sounds."

Callie thought of the blasts of the mariachis. "Even if it hurts your ears?"

Pamela laughed. "Okay, you have permission to cringe at damaging decibels. But otherwise, no. Got it?"

She caught herself looking at the door again and turned back to Pamela. "Got it," she said, trying to sound convinced.

"It's all about practicing awareness. Of how the trumpet

feels, how your lips feel, how your breath feels, how your sounds relate to those of the musicians around you.

"It's not easy to stay aware. Our minds are on the alert for danger. That saved our ancestors from being too attentive to the fragrance of ripening fruit to notice the hiss of a snake.

"But fear distracts you from playing your best. That's why it's important how we conceptualize unintended sounds. Not as snakes about to strike, but as wanderings offering wonder." She smiled. "You never know when you'll run across an apple stand."

It all sounded good, but didn't seem to stop her heart from racing when she glanced again at the open door.

"Quite a lecture, no?" Pamela raised an eyebrow. "I didn't lose you somewhere along the way, did I?"

Callie laughed. "Maybe a little. But I do know what you mean about that feeling of wonder. I have it when translating, strange as that may sound." She looked at the open door again. "But I'm not sure about being present playing the trumpet. I'm not used to being loud."

"Well, how about giving it a try?" She smiled. "Let the trumpet work its magic."

Callie took in a breath and reached for the trumpet, but she found herself looking out the door again.

"Are you expecting someone?" Pamela lowered her trumpet. "You keep looking out the door."

Caught. What could she do but confess? "Like I said, I'm not used to being loud."

"You were listening to my lecture, weren't you? About accepting the sounds your trumpet makes?"

"Well, yes, but it's one thing for me to accept the sounds, it's another thing to subject someone else to them."

Pamela laughed. "Okay, I'll shut the door." She got up.

"This time." She shut the door and sat back down. "Ready now?"

"Ready," she said, and before Pamela gave her another direction, she blew a note that sounded so loud she jumped.

Pamela laughed. "Way to go!"

Callie laughed, too, and then turned the trumpet to look inside the bell.

"Something in there?"

"That's what I'd like to know."

"Well, here's where I think it is," Pamela said pointing to Callie's heart. "The trumpet at its best—and with your willing participation—magnifies what's there."

"So that's the magic?"

"I leave that to you—and this baby," she said gesturing to Callie's trumpet. "I'll teach you some exercises to play when I'm gone. I've made a tape for you to play along with, and I'll loan you my tape of Clora Bryant's "Gal with a Horn" to listen to. You can tell me what you've discovered when I get back. How's that?"

Pamela paused before opening the door for Callie to leave. "I forgot to ask you the other day. Are you comfortable around babies? Not everyone is. I'm not sure I am, to be honest." She rushed on, "Oh, I know I'll love the little squirt. It's just that I've never spent time around babies."

She recalled her newborn warm against her chest, the smell of her scalp. "Once you have your baby in your arms . . ." She felt a lump form in her throat, and when she tried to swallow, she began to choke. She covered her mouth and turned away, coughing. She couldn't cry. Not now.

Pamela put her hand on Callie's shoulder. "Callie, are you okay? Can I get you some water?"

She turned back, tried to smile, and nodded. She had tears in her eyes, but that was all right, she told herself. Pamela would think they were from the coughing.

By the time Pamela got back with a glass of water Callie had stopped coughing. She took a sip of water. "I just wanted to say 'you'll be okay.'"

"That's what my mother says. But, you know, she won't be here. At least not most of the time. We don't know for sure yet when Ami Mai will be here. And I don't even know how to change a diaper."

Callie was surprised at how anxious Pamela sounded. It couldn't be hormones. She wasn't even pregnant yet. "You have plenty of time to learn that. And, as for your mother and Ami Mai not being here, don't worry, there's help right here in the neighborhood." She put her arm around Pamela's shoulder. "Doña Petra knows everything there is to know about babies."

"Juanito's grandmother? I met her the other day with him."

"You can depend on her."

"She seems nice, but I thought . . ."

"She can use the extra hours."

"That's an idea," she said, opening the door for Callie to leave. But Callie realized when the door shut behind her that Pamela had sounded almost forlorn.

Twenty-Six

BUT, OF COURSE PAMELA HAD NOT FELT GOOD about Doña Petra, Callie thought, as she headed to the center after her lesson to buy a new cell before her daily search for Tavelé. Pamela wasn't fluent in Spanish, nor Doña Petra in English. But she, herself, could help with translation. And there must be other things she could do, too, like make casseroles and yogurt for Pamela and purees for the baby when it was time for solid food.

She called Pamela as soon as she got home with her ideas.

"Well, that clinches it," Pamela said, sounding relieved. "Be sure to practice every day while I'm gone. Breathing, too. A month of practice."

Practice, yes. But where? She looked around her kitchen and dining area. Not there. Too many windows for sound to escape through. Some nice, enclosed space . . . Ah, the laundry room. With only one small window and that one facing away from the *callejón*. A socket for the tape player. A hook for hanging the trumpet. A basin for washing it. As Armando would say, Perfect. *Parfait. Perfecto.*

AND so early the next morning, she began a new routine, showering and dressing, breathing under the avocado tree, then practicing a few minutes. Not more than fifteen minutes at a time, Pamela had advised, and even then she was to pause for as long as each note she blew.

Even so, buzzing left her lips tingly. It wasn't unpleasant, just new. Actually, she kind of liked it. And to think she could have gone through her whole life without having had that particular sensation. How many others had she missed?

There was another new sensation, now that she thought about it, the peaceful feeling that came over her when breathing. She had thought that perhaps the breathing had calmed her father. He had always said breathing was key to playing. But the feeling after playing was still another new sensation. It was peaceful, but there was more. The resonance of the trumpet's tube and bell added warmth and fullness to the vibrations from her lips.

It was addictive, that sensation of resonance, and yet she followed Pamela's advice to the letter and took her recommended breaks, which she used to practice awareness of her breath.

She felt so at home there in the laundry room when she finished her fifteen minutes that it came to her to stay a while, savoring her tingling lips. She had plenty of time, after all, with Pamela gone, Juanito off visiting his cousin, her aunt incommunicado on a mummy adventure, and Armando away and rarely calling. Besides, Juanito's sales needed dusting. The angel with the broken wing. The cracked mirror in the tin frame. The chipped glass vase. She practiced awareness, too, when dusting them, and so she noticed new things. The way, for example, the pattern of flowers on the tin frame had been painted, one corner of the frame left unfinished, as if the paintbrush had wandered.

She had tried calling her mother every few days and expected that her mother would call her, too, as usual when Aunt

Ida was away. But she hadn't been able to reach her mother, and her mother hadn't called once.

But finally a week into July Callie came home to see her answering machine blinking. She ran to the machine, her backpack still on, to listen to the message. "Your doll now has two eyes," her mother had said, "though not the same blue as before." She hadn't been able to find a matching button for the one dangling from her doll's face.

Callie slipped her backpack off. The poor doll. It had not been her fault. She shrugged. At least now the doll was all better. But her mother. How was she? Should she be worrying about her? She put the kettle on for tea. She didn't think so. Apart from not being at home when she usually was, she sounded fine. Better than fine, now that she thought of it. Her mother had even giggled about joining the church choir. "Who would have thought?" she had said. Callie saw her mother covering her mouth, the way she did when a giggle slipped out. Her mother had joined a reading group at the library, too. She had giggled again before hanging up, "My how I've gone on, Dear," she had said. "I've got to get these things to give away over to the church."

That reminded her. She really should do something about the angel with the chipped wing and Juanito's other sales. They seemed to her, after their daily dusting, to deserve a better life. Why not have them fixed? Armando's driver, Jorge, had mentioned family members who fixed things. She had seen a flyer somewhere about an organization looking for things to sell at a bazaar. A fundraiser for animal welfare. Well, that would be perfect. She could get the things fixed and then give them away for a worthy cause. Juanito would be proud.

She got right on it and called Jorge, who came by to pick them up the next day. When they were ready, he would take them to the people organizing the bazaar. She didn't need to do anything but give him a call with the information about where they were to be dropped off.

She thought she caught the jaguar raising a questioning eyebrow when Jorge left with the stone angel, but she just returned the stare with a sigh of relief and a checking motion of her hand. One more thing off her to-do list.

SHE continued her morning sessions of breathing and then playing along with the tape Pamela had made, trying to match her sound to Pamela's. She replaced the time spent dusting Juanito's prize sales with transplanting lavender seedlings Maestro Chávez had given Armando, who, not having a green thumb, or as he had put it *la main verte*, had passed them on to her. Each day she planted a few seedlings in pots of their own.

Within a few days she'd finished tucking the last of the seedlings into fresh loamy soil and placed their pots in line with the other ones, pleased with herself for having completed the task in the full of the rainy season and weeks before Armando's expected return. Yet, when she stood back to take in the results of her labor, she felt a little sad at how small the plants looked in their pots. She shrugged her shoulders. Perhaps she had been feeling a little lonely rambling about her house without Armando coming by. And she hadn't had Tavelé to keep her company, as she usually did when Armando was away.

Armando hadn't called often either, which was a good sign, Callie thought. Things must be going well with Claude. She had finally reached her mother who talked about this and that, little details of life in a small town. Her garden, the 4th of

July fireworks. How the crops were doing. She'd been more interested before in dahlias than in soy beans or field corn. But when Callie acted surprised, her mother just laughed. "Well," she had said, "The farmers and their crops keep our little town going. I guess it's time I start thinking about them."

IN mid-July, Callie was on the patio weeding the lavender when she heard the phone. She ran to answer, expecting to tell Armando about how well the lavender was doing. But it was Pamela. She was so excited Callie could hardly understand her. "She's here. She's here," she kept saying.

"Ami Mai?" Callie sat on the side of her bed.

"No, the baby!"

"Baby?"

"The baby girl. I'm pregnant!"

Pregnant. Callie thought again of the baby she'd imagined in her own belly. A little Noah. Now, it seemed, Pamela imagined a little girl in hers. "That's . . ." She wanted to say "wonderful," but her throat closed. Her baby had been as wonderful as a baby could be, and yet she had let her go. She saw her baby's last questioning look and began to shake.

"I wanted to tell you in person. But Ami Mai thought you'd like to know as soon as possible. So you can plan for her. I mean . . ." Pamela paused, as if she didn't want to presume. "You know how Ami Mai is."

She had sung her dream to her baby. Of Daddy Noah, who was going to be a doctor and would come to take them home. But that wasn't the plan. She couldn't sing the plan. She couldn't think the plan. She couldn't admit the plan. Not when she first felt her baby inside her or when she held her to her breast. She couldn't imagine letting her go.

"Callie?" Pamela said. "Are you there?"

Pamela sounded worried. Callie shook herself. She had to think about Pamela. About *her* baby. "A baby. That's wonderful." She could plan for Pamela's baby. She knew what to do. Line up Doña Petra. "Don't worry," she said, "I'll start getting ready right away."

And she did.

SHE must be missing Juanito, she realized some days later, when she was practicing in the laundry room. Instead of relishing how clean and organized it looked, she regretted giving up his treasures, as if, with them gone, she had lost something of Juanito himself. She called the woman organizing the fundraising auction and offered a large donation to get the pieces back. "Very generous," the woman said, "but too late." The auction had begun.

And so she took off down the *callejón* and arrived at the fundraiser out of breath, but in time to race around, adding her name to the bid sheets for each item she had donated. There were so many bids for the angel, the volunteers had had to add extra bid sheets. She sighed. It had to be the angel. She didn't want to part with any of her donations and especially not with the stone angel, which Juanito had taken such pride in getting to her house. And so she stood close by, elbowing her way in each time someone wrote a name and amount on the latest bid sheet. Her stomach tied in knots at the effort, and so she tried to breathe. But she had barely a moment for breath, given how anxious other bidders were to get their hands on her angel.

She considered slipping the bid sheets into her pocket, not that she wanted to keep the price from going up. She just wanted to make sure her bid was the winning one. She kept a close eye on the clock. As the minute hand crept toward the deadline, her impulse to take the bid sheets increased. It was, after all, almost time to end the bidding, and, besides, she had to abandon her post a moment to make sure she had the last bid on Juanito's other treasures. She reached for the slips of paper, but just then one of the helpful volunteers came by. She looked the volunteer in the eye, as if she had nothing to hide, increased her own last bid, and then hurried around the room adding bids where necessary. She made it back just in time to sign her name as the last bid before the deadline. "*Perdón!*" she said to the woman whose toe she had stepped on.

Jorge, when he arrived to take her home, was surprised to be returning the items to her house. "Well, it was for a good cause," he said.

"Yes," she said and smiled all the way home, imagining Juanito's delight at seeing the newly repaired treasures.

"*Que le vaya bien,*" she called after Jorge when he left after carrying the last of the treasures down the hill.

She closed the door and leaned against it, studying the angel Jorge had placed on the opposite side of the terrace. Juanito would be pleased. But she found herself strangely dissatisfied. She crossed the terrace to take a closer look. The line where the wing had been repaired was so well hidden she could barely see it. It seemed as if the angel were no longer the one she had dusted for days. She shook her head in frustration. Still, she overcame her impulse to take a hatchet to its wing. Not that she had one anyway. And, besides, what would the jaguar— who appeared relieved on seeing Juanito's treasures returned— think then?

* * *

THE package. There it was on the laundry shelf that had held Juanito's most prized sales. The package she had never opened, nor paid attention to in her ministrations to Juanito's treasures. But once they had been removed, the package became salient in her field of vision. Still, she had not touched it. Or even reached out. She stood there, her hands on her hips, and looked at it.

She had woken that morning at daybreak and had gone to the patio, looking forward to seeing the lavender sparkling from the evening rain. But when she stood looking at the little plants in their clay pots, all she could think of was how, weeks after being transplanted, they still looked lonely. Mr. Charles's melodious voice had come to her, "Be good and you'll be lonely." She shook her head. She had tried to do the plants good by giving them space. But instead of radiating happiness in their pots large enough for them to flourish, they looked, well, lonely. "Be good and you'll be lonely." She had always smiled before when she thought of those words. But not that morning. Not when she stood back, studying the plants, wondering at their stubborn loneliness. And it wasn't Armando, Pamela, Juanito, or even Tavelé, but the package that had come to mind. The one the size of a paperback, wrapped in butcher paper and tied with twine. She shook her head, but the image remained, and so she had climbed the stone stairs to the terrace and then the iron stairway to the rooftop terrace, where she had opened the door to the laundry room. There it sat alone on the top shelf. The package Jacob had given her.

She frowned. She had never felt lonely before knowing him. Darn him. And after recovering from their breakup she had thought she never would again, but here she was, years later, imagining her lavender seedlings were lonely, and all because of him. Darn him. Darn him. Darn him.

Not that Jacob had initiated their parting. It was she who had done that. A parting she did not regret. Not once or ever. But, even so, she had felt lonely. She had grown accustomed to their weekly twenty-four hours, eight a.m. sharp Saturday, when he would arrive, his arms loaded with fruits and vegetables from the farmer's market, until eight a.m. sharp Sunday, when off he would go to catch a church service somewhere in his community.

They always passed their twenty-four hours at her place, because, though Jacob had many admirable characteristics, housekeeping was not one of them. At his place, you were likely to find newspapers, sports gear, laundered shirts on hangers and wrapped in plastic, and other miscellanea strewn about. There would be moldy take-out in the fridge—no, he didn't cook or even barbecue—and countless blinks on the answering machine. His clutter didn't bother him, he said, but he treasured the quiet simplicity of Callie's studio—"Spartan," he called it—and the meals she made from scratch. Their weekly twenty-four hours gave him, he said, respite from the social hurricane of his life.

Likely as not after she had put the groceries away, he would draw a canceled stamp from his pocket to place by the stamp she had placed on the counter. Stamps from other times and places they had given each other the week before. They would then tell each other about the envelope or parcel, the relationship between its sender and receiver, and the modes of transportation used to carry the stamp between them. The stories did not have to be accurate. How could they have known? But they did have to be plausible. And so they each, during the week, would have done some research on distant times and places. In spite of the wide variety of possibilities, their stories without exception turned out to be about how lovers overcame seemingly insurmountable odds to end up in each other's arms, which is where each Saturday morning they, too, ended up, after lowering Callie's Pullman bed, if their passion did not overtake them beforehand.

It was when Jacob's stories started turning to lovers bent on marriage that she began to get nervous. She should have ended their relationship then.

She went over to the package, blew the dust off the sprig of lavender, placed the package inside a box of the philosopher's books, and shut the lid.

Twenty-Seven

O N AUGUST 2ND, CALLIE WOKE JUST AS THE SUN began to light the sky. It was Sunday morning, but there was no time for lounging. Pamela was coming back. She would have given Pamela some time to settle in. But after realizing that it was not her lavender, but *she* who was lonely, she had decided to invite Pamela for dinner that very day. She bounded out of bed. She needed to get everything ready.

She made her bed, folding and tucking in the corners of the sheets, military style, like her father had taught her, and then opened the curtains to the patio. She looked up at the avocado tree laden with nearly ripe fruit and then hazarded a glance at the lavender plants, which stood lined up in their pots like brave little soldiers. She shook a finger at them. "There's nothing to be brave about." Then she took a quick tour about her room, noting that everything looked the way it should. She would shower. And then she would practice. She began humming "Tea for Two" from the Clora Bryant recording Pamela had loaned her.

She shivered when she slipped out of her PJs. The bathroom was cool, but she realized that wasn't the real reason. Silly as it was, she was shivering with excitement. Silly, yes, but there it was. With everyone out of touch, she had not been able to share her new enthusiasm with anyone, and, besides, no one else would understand. Not the way Pamela would.

She turned on the shower and leaned in to place a bucket to catch the cold water for her plants. She stood up. Shouldn't she jot down some notes, so she wouldn't forget? She stepped back into her bedroom and picked up a pad from the bedside table. What was most important? Okay. Here goes. She started writing. "Lips tingling less, notes sounding more . . ." How would she put it? More . . . more . . . ah, focused, that's it. "Focused." And what else? Oh, yeah. "And easier to produce." She added. "Gifts of the breath."

She ran back into the bathroom, moved the bucket, and stepped into the warm shower. She leaned back to wet her hair. Not that she had played many notes, but no matter. She foamed shampoo into her curls, then rinsed. She had started with middle C and added a note every couple of days, like Pamela had suggested. Not pushing it. She got all the way up an octave. And she had sung and buzzed the notes, too. Singing, buzzing, and playing along with the tape Pamela had given her. It was like having her there, in a way. She had liked that.

WHEN she finished dressing, she calculated the time it would take Pamela to clear customs, get a taxi to the Teatro Principal, and walk up the hill to her house. Then she filled every moment getting ready.

"Good timing," Pamela said when she called her. "I just walked in the door."

She blurted out, "Would you like to come to dinner?" And then caught herself. She hadn't even asked Pamela how she was feeling. "Oh, that is, if you're not too tired."

"I hoped you would invite me to dinner," Pamela laughed. "I haven't a bean in the house, and I'm starved."

It was only five p.m. But why not? "Well, yes, come whenever you like. How do salad, lentil stew, quesadillas, and fresh blueberries sound?"

"I'll be right there. Well, I might just take a peek at the baby things first. They're too cute to leave in suitcases."

Suitcases? How many baby things had Pamela brought with her? Callie laughed. She started to say goodbye and then had a feeling she'd forgotten something. She closed her eyes a moment to think. "Oh, I almost forgot. Do you know how to get here?"

"Didn't you say you're around the corner and up the hill from me?"

"Right. The stone house with the mesquite door."

She put down the phone and smiled, glad she had set the table. And then she noticed the jaguar eyeing the empty vase. She had meant to pick some bougainvillea. "Well," she told him. "Everything else is ready, and that will be, too." She swiped the vase off the table and skipped down the stairs to the garden.

PAMELA started talking as soon as she opened the door. "I couldn't wait to see you. I wanted to ask you right away. I knew the first time I saw you with Juanito. You didn't see me. But I saw you with him one day in the Plaza Baratillo. And then I saw you with other children gathered around asking you questions."

Callie smiled. "They like to hear their names in English. You know, John for Juan, Mary for Maria, etc."

"Well, like I said, I knew right away. But remember what I said about Ami Mai. She likes to think things through."

Like with their wedding. And planning for the baby. No problem there. Doña Petra was delighted to help out.

"It's not like there's a list of contenders, I told her. Oh, I don't mean anything by that. Even if there were, I would pick you. But still, I understood, she likes all the Is dotted and Ts crossed. And so, besides my flawless intuition, I used reason," Pamela said and laughed. "You speak Spanish fluently, and you live just around the corner."

True. But what was she getting at? Spanish lessons?

"Hey, nice angel," Pamela said, gesturing toward the stone angel she had just noticed.

"One of Juanito's sales. It arrived with a broken wing." She touched the wing. "I just got around to having it repaired."

"Oh, yeah," Pamela said and laughed. "He came to my door the day I left. I am now the proud owner of a Gorky González serving bowl with a crack down the middle."

Callie laughed.

Pamela turned back to Callie. "Anyway, as I was saying, you're kind to children. And there's more . . . Wait a minute. I was on a roll there until I saw the angel." She laughed and then paused, looking up. "What was it . . . ? Oh, yeah." She looked again at Callie. "And you don't let fear stand in your way."

Me? Facing down fear? She smiled, imagining herself in line with the brave little lavender plants.

"I saw how wide your eyes were when you arrived for your lesson."

She stiffened. Had she been that easy to read?

"It could be a hitch, your being Armando's friend. He's not exactly on my side, as you know." She frowned, then smiled. "But, on the other hand, if you can tolerate him, you must have the patience of Job."

Hmm.

"And you have a gentle voice. The more I told Ami Mai about you, the more she saw I had been right from the start. And my mother was delighted, when I told her."

"Delighted about?"

"About your being our baby's grandmother, of course. Her local grandmother, that is. My mother will be here for the birth, and so will Ami Mai's. But they don't live here. Like you."

Me? The local grandmother. Callie noticed the jaguar through the window. She knew what he would think: More like the *loca* grandmother. Or was Pamela the crazy one, asking her so soon? Still, it was a nice idea. She imagined cradling Pamela's baby. But then she imagined Armando watching her. He was scowling. Pamela was right. He wouldn't be happy about it. It was one thing to continue trumpet lessons over his objections. Another thing to grandmother Pamela's baby. Oh, dear. Lovely as the idea was, she should not accept. At least not without time to think.

"Well, what do you think?"

She couldn't say yes or no. But she had to say something. Something true. "It's quite an honor." And now she had to stall. Quickly. She gestured toward the door to the dining area. "Didn't you say you were starved?"

Pamela appeared not so easily derailed. "Okay, I'll give you some time to think it over. It took Ami Mai a while to get used to the idea, too. But now she's as excited as I am." Pamela led their way into the dining area. "Bring on the lentil stew."

Callie pulled out a chair for Pamela and then poured her a glass of water. When she came back carrying the tray with their meal, she glanced at the jaguar. Was he frowning?

"AND . . ." Pamela said when Callie was on the way back to the table with a second bowl of stew for her. "How's the trumpet?"

Up to that point, they had eaten in silence, Pamela having

been too focused on eating to speak, and Callie preoccupied with how to deal with the grandmother question. It put her in a difficult position. Not just with Armando, but also with Gwendolyn. If she were to be the baby's local grandmother and Gwendolyn came to town, there she would be rocking the baby when Pamela brought Gwendolyn back from the airport. "Gwendolyn, this is Callie, the woman I told you about. Our baby's local grandmother." She took in a breath. Gwendolyn would approach to admire the baby. And Callie would not be able to take her own eyes off Gwendolyn. Nor would she be able to speak. She coughed. Her mouth went dry at the thought. She saw Gwendolyn, tired as she would be from travel, noticing something amiss and looking at her with a quizzical look. She closed her eyes. She couldn't let that happen. She sighed. Therefore, she could not be the local grandmother. But what could she tell Pamela?

She opened her eyes and looked at the jaguar. Perhaps he had been right, after all. She *would* be a *loca* grandmother. Normally a grandmother, being a grandmother, has had the experience of raising at least one baby. But she had never raised a baby, nor had even had younger siblings. The jaguar looked skeptical. Well, she *had* tutored and, yes, there was Juanito, but that was different from having children in her care. It was only right that she not accept Pamela's offer. Kind as it was. As much as she wanted to help out, it would not be best for the baby.

She continued before the jaguar could respond. And, second, there were others better equipped than she. Doña Petra had raised numerous children. She was getting older and should be cleaning less in any case. And she would be happy to clean her own house to give Doña Petra the time off. She would help pay for baby care, too. Her thoughts began to race.

With Doña Petra, the baby would become bilingual easily. And Pamela's Spanish would improve, too. She would be on hand, of course, to answer questions. And she would help out in any way she could, when she was in town. But what with her mother and aunt getting older, she didn't know when she might suddenly find she had to be out of town. Doña Petra never left town. Appointing her local grandmother would be better for everyone concerned. All quite logical.

"Callie?"

"Sorry." She stood up. "Can I get you something else? Tea, perhaps."

Pamela laughed. "I'm fine now." She gestured toward Callie's chair. "Sit. Tell me . . ."

It's a good thing she had had time to think. She sat down and folded her hands on her lap. "Okay."

"How are you doing with the trumpet? Have you found its magic yet?"

She breathed out a sigh of relief. "I forgot."

"Not to practice, I hope?"

"No, no. My list." She felt through her pockets. "It's here somewhere."

"You made a list?"

Of course, she did, chimed in the jaguar. Callie scowled at him. She felt the paper and pulled it out. "Here it is."

"That's great," Pamela said, when Callie finished reading the list to her. "Now, did you listen to the Cora Bryant album?"

"Every day. I love it."

"Good. I didn't tell you 'Gal with the Horn' is the first record my mother gave me. She said, 'If you are going to play the trumpet, then you'd better know that you're not alone. Plenty of other women have played, too. The lady teacher I found told me that. She's white, but that doesn't matter. She plays with the orchestra and in clubs. And she's going to teach you how to play whatever you want.' My father just stood there with his mouth open a moment, and then he shook his head the way he does and smiled. 'Whatever you think, Mother.'"

Callie felt tears come to her eyes. "You have wonderful parents."

"Yes," Pamela said. "I hope I can be half as good."

"You will be," Callie said.

"And you'll be a great granny." She picked up the list Callie had left on the table. "A list-making grandmother." She laughed. "Can't wait to see you holding her in one arm to free your other for making a list." She mimicked the motion.

She felt the warmth of a baby in her arms again and then a chill went through her. "What if I let her go?"

"To make a list?"

Let her go. Why had she said that! It wasn't in her prepared speech. And, besides, there was no way she might let Pamela's baby go. There would be no reason for someone to take Pamela's baby from her arms. None at all. Imagine that. No reason at all. Her body filled with light. Not that she would have the baby all the time, of course. But, still, she would have plenty of time with the baby. She imagined rocking her to sleep, spooning apple sauce into her little mouth, reaching her arms out to catch her taking her first wobbly steps. And when the baby went to school, she would take snacks to the playground like other grandmothers. All this, she could have with Pamela's baby.

"Callie," Pamela spoke quietly. "Are you afraid you'll drop her? I am, sometimes."

She reached over and took Pamela's hands in hers. "No, I'm not afraid I'll drop her. And neither will you."

Pamela slouched back in her chair. "I hope not."

"You'll be fine." She took in a breath and sat at attention. As the baby's local grandmother, she would see to it that Pamela was fine. What would she do if Gwendolyn did know Pamela and came to town? Well, she would have to cross that bridge when she came to it. And Armando? She sighed. Armando. He would just have to get used to it.

Twenty-Eight

PAMELA HAD SAID, "PLAY A G. OKAY. NOW PLAY a melancholy G. Now a happy one. Now a frightened one. How about an enthusiastic one?" And so, after closing Pamela's garden gate behind her, Callie paused to savor how the same note sounded different—at least when Pamela played. It wasn't just the note itself, it was the repetition and rhythm Pamela added, and how the note grew louder or softer. And there was something else she could not put her finger on, something about the quality of the note itself. It sounded simple when Pamela played, but when she tried, she didn't hear much of a difference. "Try putting images or words with your notes," Pamela had said. "That can help."

She started walking, shaking her head in wonder. Would she ever be able to play like that? She stopped. Her father could. Note his stomping bulls and dancing bears. And the melodies he played that had made her cry as a child. She started walking again. Her father's sad songs reminded her of Pamela playing *"El Niño Perdido."* She thought back to Pamela's worries about caring for her baby, about dropping her. She appeared, now that she thought of it, a little lost herself. But wasn't that natural for a first-time mother, to feel not quite up to the task? Or was there more to Pamela's nerves than that? Was she afraid of losing her baby?

She was so absorbed in thought that she didn't notice Nacho sitting on the stairs. But when she heard "Callie," said emphatically the way people in the barrio acknowledged each other, she looked at him. She saw him taking in the trumpet case she carried and found herself straightening a little as if she had already learned to play.

Nacho would, he assured her, keep an eye out for Tavelé. "*No te preocupes*," he said. She repeated those words as she entered her patio. There *was* nothing to be worried about. With everyone away, she had gotten all the summer household tasks done, her current translation was going well, and now Pamela was back and Armando soon would be. She looked up. There was not a cloud in the sky, and she had plenty of time for lunch, finishing her translation, and then looking for Tavelé herself. Who knows, with the way her luck was going, she could find him that very day. She imagined the sound of a G expressing the look on Armando's face when she told him she'd found Tavelé.

She opened the door to the dining area. And in any case, there *was* news she could tell him this very day. The rumor Pamela had heard about openings in the orchestra, including one for cello. It would be perfect for Claude. She started toward the phone. Then she noticed her computer and stopped. First things first. Now that she had a cell again, she could talk to him when looking for Tavelé. She fixed herself a sandwich and then returned to her document. But still it took her a moment to concentrate, with the image of Armando and Claude arm in arm in Guanajuato dancing through her head.

WHEN she finished working, she slipped her cell in her shirt pocket, put a leash and some dog biscuits in her backpack, and then headed toward her door. Such good news about the cello opening. And here she had been worrying, worrying, worrying about how to tell Armando she was becoming a local grandmother. With Claude in town, he would surely calm down about Pamela, and, besides, he would be too busy to care if she had other commitments. Perhaps he would even pitch in. When she opened her door to leave, she saw two Jehovah's Witnesses down the *callejón* where she had intended to go. She'd have to delay her exit. No matter, she could pull some weeds to pass the time. She shut the door again and went down to the patio, patting the angel's wing on the way.

When she passed under the patio tree, an avocado landed with a thump behind her. She turned and squatted to pick it up. Squashed on one side and having left a dark mark on the tile. What a pity. She glanced around the patio. And not the only one. She looked up. And there would be more. She sighed. She would have to get out the pole with the basket Armando had had made for her to pick them. But not now.

By the time she had picked up the avocados, cleaned the stained tiles, and opened the door again, the Jehovah's Witnesses were nowhere in sight. Good. Well, no time like the present to call Armando. She took the cell from her pocket. She was glad she had put the call off. So much nicer to break the happy news when she was looking for Tavelé. It would be as if Armando were walking with her. She dialed the number as she started down the *callejón* stairs.

"Who told you that?" Armando asked when Callie mentioned the opening for a cellist. His tone sounded harsh. She stopped walking. Before she could think of an answer, he guessed. "I suppose it was Pamela. Causing trouble again."

What was going on? "What do you mean? I thought you would be happy."

"Happy to have that woman meddling in my life?"

"I mean about the cello opening."

"You assumed I had not heard?"

She sat on a low stone wall by the stairs. "Well, I thought, if you did, surely you would have called. I mean . . . It sounds like such an opportunity."

"Now look, Callie. The openings are no sure thing. Maestro Chávez has enough on his hands without auditions. Neither is it sure that Claude would win the audition. Or that he would want to audition in the first place. He's teaching in Paris, you know." He mumbled, "Where we would have been right now, if I had had any sense." And then he continued, "Who knows what the atmosphere in the orchestra will be like if Pamela gets her way about firing Maestro Chávez."

Pamela wanting to fire the maestro. Armando was getting carried away again. "Armando . . ."

"And that jerk who mocks everyone will be guest conducting the week after vacation. What if he gets hired to take Maestro Chávez's place? I couldn't do that to Claude. Put him in such a position."

"But what about Claude? What does *he* think?"

"Let's leave Claude out of this."

She stood up. "You mean he doesn't know?" She should keep going. Maybe she would come across Tavelé, and then Armando would settle down. She started down the stairs again.

"No, and he won't if I have anything to do with it."

She held the phone away from her a moment and looked at it, as if then she could see what was going on. She tried to talk. "But . . ."

"Look. I told you. The openings are no sure thing. So why tell him?"

If only she could think of a husband story. There must

have been plenty who had withheld information and lived to regret it, but she couldn't think of a single one.

"And Pamela better not either."

"Pamela? She doesn't even know Claude exists."

"Well, I wouldn't put it past her to spread the word to everyone she *does* know, and someone's bound to know Claude."

"Oh, I don't know, I think she has other things on her mind." She realized as soon as the words slipped out that she should have kept her mouth shut.

"Oh, you know her so well, it seems. But she did tell *you* about the opening, didn't she?"

She tried to direct the conversation to Tavelé, telling Armando how his driver Jorge, the other drivers, the mail carriers, the butchers, and Nacho were on the lookout for him, and how she was looking for him herself at that very moment. It was like having him there with her. And wasn't that nice? Her words did not quite ring true even to herself. And they did nothing to dissuade Armando, whose tirade against Pamela grew more insistent and veered at times toward her, too. She hadn't searched Pamela's house first thing, the way she was supposed to, thus giving Pamela the chance to hide Tavelé elsewhere. By the time he had finished and abruptly hung up, she had gotten so discombobulated that she was no longer sure where she was other than she had entered a dead-end path. When she turned to leave, there, coming toward her, were the Jehovah's Witnesses.

"ARE you lost?" they asked her. "Can we help?"

She stiffened. Then, not wanting to give herself away, she pulled back her shoulders and managed a calm, "I'm fine. I live nearby." As if to prove she knew where she was going, she turned up the hill at the corner, instead of down, the one sure way to reorient oneself, as anyone familiar with the geologic bowl that was Guanajuato knew. By heading uphill, she continued lost, and ran into the Jehovah's Witnesses several more times. Finally, she headed downhill, as she should have from the beginning, and once in the historic center easily found her way to her barrio.

When she got home, she was relieved to find that, in spite of her detour, she had time to work on her translation before dinner. Neither had her feet wandering, as Pamela would have said, been in vain, for though she had found no apples, nor had she seen Tavelé, she did have some worthwhile thoughts.

She sat at her desk, turned on her computer, and then leaned back. First, there was Armando's odd aside that it would have been better for them to be in Paris than in Veracruz. Why had he said that? And then there was his reaction to the cello opening. Had their relationship taken a turn for the worse in Veracruz? Would they have done better in Paris?

Why? Well, there was the language difference, and people tended to take on different personalities when speaking different languages. Was that it? Had Claude's speaking Spanish been the problem? She could reassure Armando by telling him about the Portuguese husband who had seen too many World War II movies and so had turned into a complete maniac when speaking German. She had had to have him hospitalized in Berlin. But once they returned to Lisbon, he became his sunny self. She would leave out the end of the story, how when climbing an olive tree to offer her a branch, her intended had fallen, and that had been the end of him. But, in any case, Claude wasn't likely to do anything rash when back in the French language. And she felt sure he would calm down in

Spanish, too. He was probably just hung up on the difference between *ser* and *estar*, as plenty of others had been. Once he got that down, he would be fine. She could see to that.

She read over the first part of her manuscript and then stopped and leaned back in her chair again. Too bad she hadn't told Armando of that husband. But she clearly had not had her wits about her, especially once Armando started in on her. And not just about failing to search Pamela's house from the get-go, but for spending so much time with Pamela that she had not even missed Tavelé. She didn't care about Tavelé, did she? Admit it! That's what he had said. She felt so hurt, she almost said, "Who has been looking for him every day? Not you!" But instead she told him how she especially missed Tavelé in the evenings. How in other summers, when Armando was away, Tavelé would lie by her chair after dinner while she was working and then rest his head on her knee so she would pet him. They would stay there like that until bedtime. Both of them missing Armando. And now she missed both of them alone.

She returned to her manuscript and then stopped again. As for telling him about being the baby's local grandmother, there was no reason to tell him right away. Pamela would surely wait to announce her pregnancy until after the first trimester. So she had months to figure out what to say. And by then Armando would have calmed down about Claude, as he had always done before. And with that reassuring thought, she returned to her translation.

Twenty-Nine

*C*ALLIE CHECKED HER BACKPACK AT THE ENTRANCE to the library, a security measure that annoyed her because it meant she then had to juggle laptop, notebooks, pens, pencils, billfold, and keys up the stairs to the reading rooms. But she climbed the stairs cheerfully enough, happy that she would have no problem meeting the deadline she set for herself, which, as was her custom, fell a day before her translation was due. That had served her well, since she never knew when Armando might appear with an emergency. Something was brewing now, she was sure.

She set up at her customary desk by a balcony overlooking Truco Street. *Truco.* Trick. Dodge. Funny, she hadn't thought of that the other day when she managed to dodge the Jehovah's Witnesses there.

She read through the document. Just the usual mining language. She should be able to get a draft done in time to catch Pamela after rehearsal and set up another lesson.

She had just finished the last sentence when she heard the clock strike a quarter past one. That gave her fifteen minutes to pack up and get to the theater by one-thirty. More than enough time. She juggled the items back down the stairs to retrieve her backpack.

On the way to the theater, she passed a taco stand. The sautéed onions made her mouth water. Which reminded her of Pamela. She should start thinking about taking good care of herself, eating well, getting plenty of sleep. She could mention that when she saw her. Oh, and see if Tavelé had turned up again. Pamela had promised to hold him, if he did. And wasn't there something else? She looked up a moment. Oh, yeah, she needed to schedule a trumpet lesson.

She paused. Perhaps she should make a list. She slid out of her backpack and opened it. Her notepad was there, but she couldn't find her pencil. She leaned against a wall and started looking through the pack. As she did so, a man carrying stacked boxes of Coca-Cola on his shoulders tried to get between her and the bus in the street. She turned to make way for him, but nonetheless he jostled her backpack as he went by, and in her attempt to hang onto it, she dropped her notepad, which fell under the bus. She would just have to remember what she wanted to ask Pamela.

Hadn't she read somewhere about using imagery? Might as well give it a try. The first person Tavelé followed home from orchestra rehearsal played the trumpet. That linked two things. She held up two fingers. And for reminding Pamela to rest. What? Ah, a hammock. She added a third finger. She imagined Tavelé lying in a hammock and playing the trumpet. That would do it.

A doorman stopped her at the theater door and said, "Musicians only." Miguel, a clarinet player, clarified as he passed by: "The guest conductor. He doesn't want anyone seeing how he treats us."

"Oh . . ." Too bad. At least Armando was spared.

Miguel turned back. "If you're looking for Armando, he just left."

"Armando?" She took in a breath. What was he doing back? She had just talked to him the day before, and he hadn't mentioned coming back early.

"He's on his way to Maestro Chávez's."

"Is he ill?"

"I don't think so."

He must be. And it must have been such an emergency that Armando hadn't time to let her know. She should call him. But there was something else she was to do. She noticed her three fingers waiting to remind her. Tavelé. Hammock. Trumpet. "Is Pamela here?"

"She's here all right." He pointed a thumb inside. "Can't you hear her?"

Callie leaned toward the door. "Is she practicing?"

"She's blasting her trumpet up to the ceiling. It sounds like she's trying to rival the firework rockets."

Like her father on a bad day.

The sound stopped. She started to push by the musicians exiting.

"You'd better wait here." Miguel said, "*No tarda.*"

No tarda could mean anything from five minutes to five hours. She looked at her watch again. It was one-thirty-five. She stepped back from the door.

Miguel went off, leaving her standing there, tapping her foot. Armando back. Was it Maestro Chávez? Or had something happened with Claude?

She heard an angry wail of trumpet. Had Pamela been insulted by the guest conductor? Callie looked at her watch. She should call Armando, but the noise of the passing buses made talking impossible. She started to walk away. Then she looked at her fingers again. Tavelé playing a trumpet in a hammock. A hammock. That's what Pamela needed. Rest. She would tell her that. Then they could walk up the hill together, and she would call Armando from home. If only Pamela would stop blasting and pack up her instrument.

A bus stopped and people piled in. More musicians came out of the theater and, finally, Pamela.

She headed straight to Callie. "Hoping to conspire with Armando, were you?"

Conspire. Oh, dear. She cleared her throat. "I . . ." She held up her three fingers. "I wanted to ask you . . ."

Pamela looked up at the darkening sky. "I've got to get a taxi."

She looked at her three fingers. "Tavelé."

"What?"

She kept her eyes on her fingers. Lying in the hammock. Playing the trumpet. She started coughing.

"So Tavelé *is* all you care about?"

Why had she started with Tavelé? "I was wondering . . ." She wanted to ask her about sleep, but she couldn't get out the rest of the sentence before coughing.

"Wondering what?"

She turned toward Pamela, who was flagging down a taxi. If only she could stop coughing. She stepped into the street behind Pamela.

"I've already told Armando all I know about Tavelé." She opened the taxi door. "If that's what you're wondering about." She slammed the door and turned away as the taxi drove off.

Callie stood there as the downpour began, staring at the taxi and holding up her three fingers.

HUDDLING at her entry door, her soaked jacket pasted against her, she regretted not having an awning. It might help, too, if she would carry her umbrella. But the weather had been so lovely in the morning. She took off her backpack and unzipped it, holding it close to protect the laptop. She felt for her keys in the top pocket, where she always put them. Nothing. She tried to remember whether they had been among the things she had juggled up and down the stairs of the library. She always had them there. She glanced down the *callejón* and then looked at the backpack. She must have put the keys somewhere else, but where? She felt around under the laptop. Nothing. She unzipped the side pockets. No keys. She slipped her hand into the side pocket of her jacket. Not there. She opened the top pocket of her backpack again. The keys had to be there. She felt and looked again. No keys. She stared down the *callejón*. Had they fallen out when the Coca-Cola man bumped into her backpack?

She zipped her backpack and cradled it against her chest. She may be locked out of her house and all wet, but she had her work, and—with Pamela so angry—she no longer need worry about being her baby's local grandmother. What had she been thinking anyway, agreeing to coddle a baby, and at the risk of meeting Gwendolyn. It was better this way. If she and Pamela were not close, she could leave town when Gwendolyn came to visit. No need to explain her absence. She would be no one important to Pamela or her baby, just a neighbor who had taken a trumpet lesson. Learned to breathe.

She closed her eyes and rested her back against the door. Had she learned to breathe? It seemed not. Not if she considered honestly how she felt now. Which was like fainting.

She felt herself falling backward. Was she fainting? No. The door was giving way. She grabbed the handle to catch herself and turned toward the opening.

Doña Petra stood just inside, her shoulder against the partly open door. "*Señora? Está bien?*"

She paused, pondering Spanish usage. Doña Petra continued to use formal pronouns and verb forms with her. Juanito and other children had used informal forms from first meeting her. Were times changing?

Doña Petra shook her keys to get her attention.

So, it was as simple as that. She had left her keys in the lock. She had never done *that* before. And then she remembered the Jehovah's Witnesses questioning her when she was leaving. No wonder she had forgotten the keys.

She let Doña Petra out and then returned to the dining room. The trumpet stood on its bell by the terrace door. She put her hands on her hips. No point in asking Pamela for a lesson now. She would get rid of the trumpet. It's what got her into this mess in the first place.

When she picked it up, it looked as if it were beaming at her. "Happy you've caused so much trouble," she said. She glanced at the jaguar, who appeared to be thinking: just like your father, blaming anyone but himself. "Well, so be it!" she said. "This trumpet is out of here." The case would go back to Pamela, if she ever spoke with her again.

She went into the kitchen for a bag, put the trumpet in it, and placed it by the entry door. She would carry it to a dumpster herself, she thought, brushing her hands against each other in satisfaction. While she was at it, she may as well get rid of the other things she had bought from Juanito. Stop kidding herself. Fixed or not, they cluttered up her house, distracting her. She had her work. Good work. That should be the focus of her life.

She shivered. She had to get out of those wet clothes. Then she noticed the answering machine blinking. She went over to the machine and played the message. Her mother. She wanted to talk to Callie about her trip. Her mother taking a trip? That was odd. Her mother resisted driving fifty miles to the closest city. She headed back toward the terrace. Her aunt must be behind this one. Where could they be going? She looked out over the garden. Maybe to that new B&B in the town down the highway, the one with the Civil War cannonball in a column of the court house. Aunt Ida had said the town was courting tourists. She smiled thinking of her aunt taking her mother to a B&B ten miles away. "Baby steps," her aunt had said to Callie when she got frustrated learning to knit. "That's how you learn. Baby steps." The same language Pamela had used. Was that what her aunt was doing, using baby steps to help her mother overcome fear of travel? Well, she couldn't find out now. She had to warm up first. When she entered the terrace to go downstairs, she glanced at the trumpet in the bag by the door and then at the angel by the stairway going down. They looked like sentinels, both of them.

Thirty

CALLIE HAD TAKEN HER SHOWER AND JUST LIFTED the receiver to dial her mother when someone pounded on the *callejón* door. Armando. She looked over at the jaguar, whose eyes filled with compassion. She put the phone down and frowned at him. Compassion? For whom?

"Callie, Calecita." Armando's voice sounded anxious. She looked at her watch. Three p.m. The personal deadline for her translation was six p.m. No time for a scene. "I listen," she heard her aunt say, when she'd asked how she calmed down families in conflict. "I listen." That's what she would do. If she had to say something, she would repeat what he said to show him she had heard. That would have to do for now.

He was still pounding on the door when she got there, and it opened so quickly she backed into a potted cactus. "Ouch."

"I told you to move that pot."

She pulled out the spines. "I'm okay."

The telephone rang. "I'll let the answering machine get that," she said, and went to turn off the ringer.

He followed her into the kitchen. "I'm sorry, Chou." He ran his fingers through his hair. "I'm just so upset. That Pamela. She won't give Tavelé back."

So he was upset about Pamela. But he hadn't come back early because of Pamela, had he? She recalled her aunt's advice again. Listen. Just listen.

She patted a stool by the center island, and he sat down, his shoulders slumped. He leaned his head into his hands. "I knew she couldn't be trusted."

"You knew she couldn't be trusted." She didn't like how that sounded. He might think she agreed with him.

"Boy, did the guest conductor lay into her." He smirked. "She deserved it, though. I've told her not to play those jazz riffs."

"You told her not to play jazz riffs."

"She plays them in rehearsals. It's annoying. I told you that before. Maestro Chávez tolerates it, but this guy set her straight."

"He set her straight."

"He told her to stop it or go back to Harlem." He mimicked the conductor pointing the way for Pamela.

She gasped. She could not repeat that. She felt sick to her stomach. "Armando . . ."

Armando looked down a moment and his voice became soft. "I've been trying to tell her for months. She wouldn't listen to me."

"Set someone straight with a racist comment!" Callie was shaking all over.

"Okay, no one deserves that, not even her."

She looked him in the eyes. "Certainly not."

"Okay, I never should have talked that way. But listen to this. When I asked her to give Tavelé back, she told me she didn't have him." Armando stared hard into her eyes. "Can you believe that? Didn't she know I would find out the truth?"

"She told you she didn't have Tavelé." She coughed. Was she really supposed to just repeat words?

"I got really angry then."

"I can imagine. But Armando . . ."

"I told her she had twenty-four hours to get Tavelé back from wherever she had hidden him and give him to me."

There was so much she needed to say to him, but not now. She looked over at her backpack.

Armando followed her eyes. "You have a deadline, don't you?"

"Six p.m."

"I'll clear out of here," he said. "Meet me for dinner at the Santa Fe?" He scooted his stool back and stood up. "I just can't get over her lying like that." He shook his head. "Who does she think she is?"

"Armando . . ."

"Okay, I'm going. I'm going." He headed across the terrace toward the *callejón* door and stopped when he saw the trumpet in the bag. "I'll get rid of this for you." He picked it up.

"Armando, I . . ."

"I know how you don't like clutter. Besides, I told Pamela you wouldn't be taking any more lessons from her."

Callie took in a breath. "You told her I would not be taking lessons."

"I told her you were helping me find Tavelé, that's why you took a lesson."

"You told her . . . What?!" Her chest tightened.

"I thought she was going to hit me." He put the trumpet under his arm and opened the door. "You can get to work now."

She walked up to him and reached out. "Give me that trumpet."

"Don't tell me you want this thing?" he said holding it away from him, as if it stank.

She took it from him. "Now, go back into the dining area and sit down." She shoved the door shut, put the trumpet back where it had been, and followed him.

Armando took a seat at the dining table, and she sat across from him, her back to the terrace doors.

"Pamela does not have Tavelé."

"But he went to her house."

"He is always running off, Armando. He ran off from you, remember?"

His face turned dark. "Whose side are you on?"

"Armando. Please." She paused, trying to control her breathing.

"You seemed to have gotten really buddy-buddy with Pamela. I suppose you made muffins for her."

She said nothing.

He leaned toward her. "Why can't you just come out and say what you're thinking?"

"Oh, so you're the model of candor?" She cringed, regretting her words and tone. But didn't she have a right to be angry with him for attacking Pamela the way he had? If only he had stayed in Veracruz with Claude the way he *should* have.

"Model of candor." He mimicked her tone. "What's that supposed to mean?"

She considered stopping before she said more things she would regret, but her tongue had other ideas. "What happened in Veracruz? Why did you come back early?"

Armando knocked his chair over standing up. "What has she done to you?"

Callie stood between him and the terrace door. It wasn't the best time, the best place, or the best manner, but she was not going to let another minute go by without telling him. "Armando . . ." She reached out to touch his arm. "It's time you were straight about Claude." What had she said? Straight about Claude. That sounded strange. She coughed. "I mean . . ."

"There's nothing to be straight about." He pushed her

aside, stalked across the terrace to the *callejón* door, and then turned to look at her. "It's over."

CALLIE stood at the open door, watching Armando walk down the *callejón*. She should follow him. But what would she say? That she, too, knew about loss? She shut the door and leaned against it. The trumpet stood there shrouded in the bag. Why hadn't she just let him take it and go? She took in a breath. She needed to stop interrogating herself. She lifted her chest. She would get back to work.

SHE had feared Claude was becoming impatient about living apart from Armando. She opened her laptop. And she had said nothing to warn Armando. She clicked the power button. Nothing at all.

She looked at the clock. Four p.m. Two hours until the document was due. The call to her mother would have to wait.

She read the first sentence and changed a word. That conversation could not be brief. And now she would have to talk to Pamela, too. But what could she say? The next line looked okay. Was Armando right? Was she siding with Pamela? Well, if she hadn't been before, she was now. How dare he call her a liar! The next line looked okay. No wonder she was angry. How many paragraphs to go? She counted them. Ten. She really needed to move on. And Pamela. So what if Armando told her Callie had asked for a trumpet lesson as a pretext for looking for Tavelé. Pamela should have given her a chance to explain instead of running off after rehearsal. Callie counted the paragraphs again. Still ten to go. She edited three lines. Didn't Pamela see how upset Armando was? Couldn't she have had some sympathy for him? She looked at the flyer of Tavelé on her desk. Where have you gone this time and why for so long?

The doorbell rang. Let it ring. She had to get her translation done. She read the next paragraph. Thank goodness it looked okay. The bell rang again. Wait a minute. Hadn't she seen the Jehovah's Witnesses down the hill when Armando left? She ran out the terrace door. The bell was still ringing. She ran back to her desk, stuffed the flyer in her pocket, and ran out the door again. The bell stopped ringing. She picked up her speed, calling *"Espérame, espérame,"* pulled open the door, and almost bumped into Juanito who was standing there holding out a plaster Virgin de Guadalupe. A gift from Armando, he said. Juanito had something else, too. Another letter for Callie that had been delivered to Juanito's grandmother by mistake.

Callie shoved the letter in her pocket, took the statue, and, looking up and down the *callejón*, asked Juanito if he had seen the Jehovah's Witnesses. When he pointed up the hill, she took off with the Virgin under her arm.

The first flight of stairs felt steeper than usual. She stopped and looked at the Virgin. How much do you weigh? She studied the hill. There were three *callejones* off the next landing. Which one had they taken? She had just started up again when she saw two men in slacks and pressed shirts coming from the *callejón* to the right and headed to the one to the left.

She had to catch their attention. "Señores, señores." They turned their heads in unison and stood looking down at her holding the Virgin de Guadalupe over her head.

SHE stood the Virgin on the dining table and then sat down at her desk, leaning back to catch her breath. She had offered the men an hour of her time to talk about the Bible, if they found the dog in the picture. They looked at each other a moment, and then the older of the two, a man close to her age, bowed slightly and said that they would be happy to look for Tavelé, but expected nothing in return. The man said she could count on them, and with another slight bow, introduced himself. "José Martín Gonzales Guzmán, *a sus órdenes.*"

She had heard the customary tag, "*a sus órdenes,*" many times before. But when Señor Gonzáles said the words, he looked at her in the eyes and smiled in such a way she knew he was truly at her service. She felt chagrined at her presumption, the crassness of the exchange she had offered. Could she do nothing right? She looked over at the jaguar, who stared back at her without comment.

Thirty-One

CALLIE NEEDED TO FOCUS ON HER WORK. A CUP of tea. That would help. She got up to put on the kettle and noticed a light blinking on the answering machine. It must be Armando. She pushed the button. "We need to talk." A woman's voice. Pamela? It had to be. She listened to the message again. Yes, Pamela. She sounded warm, almost contrite. How could that be? She looked at the phone. Dare she find out? She backed away. Not now. She had to finish the translation. And call her mother.

She was pulling her chair back to sit down when the doorbell sounded. She glanced at the translation, sighed, and then went to the terrace.

"Callie," Pamela called through the door. "Callie, are you there? Callie."

Her mouth went dry.

Pamela called again, "Callie. Callie."

She took a step toward the door and noticed the trumpet in the bag, ready to be given away. Her heart started pounding. What would Pamela think? She took in a slow breath. She could pretend she was not home. She turned to go back inside and then saw the look on the jaguar's face. She stopped. She hadn't been able to focus on her work anyway. She took in another slow breath. She may as well get it over with. She shoved the bag behind a pot and opened the door.

Pamela came rushing in. "Oh, you *are* here. Thank goodness." She gave Callie a little hug.

She studied Pamela's face. She looked friendly enough. But how could she be, after what Armando had told her?

"Do you have anything to eat? I am famished."

Pamela famished. Well, good thing she had gone to the door. "Yes . . . sure. How about a muffin?"

"Or two." Pamela laughed.

She caught herself glancing at Pamela's flat tummy. Where did she put it all?

"And some water. I'm dying of thirst."

She led Pamela through the dining area to the kitchen island, set the table, then filled two glasses of water, and got out some muffins, butter, and homemade mango jam.

"Anything else?" Callie picked up the tea kettle. "I was just going to have tea." She felt her eyelid twitch. She needed to calm down. She took in a breath. "I have fruit. Would you like a banana or an apple?"

Pamela patted a stool. "Sit down, Callie."

She set the kettle down. "Would you prefer orange juice?" She pointed to a turquoise bowl filled with oranges. "I could make some."

Pamela patted the stool again. "Take a load off."

She sat down and looked at Pamela. Her heart was racing, and she could barely breathe, but she had to say something. She clasped her hands to steady herself. "You wanted to talk, you said." She cleared her throat. "I'm sorry about Armando. He told me what he said."

Pamela picked up a muffin and rolled her eyes. "He's been on me from the beginning. First, he tried to get me to change my hair." She patted her curls. "Then he carried on about the jazz riffs." She put the muffin on her plate. "And now that

ridiculous story about you taking a lesson only to find Tavelé."
By the time she finished, she was near to shouting. She looked
at Callie. Her voice softened. "You wouldn't have . . ."

She fingered the rim of her water glass. "Well . . ."

Pamela reached for the muffin, then stopped and put her
hands down. "If you want to come to my house to look for
Armando's dog, then do it." She looked up at Callie. "I just
need you to be honest about it."

Be honest? Now she felt hot and sticky all over. She took
in a breath. "Well, Armando did think you had Tavelé. He
asked me to look . . ."

"So it was Armando's idea. That makes sense." She put a
muffin on her plate. "Ami Mai told me not to jump to conclusions about you."

She hadn't finished explaining. She cleared her throat.

"That Armando." She shook her head. "Look, Callie, I'm
sorry about how I acted at the theater. It's just that trust
doesn't come easily to me."

She understood that, and she was trying, but Pamela kept
interrupting. Callie put a finger against her pulsing lid. She had
to get on with it. "I had my own reason for taking the lesson."

Pamela put her palms against the table. "I need to get
things straight. That's how I am."

Get things straight. Okay. She took in a breath. "It wasn't
my reason. Looking for Tavelé."

Pamela went on as if she had not heard her. Her voice
softened and she looked down at her hands. "The summer I
turned seventeen, my cousin, the one who taught me to dive,
he tried to kiss me."

She leaned back. What was Pamela saying? Her cousin?
Didn't she want her to explain about the lesson? To be honest?
To tell her now? Wasn't that why she called?

"When I pulled away, he said, 'Don't worry, we're not related.'"

What was Pamela saying? "Not related? Your cousin said that?"

"He said, 'Ask your mom, if you don't believe me.'" She held out her hands and looked at them. "I am lighter than my mom, but so is my dad. I thought I'd taken after his side of the family." She looked at Callie. "But no. It was like my cousin said. I was adopted."

So, Pamela was adopted. Was that what she wanted to talk about? No. It was how she learned. Oh, my. She reached out and touched Pamela's hand. "That must have been hard, finding out that way."

"You don't know the half of it." She looked up at Callie. "But wait a minute . . . What did you say, about having your own reason for taking a lesson?"

"I wanted . . . to get to know you."

"That's why you asked for a lesson?"

She nodded. "Yes, that's why."

"Then it was me you were looking for, not a dog?" She laughed.

She smiled. "Yes, you. I heard you playing pedal tones one day when I passed your house. It reminded me of my dad, and then when you played "The Lost Child" . . . I had never heard it played that way . . ."

Pamela looked down at her hands. "Well, I guess I know what it's like. Feeling lost." She looked up at Callie and smiled. "But now everything is different." She stretched her arms above her head. "I would like some tea."

She breathed a sigh of relief and got up to put the kettle on.

Pamela started up again. "When my mother confirmed I was adopted, I told her I was a lesbian and not to expect grandchildren. I don't know why I said that. It just popped out. And here I am . . . pregnant!" She looked down at her tummy.

Callie looked at Pamela's tummy, too.

"I have an appointment with a doctor." She sat looking at Callie, as if she were hoping she would say something. Then she went on, hesitantly at first. "I . . . I also came by to see if you would go with me . . . It was Ami Mai's idea. She wanted to fly down herself. Dance through the clouds." She held her hands up over her head, dancing her fingers. She lowered her hands. "But she has performances." She took in a breath and looked at Callie, her face serious. "To be honest, I wasn't so sure about asking you. Not after what Armando said." She paused, and then went on. "But Ami Mai said I should take a chance and trust you."

Take a chance and trust her. So that's how trusting her seemed to Pamela—risky. She wanted to reassure her. She wished she could. But what could she say when she had been vacillating so? Nor had she been fully open with Pamela, or Armando, for that matter.

"That is, if you have the time . . . I know you work and all . . . But it wouldn't take long. And . . . " Her voice became soft. "It would mean a lot to me to have you there."

The scene in the Jardín came back to her again. The plaintive cry of the trumpet. Of course, she couldn't let Pamela go alone.

"So . . . " She opened her hands. "What do you think?"

She laid her hands on Pamela's and smiled. "I think yes."

Pamela laughed, sounding relieved. "Ami Mai was right again!" She took her hands back and put another muffin on her plate. "Funny, now when I think of it, what I said to Mom way back then, but I wasn't trying to be funny then. I wanted to hurt her. I said lots of other things, too."

She looked at the muffins on her plate, but did not reach for one. "The trumpet kept me sane. It balanced the darkness that came over me, seeing my mother anew. Not the woman who helped me up when I fell. Not the woman who taught me how to sing. Not the woman who loved me beyond measure. But the woman who made my life a lie. I no longer knew who I was or where I belonged."

She felt her stomach sink. Had Gwendolyn felt that way?

"Even now I sometimes feel that way. Especially when I go to a new place and don't yet have a cadre of friends or even one person, like you, whom I trust."

Could Pamela trust her? She thought of the trumpet she had snatched back from Armando. Yes, she could. She smiled. But then she thought of the loyalty Armando expected. Could *he* trust her?

"I told Mother she never would have lied like that to her own child."

Callie gasped.

"I know. My reaction was extreme, but I was a teenager, after all. I had hormones." She looked at her tummy again. "They're acting up now, too. Ami Mai reminded me of that when I was yelling about you."

"Oh." Callie felt her stomach tighten.

"Even back then I didn't yell for long. But neither did I talk to Mom or hang around her the way I had before. Mostly, I stayed in my room, practicing trumpet. I stopped seeing my friends, too. I didn't want to talk about the lie with anyone. Not even with my father. Everyone else brought him their troubles. But I could not. He was too close to my mother. I changed my college plans, too. I had been planning to stay in Chicago. But after I found out about the lie, I chose Mills College."

The kettle whistled, and Pamela paused.

"Oh, sorry." Callie'd forgotten all about the kettle. She turned it off and then poured the steaming water over chamomile leaves in the teapot. She set the pot in the center of the island.

Pamela leaned forward to smell the fragrance, smiled, and then leaned back again. "My father drove me there. To Mills. The week before we left, he came to my room. He said he had been remiss in not talking with me earlier. My mother's blood pressure had gone up, and he was worried about her—and me. He said it was not good for either of us to be estranged, and it would be worse with me so far away. He asked me to say something kind to Mom before we left. 'I suppose you want me to pretend nothing happened,' I said. 'No,' he said. 'I just want you to say a few kind words, and I want you to look your mother in the eyes when you do.'

"Before he left my room, he asked me to sit down, and then he sat beside me and took my hand in his. He reminded me that, as a rule, African Americans didn't know their history. Their ancestors, stolen from Africa, lost their language, their religion, their family connections. He said that what defined them, what defined me, was not blood relations, but actions, and that my behavior toward my mother defined me as unforgiving and unkind. He asked whether that was how I wanted to define myself." She sighed, as if hearing her father for the first time.

"Later in Paris I read Sartre." She took out a little book in French and put it on the table. "I don't think my father read him, but his lesson sounded the same. Choosing is not easy. You can't just choose to become a forgiving person any more than you can choose to become a great trumpeter. You have to take the many little steps to become one. You have to put yourself in the right environment. But it's also how you choose to see where you are, what you choose to make of where you are, what risks you choose to take. Of course, there are all kinds of limitations. And yet we have options within them. And sometimes, with attention, we can alter the limitations. At least those we have imposed on ourselves." She laughed. "That was quite a speech." She licked her lips. "My mouth is dry."

Callie poured tea into a cup and set it in front of her.

Pamela picked up the cup and blew on the tea, then set it down again. "I waited until the day we left. My instruments, bags, and boxes were already packed in the car. I thought we had everything, but my mother came out with another box. She set it on the hood of the car and turned to me with a look on her face I will never forget, a mixture of sadness and hope. 'I made something for your dorm bed. I hope you like it.' I opened the box. She had quilted together pieces of my favorite dresses from the time I was a little girl. I was so choked with tears I could barely speak, so I whispered, 'It's beautiful, Mom. You're beautiful, Mom.' We hugged until Dad said we had to go. I cried all the way to Omaha. Seven hours of crying."

Callie could feel the tears streaming down her own face.

Pamela looked up at Callie and laughed. "And now I've got you crying, too . . . and I haven't even finished." She laughed again. "But I've got to eat first." She picked up a muffin and took a bite.

Thirty-Two

WHEN PAMELA FINISHED HER SECOND MUFFIN, she brushed the crumbs off her fingers and said, "Have you read Plato's *Symposium*?"

"Some of it." It was one of the books the philosopher had left. "I liked the part where Socrates describes ascending a ladder of love, starting with passion for a beautiful body."

"Hum."

Odd. She didn't sound that interested, given she'd asked the question. But it *was* fascinating, what Socrates said. "There's passion, too, for the beauty of science—you, know, like the elegance of the periodic table."

"The periodic table?" She sounded skeptical.

"Really. I have one downstairs, if you'd like to see it."

Pamela laughed. "I'll take your word for it."

"Anyway, the seeker ends up contemplating beauty itself." It sounded like the philosopher, off by the lake in the mountains, away from the clutter of her house. Contemplating. A nice, quiet life. "What did you think of that part?"

"I haven't read *Symposium*."

"No?" Her mind strayed back to beauty. Unchanging, eternal, otherworldly beauty. It sounded blissful. She should ask the philosopher.

"But Ami Mai has."

"What's that?" She pinched herself discreetly. She should be listening to Pamela, not letting her mind wander or giving mini-lectures.

"I haven't read *Symposium*, but Ami Mai has. The story she told me was completely different from yours. Aristophanes told it. Not Socrates."

"There were several stories, I believe."

"Aristophanes's story was about the origin of love between humans, who were originally spherical. They looked like two people merged together back to back, forming a ball with four arms and four legs. They had one head with two faces pointing opposite directions. Did you read that part?"

"I don't think so." She remembered leafing through the book, drawn to the underlined parts. For some reason the philosopher had focused on Socrates. So she had, too. It wasn't just the final stage that had struck her, but an earlier one, about seeing the beauty in more than one person. She had seen that for herself. When she stood back and looked, they were all beautiful. All of the children. But perhaps that wasn't what Socrates meant. Another question for the philosopher.

"Well, there were three sorts: male-male, female-female, male-female. All equally natural. Get it?"

She paused a minute trying to capture what Pamela had just said when she hadn't been fully listening. Oh. Of course. Being gay was natural. She smiled. "Got it."

"And they were happy rolling about."

She pictured their arms and legs flapping as they rolled. But then she saw them gathering speed, bumping down the stairways of Guanajuato. That could be dangerous.

"Until, in a fit at their indifference to him, Zeus took out a sword." She raised her arm as if wielding Zeus's sword, then brought it down quickly, snapping her wrist. "He sliced them in two."

"Oh, dear." Callie winced.

"Apollo sewed their wounds." She wrapped her arms

around her chest. "But still the halves clung to their other halves, trying to unite again. They stopped eating, and became too weak for tributes to Zeus . . ."

"I thought Aristophanes was a comic writer. This story is not funny." But there was truth in it, wasn't there, the way lovers clung to each other, as if their lives depended on it. Hadn't she felt, when she parted from Jacob, as if she had lost a part of herself?

"It turned out all right." She took another sip of tea. "Zeus decided to move their genitals to the front so that they could come into contact when they embraced. They could satisfy each other that way. Soon they were happily eating, drinking, working, playing—and giving tributes to Zeus."

Happy. But for how long? Wouldn't something else come along to part them? She shook herself. Why was she being so negative? But wasn't that the deeper meaning? That loss follows from human love the way death follows from life. And wasn't it true?

Pamela reached for her teacup again, then pulled back and looked at Callie. "Ami Mai told me that's what love is. Feeling incomplete. Becoming whole with someone else."

She thought back to her attraction to Noah. How she had imagined becoming confident through him. Would she have?

"I thought 'This is it; she sees me as her other half.'"

She smiled. "Her *media naranja*."

"What?"

"Half of an orange. A Spanish version of a lover's other half."

"Oh, really? I didn't know that. But no, she hadn't thought I was her *media naranja*. She said I was like one of those spheres, self-satisfied and without need. She said I didn't know how to love."

"Oh, my." She hadn't seen that coming. She should have

been listening more closely. Self-satisfied and without need. It sounded like how Armando saw Pamela. He didn't seem aware of her vulnerability. Could Ami Mai have missed that side of Pamela, too? She poured Pamela another cup of tea. "Did she think you prided yourself on self-sufficiency? Was that it?"

"I guess that's how it seemed to her. Perhaps with reason. I admired her and enjoyed her. But I had never felt I would die without her by my side." She smiled a wan smile. "Well, not until she left." She took a sip of tea. "And then I got angry. I hated the idea of my happiness depending on her. Or on anyone, really."

She nodded. She understood the risk of becoming close to someone incomplete, changeable, fickle. Someone who altered the rules midway through the game. Someone like Jacob.

"I flew home and raged at my mother. It seemed like her fault. Her fault I had desperately wanted to be self-sufficient. Her fault Ami Mai left. Her fault I then felt severed in two. I picked up her Bible and demanded that she swear on it that she would never lie to me again."

Never lie? What did that have to do with it? Had Pamela sought self-sufficiency because of her mother's lie? Or was something else behind that hopeless desire? Something Pamela had not recovered from, in spite of her mother's love?

"She said no, she would not swear on the Bible. She told me she had waited many years to have a child. When she saw me for the first time, she wept, realizing that one day her baby would grow up and leave home. She would not leave me alone even with Dad for the first five years."

She had left her own newborn with a stranger. Her palms began to sweat.

"My parents moved to Chicago shortly after they adopted me, and everyone assumed I was their own. Mom preferred it that way. She said she loved her baby as much as any other mother, and she did not want to be treated differently from the mothers whose babies came from their own wombs. She did not want me to be treated differently either.

"Mom told me her mother had warned against keeping the adoption secret. 'You will be sorry one day,' her mother had said. And Mom was sorry. As angry and hurt as I was, I could see that. But that wasn't what made me feel safe again. It was something else, an admission she made. 'It wasn't just that I wanted us to be a normal family,' she said. 'I didn't want to share you with another mother. I wanted you to be mine alone.'"

Pamela lifted her teacup and held it in two hands. "I got it when she said that," she said. "I never wanted siblings. Remember? I'd even get my dander up if my parents showed too much attention to my friends. Mom and I. We were like two peas in a pod!" She laughed again.

Her warm, full laugh filled Callie's heart. So Pamela *had* recovered. She could love. *Of course*. She had married Ami Mai, after all. They were having a baby. She smiled. A baby she, herself, would hold.

"Mom said she would help me search for my biological mother. She admitted being afraid. But she would do it. That she *would* swear to." She shook her head. "She needn't have worried. I didn't want to know my biological mother then. What if she had been white?"

What if she had been white? She felt her stomach drop. But, of course, Pamela wouldn't have wanted a white mother. "No," she whispered. "No, I suppose you wouldn't want a white mother." And neither would Gwendolyn. That certainty turned her sweat cold. If she wasn't careful, she would throw up. She steadied herself by putting a hand on the table and stood up.

"Oh. Don't take offense." Pamela's voice softened. "I wouldn't mind now. You're going to be my baby's honorary grandmother, and you're as white as they come." She paused. "But then. When I was just beginning to feel like I belonged again, then I wanted my biological mother to look like me."

SHE had gone to the safe as soon as Pamela left. It hadn't been a year. But there were exceptions to every rule, weren't there? And she would put the photo back right away.

She leaned the photo against the mirror on her bureau. "I wanted a mother who looked like me." That's what Pamela had said. She looked at herself and Gwendolyn together. Gwendolyn's skin *was* darker than hers, but was that all that mattered? Gwendolyn had her jaw, her nose, her hands. She put a finger to Gwendolyn's hand as if to caress it. Those similarities must mean something. So what if Gwendolyn was slim, not round like her, and her eyes were brown, not green like hers? Gwendolyn's hair formed soft curls like hers. Anyway, no child looks exactly like her mother.

She picked up the photo of her own mother and held the two photos side by side. If anything, there was more of a resemblance between Gwendolyn and Callie than between her dark-haired, rail-thin mother and her. But she was unmistakably her mother's daughter, with her mother's brow and ears and those hands that Gwendolyn inherited. Surely Gwendolyn would see herself in her, the way she saw herself in her mother.

But what if Gwendolyn could not accept being born of a woman "as white as they come?" What if she had never searched for her because she was afraid of what she might find— a pasty-white woman?

She felt her stomach lurch again and leaned her head

against the mirror. She imagined Pamela telling her to breathe, and so she did. Three slow deep breaths. She straightened up and looked at herself again. She had been imagining the worst, hadn't she? And for no reason. Hadn't Pamela said the color of her biological mom no longer mattered to her? Perhaps Gwendolyn wouldn't care either.

She went to the bathroom, dampened a washcloth, and held it against her face. She wasn't so white anyway. What about her freckles? She pulled the cloth away and looked at herself again. But there, under the florescent light, her face looked more pale than ever.

She shrugged. She could not stare at herself all afternoon. She had to get the translation done. She went upstairs and started up her computer. Its clock said six p.m. She had missed her personal deadline.

Thirty-Three

CALLIE HAD A PAGE TO GO WHEN THE PHONE RANG again. She saved the document and turned off the computer. She would have to finish when she got back from dinner.

"*Bueno?*"

"Callie?"

Ah, her mother. "So you're going on a little trip." She smiled. "Aunt Ida's doing, I suppose."

"Ida?"

"She's been wanting you to join her on a trip for ages."

"Yes, but . . . Callie, haven't you read my letter?"

"Letter?" Then she remembered. "Oh, it got lost. Juanito brought it to me today. It's in a pocket somewhere." She patted her pockets until she felt it. She took it out. "I've got it. But can't you just tell me?"

"I wanted to give you time to think."

"It's not your health?"

Her mother laughed. "No, Callie. I'm fine, though I was worried when you didn't call about the letter. But now I understand. Read it. Give yourself some time to think and then call me. Okay?"

She poured herself a glass of water, and then took the envelope to the patio, where she could read away from the jaguar's watchful eye. She sat at the table under the shade of the avocado tree, opened the envelope, and took out the letter.

Dearest Callie,

You know I loved your father. I hope you will understand.

She frowned. Was this to be about her father? No wonder her mother wanted her to take time to think first. She considered tossing the letter, but she had promised to read it. She sighed and read on.

John Miller asked me to marry him.

She gasped and reread the previous line. "I hope you will understand." She laughed and noticed the leaves above her rustling, as if they too enjoyed the news. Well, why not! John Miller—Steve's favorite uncle—in love with her mother. How lovely. And she had assumed her mother was going to go on about her father. She found herself glancing up to the dining room where the jaguar lay in wait. She smoothed the letter against the patio table and then picked it up again.

His proposal must come as a surprise to you. It did to me. I had begun to suspect he was sweet on Aunt Ida because he always seemed to turn up when she was around. Then, when she was away and he offered me a ride to Wednesday evening service, I thought he was just being nice, not wanting me to have to go on my own. Afterward, when he said he wanted to talk with me about a personal matter, I said yes, of course, thinking he wanted to gather courage for talking to Ida. Then he told me he loved me, and all I could think of was how disappointed your aunt would be. But it turned out that she knew all along. I wondered then how I could have mistaken the many signals of his special regard for me. We laughed over that when Ida got back. All three of us.

She leaned back and looked up at the tree. That must have been the news Aunt Ida had suspected. She smiled and returned to the letter.

> *And so there it is. John loves me. And I love him, Callie. It came to me the moment I learned that Ida insisted John "get some gumption and propose."*

Her eyes filled with tears. She put the letter down and leaned back in the chair. So her mother had found her other half. Someone as kind as she. As thoughtful. And, by the sound of it, as humble, neither presuming to be loved by the other. She smiled. Such a dear man, Steve's Uncle John. She remembered him taking her and Steve to the city to see a Molière play though he knew no French. So unlike her father.

She dried her tears and smiled. Her mother married to Steve's Uncle John. She would be happy, truly happy. Callie could hardly wait to see them together. She read on.

> *I thought I might one day accept Aunt Ida's invitation to live with her, but it would be different living with John, being married to him. What would I do with the rings your father gave me? I want to talk with you about that and about some other things.*
>
> *I am coming to Guanajuato, Callie, so we can talk in person. I would have checked with you first about the flight, but there weren't many flights and the seats were going fast. Ida encouraged me to go ahead and buy the ticket. I arrive at five p.m., August 13.*

Callie looked at the calendar. It was only a week away. She turned back to the letter. There was nothing else other than "*Love, Mother.*"

* * *

SHE stood so quickly, she bumped the table and winced at the grate of iron against tile. What had her aunt been thinking? A flight to Mexico was no baby step. She crossed the patio to the terrace stairs, the letter in her hand. How would her mother negotiate the change of planes in Dallas? She crossed the patio. Not to mention the change in altitude—and Guanajuato's steep footpaths? Even Aunt Ida had trouble, and she was in good shape for her age. Her mother's idea of exercise was crocheting.

She ran up the stairs. Why would her mother, after all these years, become peripatetic now? If she were so intent on traveling, why not let John escort her? Why come alone when, given their ages, their time together would be short in any case? She cringed, picturing the spheres sliced in two. Her mother and John's parting now was completely unnecessary. She would be going there in a few months or sooner. In plenty of time to help her mother decide what to do with her rings. And, as for other things, the furniture her father made, for example, it would be easier to decide about those things there.

She paused at the top of the stairs to catch her breath. And, besides, now was not a good time for her to have visitors. She had her hands full with Armando. Strange. Her mother getting a ticket without asking her. It wasn't like her to be so inconsiderate. She shuddered. That was unfair. She hadn't told her mother any of her worries.

She walked across the terrace and through the dining room door. She would call her mother right away. Offer to go home soon to help her dispose of things. She would take her doll of course. And her father's trumpet, if her mother insisted. Why not? She could always give it away. And she could take her mother's rings, temporarily, to give her time to decide what to do with them.

She stood by the phone. Her mother had the chance for a happy life with John. Of course, she would do whatever she could to support that. "And I would, too," she said, turning to look at the jaguar.

But the time was so short. When did her mother say she was coming? She looked at the letter again. August 13. Well, no problem, it could be canceled or rescheduled for a time when John could accompany her mother.

She dialed her mother. There was no answer. An answering machine came on. Strange. Her mother always said she had no use for them. She listened to the prerecorded message, "Please leave a message after the beep," and then she hung up.

Aunt Ida would understand. Her mother's flight must be canceled. She started to dial the number, then checked her watch. No time. She had to meet Armando.

On the way to the door, she noticed the trumpet in the bag behind the pot. She had forgotten all about it. She pulled it out from behind the pot and left it by the door so she would remember to put it away.

Thirty-Four

CALLIE WAS PANTING BY THE TIME SHE GOT TO THE Santa Fe, but she relaxed when she saw Armando happily occupied holding the Gardners' Yorkie and insisting Jorge pick them up for their morning flight.

When he saw Callie, he handed Skippy back to the Gardners and stood to pull her chair out.

Callie nodded to the Gardners as they passed by to leave. When she sat down, she noticed the mineral water with lime Armando had ordered for her. Her throat was dry from rushing. She took a drink.

"I've ordered our usual," Armando said. He sat down, put his elbows on the table, and clasped his hands under his chin. "I want to explain." He paused. "About Claude." He looked around. With the Gardners now gone, there was no one nearby. "He was the first, and only. I assure you."

She felt her underarms grow damp. "There's no need . . ."

"I want you to understand."

"I think I do," she said.

"What does that mean?" Armando sat back in his chair and folded his arms across his chest.

She wanted to say, "You love Claude." But should she? Her aunt's voice came to her. *Listen. Just listen.* She leaned toward Armando. "Nothing. Nothing. Go on. Please."

"There are some things you don't share." He paused to look at her. "I thought you of all people would understand."

Me, why me? She opened her mouth and then shut it.

"But now . . . well, I want you to know." He looked away. "I'm not that way."

Not . . . gay? Could that be what he meant?

"I mean, here, in Mexico, I'm not . . ."

Not in Mexico? She wanted to be sympathetic, but instead she felt confused.

"In Veracruz, I reserved separate rooms. Claude didn't understand."

Really, she wanted to say with mock surprise, but heard her aunt's voice again. Don't judge. She shook herself. Why was she feeling mean? And then it came to her. Steve. Of course. Steve. Going off to Vietnam to hide his secret. "It would make a man of him," his father had said. A dead man, as it turned out. Steve hadn't had a chance at love. But Armando did, and he refused to take it. She took in a breath. She needed to calm down.

"I tried to explain ahead of time." He took a sip of his margarita. "It was different in France. I was different."

Beyond Armando's shoulder, she saw the waiter who had dropped the load of dishes the night she met Pamela. He was carrying their order. When he saw her, he nodded toward his perfectly balanced tray. She smiled.

Armando gave the waiter a thumbs up when he set their meals in front of them, then he focused on his silverware. He adjusted the spoon and knife. "I thought maybe you could talk with Claude . . ."

Talk with Claude? She felt her back stiffen. What could she say? Armando loves you, but stay away. He's nuts! She winced at the thought.

The waiter set down a basket of tortillas wrapped in a cloth napkin. She patted the napkin. The tortillas inside were steaming hot. Soon they would be cool and stiff, but she dared not open her mouth for a bite. Words might fly out. She tightened her jaw.

"Did you say something?" Armando turned toward her.

She shook her head. Had she been grinding her teeth?

"It's better this way."

She swallowed. Better without love? She did not think so.

Armando leaned toward her. "I'm thinking of entering the priesthood."

She gasped. This was too much.

"It's perfect, Callie. You must see that. I could be at peace. And I could work with the children."

She still had not taken a bite, and yet she choked and started coughing. Was she to explain *that* to Claude?

He came around the table and patted her on the back. "Choucita."

She took a sip of water. The coughing stopped, but her eyes continued to water. "I'm okay," she said.

He sat back down, cut a piece of chicken, and swirled it in mole sauce. "I wish you would eat chicken, at least. You need more protein."

How many times had she explained about combining whole grains and legumes?

"If I were in Salamanca, I would be close enough to help out Maestro Chávez . . . and you . . ."

But he would be thousands of miles from Claude. And filled with regret.

Armando put the forkful of chicken into his mouth.

How could he sit there eating chicken? She took another sip of water.

"You haven't eaten a bite . . . Do you want me to order something else?" He turned to look for the waiter.

She pushed back her chair and stood. She had to think of a way out. "I need . . ." She looked around and saw a waiter with his hand out, assuming she was looking for the ladies' room and ready to usher her inside. "I need the ladies' room."

He jumped up to hold her chair.

At the entry to the hotel, she turned back and saw him following her with his eyes.

His plan was ridiculous, as usual. There was no way she could explain his behavior to Claude when she did not understand herself. She should march on through the hotel, out the back door, and up the *callejones* to her house. But she could not just leave him sitting there. She imagined giving him a good shaking, rattling his loose screw back into place.

She pushed the bathroom door open and saw the maid dressed in blue. She sighed. She had left her purse at the table again and had not a centavo to give her. She slunk into the stall at the end, the one that felt the most private, but had a window onto a wide hallway that led to the kitchen. She closed the window, lowered her pants, and sat down. She didn't actually have to go to the bathroom when she left the table, but as long as she was there, she might as well try. Like her mother had always said.

Now that he was no longer sitting across from her, denying the obvious, she recognized the dark pain of separation in his eyes. Felt his longing. She bowed her head.

It had been hard, at first, for her to understand his love of the church. But she did, over time, understand. The quiet chanting, the flowing robes and flickering candles, the incense and lilies, the high ceilings, the cool comfort on scorching days, even the boom of rockets.

She pictured him at three years old standing at the orphanage door. How many times had Armando recounted his first moments? How Sister Ana María had put his small pack on the chair in her office and then took his hand and led him to the chapel. How she lit a candle and put it by the statue of a lady in blue. Then she put her hands on his shoulders and told him that the lady was his mother María. Sister Ana Teresa knelt with him and showed him how to hold his hands in prayer. "You can tell her anything," she said. From that day on, he crept into the chapel at dawn. He told the lady in blue everything that hurt his heart.

Would he have told her, too, of his love of Claude? Of the depth of his loss?

She felt the release of warm liquid and heard it splash into the toilet bowl. The attendant perched on a stool at the other end of the bathroom would have heard it, too.

"DID you ever think . . . ?" she said when she got back to the table. "Did you ever think the church could be wrong? About love, I mean, about love."

He hunched his shoulders and looked down at his plate. "No . . ."

She pulled herself up in her seat. "Well, it's been wrong about other things."

He looked across at her. "It's not just the church."

"It can't be Maestro Chávez."

He looked away. "No, it's not the maestro."

She reached for his hand. "Well, then . . ."

He pulled his hand away. "I would make a good priest."

She sighed. "And what would you say to a boy in love with another boy? Would you tell him to give up his love?"

He stared across the table at her. "If priests can be celibate, why can't others?"

She took in a slow breath. "Is that how you would counsel a boy in love?"

His eyes darkened. "What do you know of love?"

She took a hold of the table to steady herself, but her voice shook. "I know it's not wrong for you to love Claude. I know that much."

He sank back into his chair. "When I was twelve, an older boy hanged himself. The next day Sister Ana Teresa asked me to help her in the garden. We weeded the tomatoes. She didn't say anything to me. She just knelt beside me weeding. She invited me every day." Armando smiled. "We knelt together in the garden long after we'd pulled up every weed."

Had the boy been gay? Had the nun sensed even then that Armando was?

He leaned toward Callie. "*She* was compassionate."

"And I am not?" That sounded defensive. Why couldn't she just listen?

"Don't you see? That's how I want to be."

"By breaking up with Claude?"

His eyes filled with pain. "I thought you would understand. Isn't that what you did, retreat like a monk?" He leaned forward and looked into her eyes. "Fictional husbands don't count." He signaled the waiter for the check. "Let's go."

"I'm sorry." She reached for his arm. "I didn't mean . . ."

He pulled away, put some bills on the table, and then stood. "It's all right." He spread her shawl over her shoulders.

Neither of them spoke on the way up the *callejón* to her house. But the critical voice in her head did not cease. Why couldn't she just have listened? Why couldn't Armando accept his love of Claude? Why? Why? Why? Then Jacob's voice came to her. "There's always hope." How many times had he said that when she'd questioned him about the latest community setback. Whether it was drop-outs or prison terms, he always responded, "There's always hope." She heard the warmth of his voice and felt a wave of gratitude. And loss.

She unlocked the door. "Would you like tea?"

"No thanks. I need to practice." He went down a few stairs and then he came back up again. "Don't worry, Calecita. I'm fine. It's just that . . ."

In that moment, she saw him again as that three-year-old left at the tall wooden doors at the orphanage, and she knew. "It's just that you're afraid, isn't it? It's just that you're afraid."

She stood above him on the stairs, and he looked up to her. "Isn't it better this way, that I ended it first?"

She held out her hand as if making a blessing. "There's always hope."

"You know . . . " Armando said and smiled up at her. "You would make a good mom." He started down the stairs and then turned again. "Keep your cell by you. Would you?"

"Sure," she said, and then whispered to herself, "There's always hope."

THERE'S always hope. Easy to say. But did she believe it? She wasn't sure. She unlocked her front door. But Jacob had been sure. No matter what, he kept right on going. She pushed the door open. When she had asked him how he did it, he told her he had been inspired by Nelson Mandela. The trick was not to avoid falling, but to get up again. Every time. She entered the terrace and almost stumbled over the bag with the trumpet. Speaking of falling. She laughed and picked up the bag. Well, she had gotten up when she fell, more than once, but then what had she done? She entered the dining area. Had Armando been right about her retreating? Hadn't she taken refuge in an orderly, quiet—yes, monastic—life? She looked at the jaguar. "And it has served me well, if you'd like to know." She fingered the valves through the bag. She had forgotten all about practicing. Was it because she had given up hope? She put the bag down and shrugged. No time now. She had to finish the translation and get to bed.

Thirty-Five

SHE STOOD FROZEN AT THE TOP OF THE CALLEJÓN, clutching her translation. Her feet would not move. She leaned forward as if that would help, but no. She could not take a step. How would she get it to DHL in time? There was a bell sounding. She opened her eyes. A dream. She would make it to the DHL. The bell sounded again.

Still half-asleep and her legs feeling like logs, Callie managed to stretch far enough to answer the phone. "Hello."

"So, you know," Aunt Ida said.

"You've talked to Mother." She lay back on the pillow and tried to move her legs.

"Yes, and I've been itching to talk with you. I can't for the life of me figure out why your mother insists on traveling now."

Her aunt perplexed. She smiled. That was a new one.

"When I think of all those years she refused to travel, and now when she should be deciding what to wear down the aisle, she's taking off for Guanajuato."

"Mother said you encouraged her to go ahead and buy her ticket."

"I tried to discourage her. But she was bound and determined."

Bound and determined. Another expression she would be hearing Armando say.

"It would be different if she wanted to see the mummies.

But she's doesn't. She told me that plain enough. As for seeing you, well, you could be here in a jiffy."

"Yes."

"She was in such an all-fired hurry. I've never seen her like that. But then she's been acting strange lately."

Was her mother ill after all? She eased her legs over the side of the bed and sat up. "Acting strange?" She really should not be traveling.

"You know how I always complained about her hiding in the balcony behind the choir? Well, now she walks right down the center aisle to a front pew arm in arm with John."

How secure her mother must feel with John. She picked up her robe and drew it close around her.

"You won't believe this part. Your mother had a cat on her lap."

"In church?"

Ida laughed. "Out by the lake, at John's place. On the veranda."

She knew the cabin. Steve sometimes took her along Saturdays when he spent the afternoon with his uncle. They would sip Tang on the veranda and watch geese glide low over the lake. She didn't remember any cats. But there was a dog the day her parents agreed to go along. "Damned dog," her father grumbled when the dog would not stop following her mother around. "Damned dog." What would he say now? She felt a little sad thinking of her father all alone in the ground. She shook herself. What an odd thought. Her mother had every right to marry someone else. Especially someone like John. Damned dog. Oh, my. Her thoughts were unruly.

"There she was, sitting peaceful as could be. I saw the mass of orange and thought she was knitting, but when I got out of the car and walked across the yard, I caught the flick of a tail.

Your mother didn't get up. She sat there, pinned under that cat." Aunt Ida laughed. "Can you imagine?"

Her mother, with a cat on her lap? Strange, but not fatal.

"She never had the time of day for cats, and there she was holding one—and happy, Callie. Happy as pie."

She went on some about John, what a great guy he was, and how he had been in love with Callie's mother for years. "He loved her all along."

Had her father known? Was *that* why he would speak disparagingly of John's acreage, or was it just the usual sour grapes he spit out regarding anyone he judged more successful than himself? She sighed. Wasn't it time she stopped these ungenerous thoughts?

"One day, *years* after your Dad died, John and I were playing golf." Aunt Ida said "golf" with an ironic ring, as if she still could not believe she had taken up the sport after scoffing at those who amused themselves chasing after the small pockmarked balls. "He missed a putt on the ninth, but he looked so downcast, it couldn't have been about the putt. Then it came to me. That picture I took at your parent's wedding. John standing apart, his hands in his pockets, looking forlorn.

"I started putting two and two together. How he would stop over, 'on church business,' he would say. And it always seemed to be the night your mother came to dinner. And then how stricken he looked that day your mother swooned at the church social."

"Swooning!" Now was her chance. "Well, that settles it, Mother should not be traveling alone—or traveling at all for that matter."

"Oh, it was nothing. Her blood pressure was a little low. That's all. Dehydration. I gave her a glass of water with a pinch of salt, and she was fine in no time." She chuckled.

Her mother's health was at issue here. Why was her aunt so blasé?

"Anyway, John wanted to call an ambulance. He can be on the thrifty side, you know. But not when it came to your mother. That clinched it. It wasn't the putt he was forlorn about. It was your mother. I wondered then what he was waiting for."

John, at least, seemed to have recognized the gravity of the problem. Perhaps she should call *him*. He wouldn't want her mother swooning at thirty thousand feet, and with no companion on the plane to look after her.

"I confronted him and told him in no uncertain terms not to waste any more time. But he kept on waiting. For what? I don't know. I began to think he was like that Henry James character who would go to his grave without popping the question. What was his name? You know."

She looked toward the beams over her head. "John . . . John Marcher."

"John, you say." She laughed. "Well, the name fits. Imagine waiting all that time to propose."

Her aunt sounded incredulous, but Steve's Uncle John must have had his reasons. It would have been, must have been, a question of honor.

SHE had just undressed to shower when she heard the sound of a conga drum. She paused. It sounded as if it were in her room. Had she left a radio on? She wrapped a towel around herself and went back into her bedroom, her head turned to one side searching for the sound. The radio was off. Neither was there a percussionist hiding in her armoire. She kept walking. It was her backpack. The drum stopped. Then started again. She opened the top pocket and found her new cell. What the . . . ? Oh, Armando. He must have changed the ring tone when she had left the table at the restaurant.

"I decided not to become a priest."

Thank God. "Oh?"

"A Jehovah's Witness stopped by this morning. He asked if I'd seen a dog and handed me a flyer of Tavelé. He had not even begun his spiel yet, you know, about whether I had found Jesus."

"Perhaps you have," she said.

"Wearing a pressed shirt and slacks? Maybe." He laughed. "Thanks, by the way."

"How did you know?"

"He said a *güera* waving a Virgin de Guadalupe gave him the flyer. Who else could it be? I suppose you got it from Juanito."

"The flyer?"

"You know what I mean. And the statue is cracked, isn't it, or missing something. Like all the other things you buy from him?"

All but the trumpet, she thought, picturing it in the bag by the French doors. She should get back to practicing.

"You really need to get rid of those things, now that your mother is on the way."

"What?" How did he know?

"Your aunt Ida called this morning. Early. She's sure your mom would appreciate seeing the mummies."

"She told *me* Mother was not interested."

"She seemed to think she would change her mind. She's bound and determined that your mom see them."

Bound and determined. So Armando *had* picked up another of her aunt's phrases. She smiled.

"She said there was no way you would take your mom there."

Callie laughed. "Well, she was right about that."

"By the way, I heard about that junk of yours."

"Junk?"

"You know, all that broken stuff you bought from Juanito. Jorge said you paid to get it fixed and then bought it again." He tapped out a drum roll. "Good going, Callie."

"It was for a worthy cause."

"If you get tired of it, let me know. Meanwhile, what about the trumpet? Wouldn't you like to donate it to the home? Pamela could give the boys lessons. Better than wasting your time. Which you won't have anyway with your mother here."

He was right about that. She had enough trouble finding time to practice as it was. But she wouldn't give him the satisfaction of knowing that. "I'll manage." But how? Her mother would find it odd she *had* a trumpet, much less planned to play it. One more reason her mother should stay put.

"IT'S all taken care of, Dear," her mother said when Callie finally reached her early Saturday morning. John would be taking her to the airport, and they wouldn't have a long, early morning drive to catch the plane, as he had arranged for them to stay at an airport hotel the night before her flight. "In separate rooms, of course, Dear," her mother added, as if she would be concerned.

Callie smiled at the jaguar, but didn't say anything.

"John arranged for someone from the airline to meet me in Dallas and take me to my connecting flight, so don't worry about that. And I know to drink plenty of water. I won't get dehydrated."

It looked like everything *had* been taken care of, but still, dissuading her mother from traveling alone seemed worth a try. "But, Mother, are you *sure* you want to leave John behind?"

"Now, Dear," her mother said. "Don't *you* start giving me trouble. It took me long enough to convince John, and then your aunt Ida started up. I want to have time with you. It wouldn't be the same if John came along."

She was on the verge of telling her mother it wasn't a good time for her to have a guest, but then thought better of it. If her mother wanted to go on a lark before getting married, why not honor that impulse?

When she hung up the phone, she realized she hadn't told her mother how happy she was that she and John were to marry, and so she dialed her mother again.

Her mother answered on the first ring and laughed when she heard Callie's voice. "I knew it would be you. We hadn't finished our conversation, had we?"

"No," Callie said, "I was so worried about your trip I forgot to say how happy I am that you and John are getting married. So very, very happy."

"I'm glad you're happy, Dear. I know you've always liked John, but still I felt a little nervous. There will be so many changes."

"All for the better, I'm sure." Callie said. Her mother finally moving on with her life. There was nothing better than that.

Once she accepted her mother's visit, she began looking forward to it. She modified her weekend plans. No Sunday walk with Armando and no breathing session with Pamela. She would use the time to move forward with her next translation, to free up time during her mother's visit. She would ditch her usual Saturday and Sunday chores, too, and, instead, prepare the guest room. And she would stop by the tourist kiosk for information to make a list of things they could do together.

Armando had been disappointed when she called him, but once she assured him for the third time that she would not be seeing Pamela over the weekend either, he calmed down. Pamela seemed fine about the weekend, but then called back, sounding anxious. She wanted to make sure that Callie would be there for her OB-GYN appointment on Monday.

"What kind of local granny would miss an OB-GYN appointment?" Callie said. "Not this one."

When she hung up the phone, she looked over at the jaguar. He looked pleased for a change. Maybe she *could* do something right.

Thirty-Six

CALLIE STOOD STILL AND SILENT BY THE EXAMINATION table where Pamela lay.

When the doctor placed the ultrasound wand over Pamela's tummy, Pamela's eyes went to the monitor. Callie turned to look, too, then leaned closer to try to make out an image.

"Ask her where the baby is." Pamela's voice sounded anxious. "I don't see her."

Callie translated Pamela's question. When the doctor answered, Callie put her hand on Pamela's arm. "She says there's not much to see at seven weeks."

"What about her heart." Her voice was still tense. "It sounds fast."

The doctor explained that an embryo's heart beats at the rate of ninety to one-hundred-and-ten beats per minute and increases to one-fifty to one-sixty per minute by the time of birth.

Pamela smiled. "The rate my heart beat the first time I climbed the *callejón* to my house. Boy was I out of breath. A little like now."

Callie smiled.

When the doctor asked Callie to have Pamela breathe naturally, Callie realized that she, herself, was holding her breath. She turned to the screen again. What *did* the doctor see? She asked her, and then translated the doctor's response: "The baby is in the uterus, not in a fallopian tube."

"That's good. But what about her? Is she alone in there?"

"Alone?"

"Ami Mai has sisters that are twins and some twin cousins, too."

Callie explained to the doctor that there were twins in Pamela's partner's family.

The doctor asked whether there were twins in Pamela's family and then Callie translated the question to Pamela.

Pamela glanced at Callie and then turned to the doctor. "Sí."

How did she know?

The doctor studied the scan. Callie translated: "There's just one embryo. It's seven millimeters. Normal for its age."

"How long would that be?" Pamela asked.

"About a quarter of an inch," Callie said.

Pamela held her thumb and forefinger apart a tiny amount and studied the distance. "And she weighs?"

Callie asked the doctor, then relayed her answer: "Less than a gram."

Pamela raised her eyebrows.

The doctor smiled. "*Ligero como una pluma.*"

Callie translated: "Light as a feather."

Pamela turned to Callie. "If she's the length of a flea and light as a feather, why do I feel five pounds heavier?"

Callie laughed. "Could it be your appetite?"

Later Callie overheard Pamela phoning Ami Mai from the dressing room. "Our little flea's healthy and beautiful. Just like you. And when she moves, she dances."

Callie smiled. The embryo was barely visible, much less with distinct features or precise motions. Still it was beautiful. That she saw, too. She leaned back in her chair, recalling the tiny Noah she had imagined in her belly. Same lanky figure, same ebony skin, same almond eyes. How surprised she had been when the baby the nurse lay on her stomach was a chubby cinnamon girl.

When Pamela emerged from the changing room, she asked Callie what she was smiling about.

She coughed. "Oh, nothing."

"LET'S sit here," Pamela motioned to a table under an umbrella in the restaurant by Teatro Juárez.

Callie looked down the pedestrian street. What if Armando came by and saw them? She gestured toward the clouds forming above. "It looks like rain."

"I think we're fine. I like it here." She pointed to her stomach. "She does, too."

Callie checked her watch. Still over an hour until the end of rehearsal. Chances are she and Pamela would be gone before it ended.

When the waitress came by to ask what they wanted to drink, Pamela asked Callie to order food, too. "Something filling that can be fixed up right away." Then she started rifling through her purse. "There's something I want to show you." She pulled out a creamy white baby shoe and handed it to Callie.

"It's soft and lovely." She smiled. "But won't you need . . . two?"

"There is another one, but I don't have it. Not yet." She took the shoe back, set it on the table, and then turned again to Callie. "Look, I didn't tell you everything the other day."

"Oh?" So she wasn't the only one.

"Mother doesn't know."

"Where the other shoe is?"

"Oh, she knows that. She has it."

"Well, then . . ."

"She doesn't know I have this one."

"No?"

"No. It fell off when the social worker walked away with me. My bio-mom picked it up and kept it."

Her bio-mom. So that's how she knew there were twins in her family, too. Her hands began to shake, and she put them out of view on her lap.

The waitress returned with a plate of tortilla chips layered with beans, cheese, salsa, and thick cream for Pamela and a plate of sliced fruit for Callie.

Pamela stopped talking and focused on picking up savory tortilla pieces with her fingers. "We'll need more napkins," was all she managed to get out for a while.

Callie studied the overlapping slices of papaya, pineapple, and melon ringing the circle of banana rounds on her plate. She had been hungry when she ordered, but now she couldn't eat. Was Pamela's biological mother white? Was Pamela disappointed? The way she said "bio-mom" sounded sweet. But still . . .

"Was it, well . . . difficult . . . meeting your biological mother?" She felt her hands shaking against her legs. But she had to ask. She clasped her hands together.

"No. Some friends warned me against meeting her. 'Why open that can of worms,' they said, but Ami Mai encouraged me. We both wanted to know my genetic history. And, I don't know, I suppose I wanted my baby to have an opportunity I did not have."

Her heart filled with hope. "And so you decided to look for her."

"Yes. *She* wasn't white. But her mother, my biological grandmother, was. Is, I mean, white. That's why I'm on the light side, I guess. Anyway, my biological grandfather was from Senegal. He had fought with the Free French forces in the liberation of Southern France, and she had served in the WACS. They met in Paris. 'He was tall and black as night,' my grandmother said."

"Your grandmother?"

"I met her, too. Anyway, my grandfather told my grandmother he had never before seen a white lady walk with the grace of a Senegal woman. She was the first."

She smiled.

"She blushed when she told me that. All these years later. Imagine. It must have been love at first sight."

She pictured Noah's hands taking a book from the library shelf, and her own hands relaxed. "Lovely."

"She went with him back to Senegal when de Gaulle replaced him and the other African soldiers with white ones. But then he died suddenly the month before my mother was born, and so my grandmother returned to Detroit."

"Did she have help from her family?"

"She had no family. Her parents had died, and she had no siblings. She did have the GI bill, though, and so she went to college and got her nursing degree, toting my mother along."

"That must have been a challenge."

"A challenge. That's hardly the word. Imagine a white woman with a mixed-race baby in those days! People were nasty."

She thought of the nurse with the cross. People had been nasty in her day, too.

Pamela took a sip of water. "When my bio-mom got pregnant with me, and her young man abandoned her, her mom—my bio-grandmother—consulted with a social worker she knew. The social worker recommended adoption—for the sake of the child and to help out a childless couple. Still, her mom offered to help, if my bio-mom wanted to raise me."

"Oh, my. But . . ." She stopped herself, fearing she would give herself away if she completed her thought. Still, she wondered, how had she let her go?

Pamela must have known what she was thinking anyway. "My bio-mom wanted her baby to have the father she had never had. So, she decided to follow the social worker's advice." She turned to Callie as if she needed to reassure her. "Mom told me how grateful she and Dad were to my bio-mom, though they never knew her."

Yes, of course they were grateful. The gift of a child. She imagined Pamela's mother receiving baby Pamela, her wish come true. But how had Pamela's biological mother felt? She wanted to ask, but knew her voice would waiver.

Luckily she didn't have to ask. "My bio-mom told me that she went on with her life, and, yet, she always wondered if she had done the right thing," Pamela said.

Of course, she would wonder—especially when she could have kept her baby.

"She regretted not insisting on an open adoption so she could have known for sure that my parents loved me."

Yes, to know that, at least. Callie's hands began to shake again. "They were not common then. Open adoptions." Her voice sounded weak. Not that an open adoption would have eased her mind. She would still have had to let her baby go. She shivered. She had to pull herself together. She took in a breath.

"No, I suppose not." Pamela picked up the shoe and looked at it. "When she gave me this, she said she didn't need it any longer, now that she had met me. And then she asked for forgiveness."

Ask for forgiveness. She couldn't see herself doing that. It seemed at once too much to ask for and yet insufficient to still her regret.

"I didn't know what to say!" She put the shoe down and looked at Callie. "It's funny, I never blamed her. I know some adopted kids feel that way. But I never did."

Not blame her? When she could have kept baby Pamela? Blaming her seemed, somehow, more fitting. She checked herself. Who was *she* to judge that woman's decision?

Pamela's voice turned sad. "I reserved my blame for Mother."

She wanted to comfort her. "Maybe. But you're not blaming her any longer. At least so it seems."

"No, but that's not the only problem." She paused as if trying to decide whether to explain. And then her voice lightened. "I met my bio-mom's kids, too. Oh, she got married again eventually and had nine of them. Imagine!"

Having nine more children after relinquishing a baby. She couldn't imagine that. She could not have had even one other child. But Pamela didn't seem to mind all those other babies.

"And, you know, her mother—my grandmother—she still walks with grace." She laughed. "She's a 'graceful granny.'"

Callie smiled. "You are graceful, too."

"You know, she said that, too." She laughed. "She's nice. They're all nice. Ami Mai and I will see them again. We want our baby to meet them. But I don't feel—the way some do about their bio-families—that they are my *people*, my real family. The Fischers are my family." She pointed to her tummy again. "They are this baby's family, too."

She dipped her fingers in a water glass and then reached for a napkin. "And, yet . . ." She paused to dry her hands. "This baby will be mine, my relation, in a way that no other person is. I will have what my mother wanted, but could not have. A child of her very own." She leaned back in her chair. "You know when babies are born how people say things like, 'She has her grandma's eyes.' Well, my baby can't have *my* mother's eyes." Tears started rolling down her cheeks. "What if she has her bio-grandmom's eyes? And what if Mom sees those eyes in my baby? How will she feel then?"

Callie recalled seeing herself, her mother, and her father in the photo of Gwendolyn and felt tears run down her face, too.

Just then a hand rested on her shoulder. She turned to see Armando glowering at Pamela.

"*Now* what have you done?" he asked.

Before Pamela could answer, Juanito appeared, smiling, and carrying a lopsided music stand. He offered the stand to Callie.

Armando turned and cast a dark look at him.

"Oh," Callie lay a calming hand on Armando's arm a moment and then reached out for the music stand.

"Now, Callie," Armando said, reaching out to intercept the music stand. "You don't need this."

Juanito pointed to the listing side of the stand. A piece was broken, but Juanito said he knew someone who could fix it.

Callie smiled at him. Well, that would be nice—for Juanito himself to see about getting the broken stand fixed.

"I think it can be made good as new," Armando said, turning the music stand this way and that to check it out. "I know a student who can use it and that trumpet you'll never play."

Pamela turned to Callie and asked, "Were you thinking of giving your trumpet away?"

"Well," she said. She looked at Armando and hesitated and then turned back to Pamela.

"I would like . . ."

"Another lesson. Sure. I meant to talk with you about scheduling one." She looked down at her stomach. "But there's been so much going on."

"Why would you want to do *that*? You told *me* you didn't have time for anything because of your mother's visit!" Armando said to Callie. "Tell her 'no.'"

Pamela stood up and went to stand by Armando. She pointed at him. "Tell him 'no.'"

Callie turned to Pamela. "Look, to be honest, I have been busy. I haven't had time for practice or the breathing exercises."

"Which you could use," Pamela said. "I noticed you were holding your breath a little while ago."

Callie turned to Armando and said, "But, no, I am not thinking of giving the trumpet away."

"Well," Armando said, and set the music stand down beside Callie. "Then you might as well have this piece of junk, too."

Pamela leaned over to gather up her things. "I've got to go." She turned to Callie and said, "But I wanted to check with you about your mother. Didn't you say she was coming in on Thursday? Mine is too. I could drive us there."

"No, you can't." Armando said. "I am taking Callie to pick up her mom." He turned to Callie and asked, "What time did you say she's coming in?"

"Five p.m."

"Oh, well, then," Pamela said. "My mother arrives in the early afternoon."

"I suppose you're planning to skip out early on the rehearsal?" Armando said. "Why weren't you there today, anyway?"

"That's none of your business."

"Well, at least you weren't distracting Maestro Chávez for a change."

Pamela turned to Armando. "You do him no service by

ignoring his lapses. He needs medical attention, not cover-ups." She turned to Callie and asked, "I'm right, aren't I?"

"Well . . ." She looked from one to the other.

"Don't say anything," Armando said to her and then turned to Pamela. "And *that* is none of *your* business."

"It's orchestra business. He needs to resign. And I am not the only one who thinks that."

"Well, you are a *pinche metiche*, and I am not the only one who thinks that."

"Call me names if you like; it doesn't change the facts." She slung her bag over her shoulder and stormed off.

"Good riddance to bad rubbish," Armando called after her.

Pamela turned and flipped him the bird.

"Did you see what she did?" Armando asked, his voice rising.

"Oh, Armando," Callie said gently.

"And him," Armando said, nodding toward Juanito. "He started it all. Can't he find anyone else to buy the junk he comes up with?" He lifted his hands palms up. "I really don't understand you, Callie." Then he picked up the music stand again and rattled it. "Look at this thing. It's not worth a peso." He threw it back down and looked at his watch. "I have to get out of here." And then he walked off.

Juanito stood there, looking puzzled. He wanted to know if Armando was angry with him.

She told him not to worry. She looked down the street where Pamela and Armando had disappeared. He could leave the worrying to her.

* * *

BY the time Callie climbed up the *callejón* to her house, there were two messages on the answering machine. She took off her backpack, pointed for the jaguar to notice the folded music stand sticking out the top, and then pushed the play button.

"It looks like I got there just in time. She had you crying. Calecita. Crying! I told you she was trouble." His voice turned soft. "I know how difficult it is to put up with her, but I have to. I work with her. You don't. And, besides, I need you."

A wave of weariness washed over her.

"You have always been busy. Your work, your dusting, your garden, your aunt, your mother, Juanito. But did I ever complain? Never. And now when I need you the most. With Claude gone, the Maestro Chávez fragile, Tavelé missing, and your mother on the way . . ."

She heard him, drumming in the background, ending with a roll, before his final point. "It's Pamela you spend time with."

He paused. It sounded like he was taking a drink of something. She sat down.

"I understand about your mother, Calecita. I would be in constant contact with mine, if I had one. But I don't, you know. I don't have a mother. I never really did. Not one I remember anyway. You know that. And yet, after all I told you about Pamela, now, of all times, you are giving her your precious time. *Je ne comprends pas.*"

How *could* he understand? She hadn't exactly been forthcoming with him. She sighed. She didn't know what to do about that.

There was a pause, and then he added, "What were you doing in the center this morning anyway? Didn't you have work to do?"

She breathed a sigh of relief that she had not been at home to answer *that* question.

The next message started up.

"Hi Granny, it's Pamela. I don't know how you put up with that guy. I was so mad when I got home, I poured a glass of ice water on my head to cool down." She laughed. "In the garden. Don't worry. I didn't make a mess. Anyway, then I called the person I know best in the brass section to see if people are calling me names. What was that M-word Armando used?"

Metiche. Busybody. A favorite of Armando's.

"Well, anyway, according to her, they're not calling me names. And neither am I the only one who's worried about Maestro Chávez. That's just Armando's denial talking. I asked my colleague to say something to him tomorrow."

She paused, and then added, "It was so annoying of him showing up when he did. I wanted to run something else by you before my mother got here. And now I don't know if there'll be time."

Run something by her. What could that be?

"Anyway, thanks for going along with me today, Granny. I can call you that, can't I?"

She nodded, smiling.

"Oh, and one more thing. I think Mom and I will stop on the way back from the airport to get one of those wooden highchairs they sell by the road. I know, the baby won't need one for a while. But I like the idea of having one in the kitchen. I can imagine her here already, eating Cheerios from the tray."

She felt tears roll down her cheeks again.

Thirty-Seven

CALLIE AND ARMANDO STOOD BEHIND THE CORD that blocked entry to the corridor where passengers exited customs. Jorge waited nearby, chatting with another chauffeur holding a sign with a passenger's name.

She should have made a sign with her mother's name in case her mother swooned in customs. She wiped her hands on her shirt. Shouldn't she have insisted that her mother stay put? That question had kept her awake all night. She was exhausted, and it didn't help that Armando kept whispering in her ear. But she would not stop him, hoping he would get it out of his system before her mother arrived.

"And now that's she's gone and gotten herself pregnant. She'll be impossible."

So, Armando knew! Hadn't the gynecologist counseled to wait until week thirteen to share the news?

He leaned forward to see if anyone was coming through the doors and then bent to whisper in her ear again. "Oh, and I heard she picked out a local *abuela*. Who would want *that* job?"

I would, that's who, she thought, but kept her mouth shut. Was she beginning to side with Pamela, like he thought?

"I can't imagine her a mother, but at least now that she has a bun in the oven, she'll give Tavelé back."

She frowned. *A bun in the oven.* Not an expression her aunt would use. He must have gotten that one from someone else.

"You know she's a lesbian. *Everyone* knows. She's not exactly discreet. All she ever talks about is Ami Mai. And now with a baby coming, the whole brass section gathers around her at break, hanging on to every word. Pamela of all people."

He leaned forward and then back again.

"I don't see how she'll have time for the orchestra. Maybe she'll resign." He snapped his fingers. "That would be sweet."

But it would not solve the problem of the maestro, she thought. Even Jorge had noticed. He mentioned it on the way over, how Maestro Chávez had recently paused when he got out of the cab, as if he had to think about which direction to go. Armando had brushed off Jorge's concern, saying the maestro had a lot on his mind. "Pamela," he had mouthed to Callie.

Passengers began streaming out, laden with luggage. Where was her mother? *Had* she swooned? She felt her heart begin to race. She should not have let her mother chance the trip.

She was on the verge of interrupting Armando's monologue when her mother walked through the doors. "There she is!" Callie waved both arms above her head until her mother saw her.

She followed her mother's approach. There was something new. Not her hair pulled back into her customary bun, nor the A-line that fell just below her knees. It was her posture, which had always been perfect, if somewhat forced, that now looked effortless, as if a yoke had been lifted from her shoulders. Callie frowned at the thought of the yoke that had weighed her mother down, even from his grave.

"Aren't you glad to see me?" her mother asked.

"Of course!" Callie smiled and put her arms around her mother. Her own body felt soft and squishy against her mother's ribs. She breathed in the familiar fragrance of violets and felt tears come to her eyes. "I am so glad you are here."

"Hey, give me a chance," Armando said, pulling her away and bending down to kiss her mother. "I'm Armando."

Her mother smiled up at him. "I've heard so much about you."

Armando glanced at Callie.

"Not everything," she said and laughed, trying to reassure him without giving anything away.

He took her mother's hands. "And I've heard you're soon to be married." Callie looked at the two of them together. Her mother beaming. Armando smiling, but tired around the eyes. He looked in a way older than her mother.

He nodded to Jorge, who came for the bag, and then offered Callie and her mother each an arm. At the car, he insisted that Callie sit in front by Jorge. "You will have your mom to yourself soon enough," he said, opening the front door for her and the back door for her mother. "And, besides, I'm on a mission from your aunt Ida." He walked around the car and got in the other side.

Callie's mother turned to him. "Oh, I know all about that. And I might just take you up on it, young man."

Callie turned from the front seat. "You want to see the mummies?"

"Of course she does," Armando said.

Callie didn't think so. "But Aunt Ida said . . ."

"I wasn't enthusiastic about seeing them, I admit. But on the way here, I thought, why not go see them? It would make your aunt happy." She turned to Armando and said, "But first I want some quality time with my daughter."

Quality time? Where had her mother picked up that expression? Callie leaned back against her seat, stifling a sigh. Whatever could she mean?

* * *

"YOUR mother," her father had always said, "is part sparrow. She's always hopping about." But at seven thousand feet, even her mother slowed down. Callie had led her to the guest room off the kitchen and expected to continue showing her around, but her mother sat on the chair by the daybed and leaned down to take her shoes off. "I'll have to tour later," she said.

So Callie had pulled back the daybed cover and gone for a pitcher of water and a glass. By the time she got back, her mother had changed to a flowered flannel gown and was sitting on the side of the bed, unwrapping a framed photo of John.

Callie poured a glass of water for her mother and kissed her on the cheek. As she was leaving, her mother called her back. "I almost forgot. Your doll. She's there, in my suitcase."

Callie bent to open the suitcase, and there, on top of her mother's folded clothes, was the doll, her new eyes shining. They reminded her of her father's eyes, shining with hope.

THE next morning Callie found her mother sitting at the kitchen island already dressed and looking through a stack of tourist brochures. On hearing Callie, she looked up and said, "What's for breakfast?"

Callie smiled. The sparrow was back.

ARMANDO called every day to let her know how the search for Tavelé was going, but he left them mostly to themselves, saving his energy for *la pièce de résistance* of her mother's visit. The mummy museum. Pamela, who was occupied with her own mother, wanted to meet Callie's mother, referring to her as "Little Flea's great-granny," but insisting there was no rush.

And so Callie and her mom had plenty of time on their own, "quality time," Callie supposed, for visiting Diego Rivera's childhood home and the Alhóndiga with Chávez Morado's murals depicting local scenes from Mexico's war of independence. Jorge took them to Dolores Hidalgo, where Father Hidalgo raised the cry of independence, and then to San Miguel—"so you can practice your English," Armando quipped. At her mother's insistence Jorge drove them several times on a loop through the historic center, going one way on the plaza-level streets and then back on the Subterránea underneath.

Her mother sampled *gorditas* and *tamales*—"nothing like the canned ones I bought for your father to heat up when I had a church meeting"—and one evening even dared a sip of Armando's margarita.

Amazed by the sweetness of fresh papaya, not a meal could go by without her mother asking, "Will we be having papaya?" And they always would, since Juanito, who came by every day asking to do errands, happily ran up to the fruit stand to buy them.

In the evening, her mother would take the portable phone to her room to call her dear John, and Callie could hear her laughter through the door. She would tiptoe away, grateful her mother hadn't been persuaded to stay home.

"I've gone on so about Guanajuato," her mother told Callie one morning, "that John asked me if I wanted to be married here."

"Do you?"

"No," she said. "I want to be married in our church. But I did say that maybe I would go on another trip, if he liked. You know what he said? 'I would take you around the world.' And I believe he would, Callie. I believe he would."

From what Aunt Ida had said, John would do anything for her mother. But then, knowing her mother, she wasn't likely to ask him to do anything he didn't want to do in the first place.

Thirty-Eight

CALLIE EXPECTED TO TAKE A TAXI UP THE HILL TO the enormous statue of the Pípila, the independence hero who died blasting open the door to the Alhóndiga. But Armando insisted she take her mother in the funicular so her mother could take photos of the spectacular views of Guanajuato's historic center and surrounding hillsides on the way up. So, one afternoon, when they had seen every other tourist attraction, except the mummies, they bought their tickets and then waited on the platform at the base of the tracks. While her mother got her camera ready, Callie relived the steep ride up and the jar a few meters from the top, when the car came to a stop and then inched to the end of the line. She shuddered, remembering there being fewer bolts clamping the cable the last time Armando talked her into taking the funicular.

Soon the approaching car entered the platform, and the door slid open. Her heart, already pounding in anticipation of the ride up, felt as if it would break through her chest wall at the sight of Pamela stepping onto the platform, followed by a woman that she recognized as Pamela's mother from the photo in her living room.

Pamela looked radiant, and, in normal circumstances, Callie would have been delighted to see her. She had at first started toward Pamela, her arms outstretched and a smile on her face. But then it came to her. The trumpet. If only she had thought up something when she noticed it still in a bag by the terrace door when she showed her mother in. At least she had put it back in the case and taken it up to the laundry room right away. But still, with all her planning, why hadn't she taken care of that detail before her mother arrived? What if Pamela said something about her taking a trumpet lesson? How would she explain *that* to her mother? She dropped her arms and turned away, hoping Pamela would not notice her.

"Callie."

She turned to see Pamela coming toward them.

"*You're* going up the funicular?" she said to Callie and then turned to Callie's mother. "You must be Callie's mother."

"Evelyn, Evelyn Quinn." She offered her hand, which Pamela took before hugging her.

She stepped back and gestured to the woman by her side. "This is my mother." She glanced at Callie and then looked back to her mother. "Pearl Fischer."

As the arriving passengers finished exiting and the departing passengers approached the funicular doorway, Evelyn and Pearl went through the usual "How long will you be here?" and "Where are you visiting from?"

Callie, meanwhile, felt sick about having turned away from Pamela. How *could* she have! At least it appeared that Pamela hadn't noticed.

When Evelyn learned that Pearl was from Chicago and that Pamela grew up there, she turned to Pamela and asked, "Did you know Callie there?"

Pamela turned to Callie. "You didn't tell your mom?"

She braced herself. Tell her what? About Pamela remembering seeing the woman wearing a black scarf in the back of an auditorium? No, she hadn't told her any of that. She shook her head no.

"Well, I'm not surprised." She laughed. "The first time I

met your daughter was right here when she tossed a margarita at me."

Callie laughed, too, then froze. Would Pamela mention the trumpet?

Noticing Callie's discomfort, Pamela put an arm around her shoulders. "And in spite of that—no, *because* of that—we became friends. Right, Granny?"

She glanced at her mother, who looked surprised, but didn't say anything, and then back to Pamela. She tried to make her voice sound calm. "Right," she said. She slipped out of Pamela's embrace and stepped through the funicular doorway.

ON the ride up the hill, her doubts about the bolts gave way to the certainty that when her mother learned, as she inevitably would, about the trumpet lessons, nothing would stop her from putting two and two together. Pamela was around the same age her baby would now be. They may have known each other in Chicago. And *that* had drawn Callie to the trumpet. There was no other reason for Callie to take up the instrument. It had to be because she thought it would lead her to her child. Standing there, holding onto the rail and avoiding the view, Callie felt the eyes in the back of her mother's head trained on her.

When the jolt came and then the car eased into the platform, she relaxed. Once she stepped onto firm ground again, she realized how crazy her thinking had been. Her mother could not have figured out from one spilled margarita why she approached Pamela. She took in a long, slow breath. And if her mother did ask, Armando would save her. Armando and Tavelé. All she had to do was tell the truth. Well, part of the truth, anyway.

* * *

THAT evening after dinner, she got her chance. Juanito, hoping to please Armando, but afraid to approach him himself, stopped by with another music stand. When he left, her mother said, "Didn't I see a trumpet in a bag by the terrace door when I first got here? Was that for Armando, too?"

So she hadn't put the trumpet away in time. She drew in her breath and told her mother the story she'd prepared. She had bought the trumpet from Juanito not knowing what she would do with it. One evening in the Jardín, Armando asked her to take a lesson from Pamela as a pretext to look for Tavelé. She was, of course, nervous about approaching someone new and unfortunately spilled a margarita on Pamela. But she did, nonetheless, ask her for a lesson, just as Armando wanted. Callie looked over to see the jaguar frowning at her.

Before Juanito's arrival, her mother had been chirping away about how lovely it was that Callie would be a local grandmother. It reminded her of how much fun she had been having at the lake when John's great-grandniece came to visit. Callie had been enjoying her mother's breezy manner. She felt relieved that, after years of avoiding any mention of babies, her mother spoke freely, not just of children, but of babies, too, as if she had never remained silent on the subject.

But then, after Callie told her the "truth" about the trumpet, her mother paused a moment, and then said, "Let's get these dishes washed." They stood side by side, like they had each night, her mother washing and she drying and putting away. Callie turned the conversation back to John's little niece, questioning her mother about her, and her mother answered, but without her earlier enthusiasm.

When they finished the dishes, her mother dried her

hands. "It's been a long day." She picked up the phone to carry it into her room. Before she closed the door, she turned back toward Callie and said, "Your aunt said something to me about you taking up the trumpet because of Armando. From what you've both said about him, I understand he needs your support. But tricking Pamela. That doesn't sound like you."

She sat on the floor and leaned against the closed door. She thought of what Pamela had said, about defining yourself through your actions. Was it not her, not the way she acted, but how she told the story that made her sound deceptive?

She could have told the story differently. How she had been drawn to Pamela by her vulnerability and poise when she played "The Lost Child." How apparently going along with Armando's crazy idea that she take a lesson to search for Tavelé was just a ruse. That she had gone to the lesson to get to know Pamela. How Pamela had become as dear to her as Armando. How honored she was that Pamela would entrust her with her baby. But with that story, she would come off no better. Then it was not Pamela her omissions misled, but Armando.

There was another story. About how she had been drawn to Pamela first because of the caramel color of her skin. About how, at her first lesson, when Pamela led her in a breathing exercise, images of Gwendolyn came to her. About how, when she saw the photo of Pamela's graduation, she realized Pamela and Gwendolyn had gone to the same high school. How she had fantasized that they were friends and that she would one day meet her daughter because of Pamela. She didn't think she would come off better telling that story. Not that it mattered, if she would. It was a story she couldn't tell.

She sat there listening to the sound of her mother's muffled voice. It went on longer than previous nights and, this time, without laughter.

Thirty-Nine

ALLIE OPENED THE DOOR A CRACK. "MOTHER'S sleeping."

Armando whispered, "I have to talk with you."

Now was not the time. "Oh, Armando, can't it wait?"

"No, I have to talk. Now."

She tensed. Had he learned Pamela had selected her as her baby's local grandmother? She pulled the door open and led him up the circular stairway to the roof terrace. On the way up, he started to talk several times until shushed, but once there all he did was look away, his arms dangling by his side.

She stood beside him looking across her patio and recalled the pile of rubble outside her wall. How Armando had worried that kids would use the rubble to climb in. She *should* ask him to have someone remove it. But not now. She looked over at him standing there, staring off to the northeast. To Paris?

He turned to her. "I didn't tell you everything about Veracruz."

Veracruz. So, it wasn't about her being Pamela's local granny.

"About how Claude and I danced in my room. He could move to Latin rhythms okay, but so stiffly that even those perfect wrists of his seemed made of wood. I didn't care. Honest. And he didn't either. We laughed. It was the most fun dancing I have ever had. Ever."

She pictured them together. Claude's left hand on Armando's shoulder. Armando's right hand on Claude's back. Their beautiful heads tossed back in laughter.

"Later, at the bar, I danced with the waiter's sister. It took me a while to talk Claude into asking her to dance. But he finally did and—you won't believe this—when he danced with her, he danced as if he had been born in Havana. Afterward, a woman passed by our table and glanced over at him. She said nothing, as she was on the arm of a partner who watched with jealous eyes. But the way she looked at Claude, I knew she wanted to dance with him, too.

"He didn't seem to notice her or the other women who watched him dance. But I noticed. It seemed all the women's eyes were upon him."

He paused and placed both palms against the top of the half wall that rimmed the terrace. "It was bad enough imagining him with other men, Callie, but with women. There are so many of them. He only danced with the waiter's sister, and she's just a kid, really. Still in high school. But I cannot stop thinking of his hand confident against her back and her skirt, slinky and short, shimmering when her hips moved. I swear, Callie," he said turning to her. "He danced like a Cuban. You would not have believed it."

She did not believe it. Claude had probably been more ill at ease with the girl than with Armando. But she would have been dancing the way she always did, and that's what Armando noticed: her rhythmic hip movement, the lightness of her steps, the grace of her arms. She had made Claude look like he could dance, the way Armando made any partner look good. He would have made Claude look Cuban, too. But, of course, no one could have told him that. No one would have seen them dancing.

Armando went on. "After that evening I noticed other

women looking at Claude when we took our morning strolls." He gestured toward his neck. "He always wore a scarf—you know how Parisians are. But they weren't wondering who would wear such a thing in the heat. It's lightweight, and, besides, their look wasn't that kind of look. They looked as if they wanted to rid him of the scarf and his shirt and the rest of his clothes, to lie next to him with those perfect wrists."

He paused, and then continued. "Dark glasses hid his eyes." He smiled. "Gray with golden flecks that you see only if you look close. No one would notice those warm flecks on the street, even without the dark glasses. But I knew they were there, and I knew those beautiful eyes were looking back at the women."

He shuddered, and she reached out to touch his arm, but he pulled away. "After breakfast, when we walked along the boardwalk, Claude would tear off chunks of *bolillo* and throw them in the air for the seagulls. They swarmed above him squawking and flapping their wings. He laughed, but all I could see, looking up at them, were pointy faces of women vying for his attention."

She resisted reaching out again.

"I can't stop thinking of him. In the middle of a concert, when I hear a cello solo, I imagine Claude there. And I get lost, Callie. I lose the beat." He slapped the top of the wall.

"I took down the poster above my bed weeks ago, but when I lie there and look up, I still see him."

He looked into her eyes. "You don't know what it's like. To see images as if they were real."

She wanted to say such images could be comforting. It could have been yesterday when her baby rested in her arms with complete trust. She cherished that image. But if she told Armando that one day he would have his memories, but without the pain, it would not be true. It could have been yesterday, too, when her baby was taken from her arms. So all she could muster was the cliché, "You will meet someone else." She looked away.

"Really?" he said, putting his hands to her face to hold her gaze. "Did you?"

When she said nothing, he dropped his hands and started toward the stairs.

She wanted to stop him, but what could she say? She followed him to the door. He stood back while she opened it.

He stepped toward the opening and then turned toward her. "Tell me, Callie, how would you feel if Claude came here, if you saw us walk hand in hand through the Jardín de la Unión? Saw us kiss in the Callejón del Beso. It would make your stomach turn, wouldn't it? Admit it, Callie. Be honest."

She would be honest, but she had to gather herself first. "No," she said, finally. "My stomach would not turn."

"I don't believe you!"

He deserved her honesty. "But my eyebrows might go up or I might cough."

"See. I told you!"

"But only because I am unfamiliar with men kissing in public. Not because I disapprove."

"Oh, yeah."

"But what if I did disapprove? What matters is not whether I have eradicated all the roots of homophobia. What matters is, have you?"

"You really don't understand, do you? I am Catholic, Callie. A good Catholic."

That wasn't right, what she said. She tried again. "What matters is, can you love regardless? Can you risk your faith for love?"

"You sound so high and mighty. But you have no idea what I'm dealing with. What I've given up to be with Claude. And neither did he."

He put his hands on her shoulders. "The last night in Veracruz, when we came back from dancing, I confronted Claude about the women. How they looked at him . . . How he looked back . . . But he only laughed. He laughed, Callie." He dropped his hands to his sides and bowed his head. "And I hit him. I hit Claude." He looked up again, his eyes intense and tired. "Hard."

"Oh, Armando," she said as softly as she could and put her hand on his shoulder.

"Don't worry." He put his hand on hers. "It's better this way." He went through the door and then turned. "Tell Pamela she can have Tavelé."

SHE stood watching him walk through the shadows cast by moonlight. He didn't turn to wave, the way he usually did, before disappearing around the corner below. She closed the door behind her and then went down to the patio. Seeing her reflection as she passed the window of her bedroom, she noticed her shoulders drooping the way Armando's had when he walked away. She took in a breath and stood straighter. He hadn't meant that about Pamela having Tavelé. But his saying it showed how he must be feeling about himself. She went to her room for a sweater and then sat at the table under the avocado tree. She unbuttoned the sweater. Bad enough to hurt himself more. She pushed her hands out the sleeves and shook the sweater into place. Wasn't it enough that he thought he had lost Claude? Or had lost Claude? She put her elbows on the table and rested her chin against her cupped hands. Or had given up on having Claude? Or had given up on himself? That was more like it. She flattened her hands against the table and tapped her fingers. He couldn't trust himself to treat Claude well. And so, he let him go. It was, wasn't it, a question of honor?

But there must be another way. A path she could help him find. If only she could think of a husband story. She leaned back in her chair and looked up at the whispering leaves of the avocado tree. But all she heard was *Jacob, Jacob, Jacob.* She frowned. There was nothing comforting in *that* story. And neither had the end come just when they were to be wed. She closed her eyes and put her face into her hands.

"WHAT happened?" Her aunt had asked. Callie and Jacob's twenty-four-hour dates each weekend had gone on long enough that her aunt had thought they were for good.

Callie, too, had thought they were for good. But then one night she realized that was just one more of her fantasies. She chided herself. Years older and yet as naïve as she had been at seventeen, imagining that Noah, smelling of cinnamon and hope, would find his way to her hospital room, and they would raise their baby together. Years older and yet immersed in the fantasy that she and Jacob could go on indefinitely, neither asking more than the other offered.

There had been, after all, plenty of clues that the end was near. Jacob's stories of the couples set on marriage. His saying she must have had plenty of beaus and showing surprise that none them had carried her across the threshold. He had even asked at one point, "Had you taken a vow of some sort?" But she had willfully ignored the hints.

She should have known something was amiss when Jacob called to ask her to meet him at the jazz bar of their first date. It wasn't Saturday, nor was there a special group he wanted to see. There weren't any musicians at all that night. Nor were there other patrons when she arrived. Just Jacob at a candle-lit table in the corner.

He rose to help her with her chair and then called the waiter over. "Champagne," he said. When she looked at him in surprise, he said, "I've thought it over. It's time for a change."

"Well," she had said, "I suppose a glass won't hurt."

He didn't say anything else until after the waiter returned with the Champagne, and then when he started in, she felt comfortable enough, sipping her Champagne while he talked.

"I always put work first, and so I never offered a ring to any of the women I dated. One by one, tired of waiting, they left me, and I started all over again. I was relieved, then, when you appeared to have no interest in marriage."

The word "ring" had given her pause, but she had relaxed when he said that about being relieved she wasn't interested in marriage. She wanted to say how glad she was about that, but before she could get the words out, he went on.

"I had been relieved until I realized it was time for a change." He hesitated and then continued, "I hope you are ready for that."

That confused her for a moment. Hadn't she already agreed to a change? Wasn't she sitting there before him sipping champagne? She held up her near-empty glass, in case he hadn't noticed.

He signaled to the waiter for more and then went on. "It's not just because my family has been pestering me."

The waiter filled her glass.

They had teased him about being a teetotaler, she knew that. But pestering him about Champagne? She held her glass up and looked at the sparkling bubbles. Well, why not. There was something charming about it. She took another sip.

"I realized that our bond took me out of myself as nothing else did. There is something sacred in that."

She put her glass down and stared at him. She wasn't sure what he was getting at, but she was pretty sure it wasn't Champagne.

He took a little box out of his pocket and opened it, showing a gold band.

The ring shone in the candlelight. Simple. Lovely. And impossible. She could see that clearly enough, in spite of feeling dizzy from the champagne. A change she then realized she should never have agreed to. Why *had* Jacob offered her champagne? Her face felt flushed. Had he wanted to confuse her?

He apparently sensed her reluctance, because he went on explaining how she could stay the private person she was. "You can go or not go to social events, as you wish. I'm not planning to run for president, after all." He laughed at the idea and then became serious. "I want to devote more time to you, to us, to who we are together. And, besides, you are a good cook." He laughed again.

But she had not been amused. "You seem to have it all figured out. You like my cooking. But what about me? Why would I marry *you?*" That sounded harsh. Maybe she was jumping to conclusions. She had to be. "Uh . . ." She coughed. "I mean . . ." She looked from the ring to him. "What *did* you have in mind?"

Jacob smiled and started to stand up. "Would you prefer I got down on my knees?"

She put her hands out, palms facing him. "Oh, no. Stay where you are. Please. I get it."

Jacob smiled and settled back into his chair. "You give me a quiet space to rest, to dream, to feel myself open up, to want

what we have to go on until death do us part." He took her
hands in his. "But I'm good for something besides a weekly bag
of groceries." He winked. "We could have children."

Children? Not just one child, but a host of them. She
pulled her hands away. What had come over him? He had led
her on, Saturday after Saturday, led her to believe she was safe
with him. She shivered. He had even said he had been relieved
she did not bring up marriage. And then he had turned the
tables on her. After first dosing her with Champagne. Well,
she would tell him a thing or two, if only she could think of
something. She finished her glass and set it down on the table.
She looked over and saw that look in his eyes again, the look
he had given her the night they met. And the words just
popped out. "If it's children you want, look for some other
broad-hipped woman."

A gust shook leaves from the avocado tree. She pulled her
sweater closer and stood up. She never told her aunt what
happened that night. And she wasn't about to tell her what she
realized once she sobered up, that if anyone had led the other
on, it was she. She had loved Jacob fully, but not well. She had
not told him why she could not have children. Nor why she
could not marry him. She couldn't explain without breaking
her commitment to her daughter's privacy. And so, when Jacob in disbelief had asked, "What is it, Callie? I thought we
were good. It's not someone else, is it? It couldn't be that?" she
was relieved that he had offered a way out and she took it.
"Yes, Jacob, that's what it is. I'm sorry." So, that's what she told
her aunt, too, that there was someone else. And she had left it
at that.

Forty

ALLIE WOKE TO THE RING OF THE PHONE. HAD IT woken her mother? She frowned. Who could be calling so early?

"Callie?" It was Armando.

She looked at the bedside clock. Seven a.m.

"She doesn't have him."

Him? Claude? She rubbed the sleep from her eyes. "Who doesn't have him?" A pencil and her latest translation lay on the bed beside her. It wasn't due for some time. But starting it had been the only way she could get her blunders of the evening before off her mind.

"Pamela."

She sat up. "Pamela?"

"Of course. Who else?"

She flopped down. "I told you so" went through her mind, but she resisted saying it. "Oh, so you've found Tavelé?" Not Claude. Too bad. She yawned and stretched her free arm. "That's a relief." She picked up the pencil.

"Señor Gonzáles, you know, the Jehovah's Witness. He found him. And, no, it's not a relief, Callie."

Her chest tightened. "Not the . . . the . . . pound." He had told her of the cement floor, the scarce food, the cages of hungry dogs.

"Worse, Callie, worse. If he were there, I could get him back."

She wrote "Dead" on the manuscript. There was no way back from there. Her eyes filled with tears. "I'm so sorry, Armando."

"He's in the country."

She saw Tavelé running across a gravel road, his tongue flapping and his eyes dancing, and then a car, the squeal of brakes, a thud. "How did it happen? Was he hit . . . ?"

"They would never hit him."

"They? Who?"

"The Petersons. A New Orleans family. Friends of Samuel, the tuba player who left for the summer to play jazz in The Big Easy."

"Tavelé's in New Orleans?"

"No. The Petersons are staying at Samuel's cabin. You know, the place near a village way out in the country. Where we sat by a stream, eating pizza baked in a brick oven. I took you there a couple of years ago. Remember? Tavelé loved the pizza."

"I remember him stealing mine." He had been a scamp, that Tavelé.

"The Petersons are looking after Samuel's dog. She's Tavelé's mother. That's why Tavelé's there."

"So, he's okay?"

"Yeah. He's okay. He jumped in the Peterson's car last month when they came in for some supplies they couldn't get locally."

She scratched out "Dead."

"I'm going out there to see him. But I'll never get him back, Callie. After being there, he won't come back to me."

Hadn't he just talked about giving Tavelé away? To Pamela, of all people. She put the pencil in her mouth. Bit into the rubber tip.

"He'll want to stay there with his mom."

She spit out the pencil. "Remember those other times he ran away? He always came running when you found him."

"But he wasn't with his mom, then, was he?"

He sounded bitter. But why? "It'll be fine. You'll see." She glanced through the draft. Just a question of typing in the changes. "I can be ready in no time."

"Oh, no, you're *way* too busy. What with your mother there. And Pamela's baby."

"Pamela's baby?"

"When were you going to tell me, Granny Callie?" He sounded dejected. "So, no, I'll just go on my own. I might as well get used to it, with you chumming around with Pamela."

Oh, dear. She bowed her head and put a hand over her eyes.

His tone turned determined. "But if I *do* get Tavelé back, *she* can't have him." He hung up.

With the phone still in her hand, she thought of the jaguar. She imagined him looking back in disgust.

SHE took a papaya out of the refrigerator. Her mother had been right. Armando needed her support. Especially now. She cut the papaya in two, put one half cut-side down on a plate, and put it back in the fridge. But instead, she had betrayed him. No wonder he was angry. She scooped out the round, black seeds, and discarded them in the compost bucket. At least he would get Tavelé back. She smiled, thinking of Tavelé running to Armando the way he always did. How she would like to be there. She slid a paring knife under the papaya skin. But she couldn't, because of her own selfishness. She peeled off smooth strips of skin. Attaching herself to Pamela when she knew from the start that would hurt Armando. But she hadn't been able to stop herself. And now there was no way she could give up Pamela. She sighed. If only she could have been candid with him. Maybe, then, he wouldn't be so angry. She cut the papaya into slices and then cut the slices into chunks. She had lost her mother's respect, too. She divided the chunks into two azure bowls and set them on the table by the place settings, where she had already placed tea, cereal, and soy milk. All because she had been drawn to Pamela. Mesmerized by how she played "The Lost Child." Now she felt lost herself.

Forty-One

HER MOTHER CAME TO THE TABLE WHEN CALLIE called. She looked down to spread a napkin across her lap and then up at Callie. "I had a long talk with John last night."

A long talk. Without laughter. "I am sorry, Mother. I don't expect you to understand."

"No, Callie, I'm the one who's sorry. I should not have said what I did." She smoothed the napkin across her lap. "I needed to look at my own behavior, the words I left unsaid, the deeds I left undone. All those years you lived in Chicago, and I never went once, even after your father died. Not once. But what I regret most is not being there with you when your baby came. Leaving you alone like that, Callie. It is unforgiveable."

"That was a long time ago, Mother. It's all right." She couldn't say she had not wanted her mother there. She had not even let Aunt Ida come to the hospital. "I understand. It was Dad. He made you promise. You had no choice."

"Let me go on, Callie. That's why I came here." She pushed her chair back a little from the table, turning toward Callie. "They say you can't go home without reverting to who you were. You were always a good girl, Callie. Quiet. You did your homework, helped with the dishes. You did what we asked. Your father and I." She took in a breath and then went on. "It's no longer necessary for either of us to please your father. That promise your father extracted from me, from both of us. You don't have to keep it." She looked into Callie's eyes. "You don't need to be that 'good girl' now. You don't have to hide."

So *that* was her mother's idea of quality time with her. Bringing up her past. Encouraging her not to hide. Not hide? And expose Gwendolyn. That was not an option. But she knew her mother meant well. She reached out to touch her mother's hand. "It's in the past, Mother."

Her mother sat up straighter as if to give herself courage. "I never told you what happened the morning your father died." She paused a moment and then went on. "Pastor's daughter had been in church the Sunday before, back visiting her parents. 'Why couldn't Callie be like *her*,' your father said. 'She honors her father and mother.' It wasn't the first time he'd made a comment like that. I never told you that either. Things he would say about you not coming home." She looked away and then back at Callie. "I'm not sure what came over me that morning, but I told him it was *his* fault you didn't come home. What did he expect the way he had talked to you? The way he continued to talk. As if *he* had been a victim."

"I suppose he apologized right then and there." Callie could not keep the sarcasm out of her voice.

"Callie, please." Her mother looked as if she would cry.

And then it came to her. Her mother would have felt responsible for her father's death. She took both of her mother's hands into hers. "Dad's fall. It *wasn't* your fault."

"Maybe he was distracted by what I had said. I don't know. But that's not what's worrying me. It's that I hadn't been fair to him. It wasn't *all* his fault that you didn't come home, or that, in a way, we had lost you."

She sighed. Would her mother *never* stop defending him.

As if she had read her daughter's mind, her mother went on. "I won't make excuses for your father. I'm done with that. But it's not his behavior I want to talk about. It's mine." She took her hands from Callie's and sat up a little straighter in her chair. "After he died, I realized my silence wasn't just protecting him. I was protecting myself." She leaned forward. "I was afraid, Callie. I was afraid of his temper. I was afraid of his tears. But more than anything I was afraid he would leave me, and I would be alone." She paused a moment and then went on. "When he died, I thought I would die, too. I wanted to die. I waited to die. And then one dawn, I heard a robin singing in the garden. It was four years to the day he died, and the first time I woke without reaching to feel him by my side. I had stopped being afraid. I still missed him, but I was no longer afraid of being alone." She paused again. "I sometimes wonder, Callie, if you are afraid? Not of being alone. It's not that. It's that I wonder if there are things we would have talked about, if I had not protected Dad—not protected myself—for so long."

"It's all right, Mother. It's better this way. Truly." Her hands had begun to perspire. Didn't she have a translation she could do? She started to stand up.

"Callie, please. Stay."

She wiped her hands on her shirt and settled back in her chair.

Her mother leaned toward her. "I was overjoyed when I found I was pregnant. If someone had taken you from me, I don't think I could have gone on. And yet I made you give up your baby. It wasn't just Dad. I said you could go stay with Aunt Ida. That no one would have to know."

She reached out a hand to her mother. "Please don't worry about that."

Her mother took her hand between hers. "And then, afterward, you and I never talked about it. Even after your dad died. I never once asked how you felt. I never told you how sorry I was."

She thought again of how her mother had avoided the topic of babies. Tears came to her eyes. "Please don't feel bad, Mother. Maybe you were protecting yourself and Dad, but I felt protected by you, too." If her mother had pried, it would have been more difficult to keep her promise to her baby and to Gwendolyn, the woman her baby had become.

And she had never wanted to talk about how she felt about letting her baby go. It was one thing for her mother to have expected her teenage daughter to give up her baby. It was another for her to give up her own baby. She's the one who did that. She, herself. Her mother did not steal the baby from her. She just left her alone to do what she would do. And that's what she did. She opened her arms and let her baby go.

She took her hand from her mother's and then sat back and picked up her fork. "Shall we eat?"

Her mother looked taken aback. "Oh, well, I thought . . ." But then she recovered. "Yes, of course." She started to reach for her fork and then paused. "Do you mind, Callie, if I say grace?"

Her mother always said grace at home, but had not since her arrival in Guanajuato. She put her fork down. "Please do."

"Thank you, Lord, for the food before us. Thank you for giving me the daughter who served this food. And, most of all, dear Lord, thank you for making it possible for us to share this food, mother and daughter, together. Amen."

Mother and daughter together. She was not a believer, but she would thank the Lord for that. Mother and daughter together. Tears came to her eyes again. "Amen."

IT didn't take long to finish breakfast and wash up, not long enough for her to decide how to distract her mother, who had begun to ask questions about Armando and Pamela. She felt comfortable enough telling her mother about Armando's resistance to Maestro Chávez retiring. About how he blamed Pamela's hair for the maestro getting lost. But then she was stymied. She couldn't relate Armando's wild theories about Pamela being responsible for Tavelé's disappearance. Her mother might bring up her deceiving Pamela again.

To her relief, her mother didn't seem to notice her uncomfortable silence. When the dishes were done, she dried her hands on her apron and said she wanted to get on with the booties she had started making for Pamela's baby.

After helping her mother settle in the shade of the avocado tree, Callie made herself another cup of tea and went to her desk. She looked forward to finishing her translation.

Just as she was opening her document, the phone rang.

"You won't believe this." Armando said. "At rehearsal break I was talking with this sweet elderly lady in the Plaza Baratillo. We were watching a couple of dogs chase each other around the fountain. One of them was brindled, like Tavelé, and I started telling the lady about him."

His voice sounded light. Was he no longer angry? Or was he just rubbing it in? That he had found someone else to share his troubles with.

"I told her how worried I am that he won't want to go home with me when I see him this afternoon, and with you busy with other things, I had to go alone."

No hint of sarcasm. That was good. Or was it?

"And do you know what?"

"No. What?"

She heard a drum roll and then he said, "*La bonne femme* offered to go with me. Just like that."

So, the good woman was taking her place. What if she also spoke French?

"And then when we were discussing where to meet, Pamela showed up."

Pamela did speak French, but that would probably only annoy him.

"I ignored her, of course."

Of course. Should she say how sorry she was about Pamela now? Before it was too late.

"But the lady put her arm around Pamela and asked me if I knew her daughter. I almost fell over. That sweet lady with her tailored suit and her hair pulled back into a chignon was Mrs. Fischer."

Pamela's mother offering to go with Armando. She couldn't have picked a better replacement. But, still, she wished she could go herself.

"Can you imagine? She didn't seem anything like Pamela."

Perhaps not. Superficially, anyway.

"You should have seen the shoes Pamela had on—you could puncture a tire with the toes, and those crazy red curls sticking out all over her head."

So, some of Armando's feelings hadn't changed.

"Of course, she tried to go along with us."

How was she supposed to be on his side when he said things like that?

"But when she offered to postpone her lesson and take us in her car . . ." another drum roll came from Armando. ". . . the dear lady said 'No, Dear. You mustn't upset your schedule. Armando has arranged transportation.' Then she took Pamela's arm and they started to walk off. Oh, but then Mrs. Fischer turned to me and said, 'Now don't you worry, Dear. Everything will be okay. You'll see.'"

When she, herself, had said that, he hadn't been convinced. But now, quoting Mrs. Fischer, his voice sounded calm. She would have been the one to go with him, if it weren't for Pamela.

Before hanging up, he said, "You're okay, aren't you? Everything's okay there, isn't it?"

So, he hadn't been trying to make her feel left out? He did care? She looked out to see her mother take a break from crocheting to wave at her. She lifted a hand back. "Yes, of course." She would be okay—once she got to work.

SHE had just finished one translation and started another one, when the phone rang again.

"You won't believe what happened." Pamela sounded worried.

That Pamela's mother was going off with Armando. Yes, she would believe it. "Armando told me."

"Does he know, too?" She sounded incredulous.

That Pearl was going with him to pick up Tavelé. "Well, of course."

"But how could she have told him, when she didn't say anything to me?"

"I thought you knew. Armando said you came by when he and your mother were talking about picking up Tavelé. He said you offered to take them."

"Oh, that. I wasn't too happy about her going off alone with him."

She frowned. She hadn't been as happy as she should have been either.

"But it was clear he didn't want me along. He got his way on that one. But that's not what I called about."

"No?"

"No. I was rifling through my backpack to look for a hat

for Mother to take with her, and the baby shoe came out with it."

"Oh, dear." She thought of the leash that slipped out of her backpack at her lesson. Pamela had noticed it. Had Pamela's mother noticed the baby shoe?

"I grabbed it and slid it back in the pack, but I think she saw it. She didn't say anything then, but just before she left, she said, 'Is there something you want to say before I go?' and all I could think of was, 'Armando's a handful.' I didn't know what else to say. It just wasn't the time to bring up the past."

"I know what you mean." She wished her mother felt the same way.

"There wasn't time to go into it, not with Armando champing at the bit to get Tavelé. He'd already called three times. I wish I'd never given him my cell number. And so she left—with that image of the shoe in her head, and she's with Armando of all people."

"*À cœur vaillant rien d'impossible.*"

"French. Let's see, that means... ah, it's been a while . . ."

"It just came to me, Pamela. I'm not sure why. But it's true, I think. The saying. To a brave heart, a brave love, nothing is impossible. You're worried about your mother. You're afraid she will suffer. I understand. But you can tell her what happened just the way you told me, and she'll be fine. Your heart is brave, and, from what you've told me about your mother, so is hers. So you'll be fine, too. You'll see."

Forty-Two

THE DAY WENT WELL. HER MOTHER FINISHED the booties, Callie made progress on her translation, and Juanito brought them fresh papaya. Callie had even thought up some safe topics for their dinnertime conversation.

She filled their plates with beans, Spanish rice, sliced avocado, and tossed green salad, and then arranged their trays to take down to the patio. It looked like the rain would hold off long enough for them to finish dinner under the avocado tree.

Her mother had already talked for hours about her wedding plans, how they would be married on a Saturday evening, the entire congregation invited, as was the custom, and then there would be a reception in the church basement. The next day after church, there would be a gathering for family and close friends at John's house. They had not planned a honeymoon. Yet. John wanted to take her somewhere, anywhere. But she was happy to stay at his place, sitting on the porch, watching the geese fly low over the lake. Luckily, questions remained. What would her mother wear? What songs would be sung at the service? Was there anywhere her mother might be persuaded to go for a honeymoon?

The sun had set, and they were still talking about the wedding. Callie got up to turn on the patio light. Soon it would be time for her mother to go to her room and call John. She could relax now.

Her mother seemed in no hurry to retire, so Callie began

asking about how she could help her mother. She expected to have a translation deadline a few days before the wedding. But she could help serve the Sunday lunch. She would take charge of cleaning up, too. And she could stay for a while to help her mother clear out her house.

Her mother thanked her. "You are such a help, Callie."

"Oh, that's nothing, Mother. Really. I am so happy for you. And John. I would do anything to help you start up your new life. Anything at all."

"Well, there is something," her mother said. "The ring John gave me. When I saw it, the first thing I thought was, 'Where would I put it?' You see, I still wore the ring your father gave me. I had not even put it on my right hand, the way some widows do."

As a child, she had loved that engagement ring. The pearl's smooth surface, its warm glow.

"I don't know. I can't explain it. I had that ring on my finger for so long. It felt like it belonged there."

Over time, it had come to symbolize her father's hold on her mother, his guarantee of her loyalty.

"I took it off to try on the diamond John gave me, but my finger didn't feel the same."

Surely not.

"Do you know what your aunt said? I should put John's ring on my right hand and leave your father's ring where it was. What ideas your aunt comes up with!" She started laughing and put her hand over her mouth as if she should not be laughing at such a sacrilege. "I got used to John's ring eventually." She held up her hand. "It looks like it belongs there now."

"Yes, it does." That thought she could say out loud.

"I didn't know what to do with Dad's ring. And then I thought of you."

Well, she could always put it on a laundry room shelf.

"It's been in your father's family for some time. His mother wore it, you know."

It sounded like her mother had been practicing reasons for her to accept the ring.

Her mother took a small white box out of her pocket and opened it. She looked at the ring a moment herself. And then turned the ring toward Callie.

The ring looked different off her mother's finger. There, nestled in the plush black lining of the box, it looked forlorn. Like her father sometimes did after one of his rants. When he would sit in his reading chair, but not reading. Just sitting. While the room turned dark.

He would sit there until her mother called them for dinner, when he would go to the kitchen. He would sit in silence there, too, not even joining in when they said grace. But then, when they finished eating, he would thank her mother for the meal. And thank her, too, for being a good girl. His voice soft and his eyes sad.

And now he was gone. And her mother was giving away his ring. Had she no heart? She looked at her mother, sitting there before her, expectantly. The vulnerable bride to be. Offering the ring to seal her fate. Expecting her daughter to collude. She shook herself. Goodness, what was she thinking! There was no Shakespearean meaning in her mother's offer. Nor was her father a tragic figure. Be reasonable.

She accepted the box and took out the ring. It was just a ring. Gold and pearl. Lovely like multitudes of others. No more, no less. She slipped it on her finger.

"There's something else I'd like to ask you, Callie." Her mother put her hand on hers, covering the ring. "I'd like permission to talk with John about the baby."

Callie gasped.

"I think he already knows. He must have heard things."

She remembered when she was a freshman, hearing girls in the high school cafeteria whisper about an older girl who went away, supposedly to stay with a bereaved grandparent, but the girls thought there was more to the story. She pulled her hand away. "Has he told you he heard something?"

"No, and I don't think he would."

"Rumors abound in a small town, but you don't have to confirm them." Her voice sounded breathless. She willed herself calm.

"John's been open with me about burdens he carries in his heart. He's talked with me about Steve, how bad he felt about letting him go off to Vietnam."

Poor John. If only he knew. There was no way he could have stopped Steve. But she would not hint at the secret Steve told her, when she shared hers. How he had laughed wryly at her father thinking *he* was the father. *He* would not have been the one to spread the rumor, and she must keep her word, too.

"I started doing the same. Lightening my burdens by sharing them with John." She paused. "I felt uncomfortable, especially at first."

"Well, yes, I understand." Some burdens weren't meant to be shared.

"But, Callie, I can't tell you how different I feel now. How much more at ease. And how much closer I feel to John. It's almost like we are one." She smiled and put her hand over her mouth. "And we're not even married yet." She lifted her shoulders and then let them settle. "I told John what I said to your father, that it was *his* fault you didn't come home."

Her mother must love John dearly to be so open with him.

"But I didn't tell him the whole story. I didn't admit that

the gossip was true or that *I* had been the one to suggest you go away. That's what I want to tell him now."

"So you can feel better? You and John." Was it happening again, her mother siding against her? She felt the ring burning on her finger.

"It's not about feeling good, Callie. It's something else. It doesn't feel right, not telling John. He's to be my husband. I want him to know what I've done. Who I've been."

Of course. Callie had wanted to tell others, too. Had wanted to shout from the rooftops from the time she first saw her baby's sweet face. But *she* had resisted. Over and over.

"Callie?" Her mother said softly. "May I?"

The softness of her mother's voice didn't fool her. Her mother was determined to tell her dear John. There was no way she could stop her. "Go ahead. Tell him." She felt the ring burning on her finger. "And while you're at it, tell your neighbors. Announce it at the wedding." She tugged at the ring. "Meanwhile you can tell Armando, Pamela, her mother, Juanito, the *gordita* ladies. Oh, and don't forget the Jehovah's Witnesses." She pulled again on the ring. "You could hand out leaflets to save time." She saw the look of horror on her mother's face, but she could not stop. "Or would you rather I brand my forehead?"

"Callie, please. Times are different. You don't have to keep your baby a secret. Not even your father would expect that of you now."

"My *father*. Do you think *he* could keep me from my baby? Do you think I would give up one minute, no, one second, of time with her for him? My loyalty is not to him, or to you, and certainly not to John. It is to my baby."

"Of course, and we could help you find her."

"No. I made a promise to myself, to her, never to disrupt

her life again. Never. And I will not. I will never contact her. And you will not either. You and John." She was almost shouting. "Promise me that you will not look for her."

"We would never look for her without your permission."

She was firm. "No. Promise you will never look for her. Period."

"Okay, Callie. Okay." Her mother sounded tired.

Her heart was racing. She couldn't think. She had to calm down. Figure out what to do next. She focused on Pamela's instructions. Take in air, like a pitcher filling with stream water. "All right then." She pulled again on the ring, and this time it came off.

Her mother was watching her, and so was the jaguar, warning her with his eyes. They needn't have worried. She was calm now. No more scenes. She opened the box and slid the ring into the velvet slot.

Forty-Three

CALLIE PUT DOWN THE RAG SHE HAD BEEN DUSTING with and answered her cell. "Bueno."

"It's late. I thought you might not answer."

Late. What time was it?

"It's midnight."

So, she'd been dusting and organizing the philosopher's books for two hours? Well, she'd gotten a lot done, separating the books into categories. She had put Jacob's package in the box she'd marked "Ancient." Jacob and Socrates side by side. She looked over at the box. What would their dialogue sound like?

"I'm sorry to call so late, Calecita, but I had a gig."

Calecita. She smiled. He hadn't called her that for a while. "I am tired, but happy to hear from you." She crossed her legs and sat down on the floor by a box she had marked "Medieval." "How's Tavelé?"

"I was so worried that he wouldn't come to me. Before we left, I went by the bakery for his favorite cake, you know the one, orange with cream cheese frosting."

Food. That would revive her. She looked around. Where was that egg sandwich she'd brought upstairs for a snack?

"When we got there, and I saw Tavelé playing with the other dogs, I ran to see him. Jorge took off before I remembered the cake. I ran after his taxi, but he didn't see me. Mrs.

Fischer was still standing there under the pepper tree where the taxi had been. She's such a lovely *viejita*."

Viejita? Pearl was not much older than she was. Her stomach growled. Where was that sandwich?

"She told me not to worry about the cake. Everything would be all right."

"And was it? Was everything all right?" All right without her there. She sighed.

"Someone else had brought a cake, so it didn't matter. And we baked pizzas in the Petersons' new brick oven. The oven gets so hot, they bake in seconds. It's amazing."

It hadn't taken long to fry the egg, either, and spread the bread with mayonnaise. But little good did it do her if she couldn't find it. She looked around.

"We each rolled out small balls of dough—whole wheat, you would have loved it—and filled them with whatever we liked. Mrs. Fischer likes chorizo, and so does Tavelé."

Everything must be all right, but Armando was clearly not in a rush to tell her. She tried to stand up to look for the sandwich on an upper shelf, but one of her legs had gone to sleep. She settled back down and shook her leg against the floor. "So, he was fine?"

"Oh, I guess I forgot to tell you. He came to me as soon as he saw me. He jumped up to my chest, the way he does, and then let his front feet slide back to the ground."

She looked down her body, remembering the line of bruises from her chest to her toes left by Tavelé's nails.

"But then he ran away again to play with the other dogs, as if he'd forgotten all about me. I was so nervous I could barely finish my pizzas."

"Pizzas? You mean slices?" She pushed herself up and looked around, but didn't see the sandwich. She sat back down.

"No. Pizzas. Three of them."

"Three?" She would be happy with one.

"They were small."

She would have to make herself another sandwich and get to bed. "It's late, Armando."

"But I haven't told you about Mrs. Fischer. Did you know she sings? She has a beautiful contralto voice, warm, rich, and deep. When we finished eating, we started playing music. I remembered what Pamela had said, about her mother singing, and so I asked Mrs. Fischer to sing. At first she refused. She didn't know the songs we were playing, nor we hers. I said it didn't matter. She could sing a cappella. And so she did, standing there erect and solemn, with her hands clasped at her waist, she sang, 'He's Got the Whole World in His Hands.' The way she sang it, it sounded like a prayer, reminding God that he had all of us, the Petersons, me, Mrs. Fischer, Tavelé, all of us in his hands."

It would be nice to feel that way. In the hands of someone you could trust.

"No one moved. The dogs stopped playing. Even the leaves of the pepper trees became silent. And then, when she finished, she opened her arms out wide, and we all stood and did the same and made a circle with the dogs inside. The Peterson's little girl said, 'Look, we're making a pizza.' Everyone laughed. The dogs started barking and jumping. The breeze came up again, and peppercorns rained from the trees on all of us."

"That's lovely." More lovely than if she had been the one with Armando. Tears came to her eyes. She should get off the phone. She willed her voice steady. "I'm sorry. I need to go."

"But that's not all. When Jorge came back, I helped Mrs. Fischer into the taxi, and then I called Tavelé. When he came running to me and jumped into the taxi, Mrs. Fischer said, 'Bless you God, bless you,' and started to cry. She cried and then she laughed and then she cried some more. I've never seen anything like it. The cake was still there in Jorge's taxi, so I offered her a slice, but she couldn't eat it for crying. So Tavelé ate it. Anyway, when Mrs. Fischer stopped crying, you know what she told me? She had been afraid of losing Pamela. Just like I had been about losing Tavelé. Imagine that. Did you know Pamela was adopted?" He didn't wait for an answer. "I sure didn't. Pamela didn't know either until she was in high school. She was furious when she found out. Wouldn't speak to that nice lady for months."

Pearl had told Armando all that?

"After she told me that, about Pamela not speaking to her, she started crying again, and I thought she would not stop. Tavelé was worried, too. He put a paw on her lap. Then she smiled and calmed down some."

Tavelé should put his paw on Armando's lap.

"She told me what a wonderful daughter Pamela was, how she never stayed angry for long. Well, I don't know about that. But, anyway, that's what she said."

She heard him starting to swish his drum. Her head felt as if it were spinning, too.

"When we got to the parking lot below Pamela's house, Pamela was there waiting. Before Mrs. Fischer got out of the taxi, she said, 'Thanks for taking me along.' Isn't that funny? Her thanking me—when she's the one who helped me."

Armando needn't have worried, and neither should Pearl. She had been the one Pamela had come to depend on. Pamela would always come back to her. And now so would Armando.

"Callie? Are you there?"

"I need to get to bed." When she pushed herself back up again, her sleeve brushed something off a shelf. She reached down to pick it up. The postcard the philosopher had sent about the silent retreat. She'd forgotten all about it. Doña Petra must have found it in her pocket when doing the wash. She should write the philosopher a note. Tell her about the lavender. She slipped the postcard into her pocket as a reminder.

"Okay, just a minute. I'll be right back."

"Armando . . ." Too late, he had already gone off somewhere. She looked at the shelves again. Lifted an extra dust rag. Ah, the sandwich. She took a bite.

"I'm back. Tavelé wants to say hello . . ."

"Armando, I have to finish up here."

"Say something to him."

She swallowed and then said, "You need to wear a leash."

She heard Tavelé sniff into the phone as if he understood.

"You can finish up now, Chou," Armando said and hung up.

She had just finished arranging the boxes when the phone rang again.

"I forgot to tell you. I told Mrs. Fischer how Maestro Chávez stares at Pamela, and she said she wasn't surprised. When I asked why, she told me he had shown her a photo of his wife when she was young. One I'd never really paid any attention to. And guess what? According to Mrs. Fischer, she was the *spittin' image* of Pamela. Imagine that." He sounded pensive. "Maybe Pamela wasn't trying to distract him after all."

"No, I don't suppose she was." Why hadn't she told him that a long time ago? But she hadn't, had she? So it was Pearl who had come to the rescue. "Armando, I really must go."

"I just wanted you to know that," he said and hung up.

She was pulling the door shut when the phone rang again.

"There's something else."

"What?"

"I've been thinking."

"Okay."

"Well, if Pamela isn't so bad and wouldn't have intentionally distracted Maestro Chávez, then she wouldn't have stolen Tavelé, either—well, not intentionally."

He was, it seemed, finally coming to his senses. No thanks to her.

"And you would have known that. Right? I mean, you don't usually go along when I'm suspicious, you know. You've never once called a Paris hospital, for example."

"No . . ." She closed her eyes. She still felt lightheaded, even after finishing the sandwich. She needed to get to bed.

"And at first you didn't want to go along with my idea that you search for Tavelé at Pamela's. I know you don't like to meet new people. So now I wonder. Why did you?"

She looked around the laundry room, as if looking for an answer. The box with the pearl ring sat alone on the top shelf. Forlorn, like her father. He had been a lost child, hadn't he?

"Callie?"

"She reminded me of someone."

"Maestro Chávez's wife?"

"No. Someone else." She picked up the box.

"Someone you loved? Like the maestro loved his wife?"

Someone she loved. "Oh, Armando, I can't talk about it now. I'm too tired." She opened the box.

"Will you tell me sometime, Callie?"

"Maybe." She took out the ring. An engagement ring. A promise. "I don't know."

"I tell you things. I told you about Claude."

Her father had kept his promise. "It's a long story, Armando." And she should keep hers. She put the ring on her finger and touched the pearl.

"And you're tired, Calecita."

Tired. "Yes." She needed a long, long rest.

Forty-Four

THE BELLS WERE RINGING THE TIME, AS THEY had every quarter hour since Callie had lain down. When was that? Around one-thirty a.m.? And now they were striking two-fifteen. They must strike all day, too. But she only heard them in the darkest hours of the night when everything else—even the rooftop dogs—quieted down. She sighed. If only her thoughts would quiet down.

She felt for the pearl on her finger. Perhaps her father had never forgiven her for her pregnancy. But he had been right about one thing. No one should ever know.

Her feet felt ice cold. Her hands, too. She really should try to get some sleep. But she had to figure it out first. How to keep her promise. It wouldn't be easy. Not with her mother pressuring her. And Armando asking questions. And then there was Pamela. She *had* deceived her, hadn't she? Was *that* the kind of granny she was to be? She shivered.

She cupped the ring hand in the other and moved the ring up a little and then back down. She wished her mother would just drop the subject. But how could she expect that when she herself had never fully let her baby go? She should have forgotten all about her, like the social workers said she would. But no, not her. She thought herself better than that. She had given up all her rights, but she would never forsake her child. *Her* child. So she had thought. How foolish she had been. Imagin-

ing someone else's daughter her own child. Foolish. And self-
ish. Instead of protecting her, as any real mother would have,
she had tracked her down. Had her watched. Accepted a clan-
destine photo.

She should never have seen the image of the woman her
baby had become. Never imagined hearing her voice. Seeing
her face to face. Taking her hand in hers.

Her stomach felt a little queasy. Lack of sleep? Or the
thought of Gwendolyn's voice, if she were taken by surprise,
called against her will. Polite at first. Then cool. And finally
sarcastic. Like her father's voice. But then what else could she
expect? She shivered and shifted lower into the covers. It was
time she faced facts. She felt the pull of seeing Gwendolyn only
when she could not. The real possibility of meeting her, even
talking with her on the phone, had made her ill. She recalled
that day in Chicago when she had sat by the phone all afternoon, waiting for the perfect time to call. Not too early. Not
too late. Just right. The moment the sun began to cast long
shadows, she reached for the phone. She had dialed the number. Waited while it rang. But the moment she heard it picked
up, her baby's face came to her. A question mark, wondering,
Why? Nausea had overcome her. She had hung up before the
person spoke. She pulled the covers over her head and curled
into a fetal position.

She had comforted herself then with the thought that it
would be different, that voice. Warm and sweet, it would
sound, if Gwendolyn reached out to her. And, so, that's what
she had wished for. Every time the phone rang. Even after
moving to Mexico. That's what she wished for. That it would
be Gwendolyn calling. But now as she lay there in the dark,
images from "The Monkey's Paw" filled her mind. The son
who had died mangled by a machine. His mother in despera-

tion pleading with her husband to wish their son alive, using a magic paw. Their realization, when they heard the knock at their door, that they had sentenced their son to suffering they could not ease. She pressed her face against her knees. She had to let her daughter be. Whatever it took. She had to let her be.

She dozed and drifted and dreamed. Something half hidden. Her heart racing. And then peace. A stream. A ripple. She stirred. A lake. Still. But not silent. She could hear something. She woke. Rain. Gentle rain. Washing the dust from the avocado leaves. She sat up. What had she been dreaming of? A place of peace. A lake. And then it came to her. The postcard. That was it. Her answer. She touched the ring on her finger. "I can do it," she whispered. "Thank you."

BY the time she finished showering and dressing, she had it all figured out. She took the file of information about Gwendolyn from the safe and went back to her bedroom for the hand-painted box on her bookshelf. When she dumped her socks out of the box, the key fell out with them. She put the file into the box, locked it, and took it to the garden.

It was easy to shovel the ground after the rains. She made a hole eighteen inches deep and rectangular with straight edges, just the right size for the box.

She would go to the philosopher's retreat. She felt light-headed. But she had all her wits about her. She would be living in silence, meditating. She could fit everything she needed in her backpack.

She emailed her translation supervisor, explaining that an emergency had come up. And then she wrote out notes. To her mother:

*Please forgive my outburst last night. It will never happen
again. I have been under stress, but I will be all right. Please
do not worry. I love you. Jorge will take you to the airport.*

She reread the letter. And then added,

*Thank you for coming to visit me here. I am grateful we
had this wonderful week. I do not want to inconvenience
anyone, least of all you. But I must go. Please give my love
to Aunt Ida. And to John. I am happy knowing you will be
with him. Love, Callie*

To Armando she wrote:

*I need to go away. Don't worry. I will be fine. I just need
some time. Please have Jorge take Mother to the airport and
pay Doña Petra. I've left some things by the door for Juanito
to sell, if he likes. Pat Tavelé for me. Un abrazo, Callie*

She tucked pesos in Armando's envelope for Jorge and Doña
Petra and then wrote to Pamela:

*I am sorry to be leaving in such a rush, but I have to. Doña
Petra and Armando will help you. Thank you from the
bottom of my heart for asking me to be your baby's local
grandmother. Please tell your mother goodbye for me.
Callie*

She put the notes in unsealed envelopes, wrote their
names on them, and left them in a row on the dining room
table. She had not told them when she would be back. She
didn't know how long it would take for her to trust herself.

As for the house, it could be left as it was. Maybe one day

she would sell it and everything inside the way the philosopher had, but in the meantime, she had left money for Doña Petra to come clean the way she always did. Enough for a year. She hoped that would be enough time. But she thought of the four years it took her mother to accept her father's death. It could take her longer to stop imagining she had a daughter.

SHE checked her watch. Five-fifteen a.m. All she had to do was find some things for Juanito. There wasn't much for him to sell other than what she had bought from him. He would be disappointed if she cast them off. She went to the laundry room, opened the box of Greek Philosophy, and took out Plato's *Apology*. Not a bad book. But it was in English. Who would buy it? She didn't have the time to think about it. She put *Apology* back into the box and closed it. What about Jacob's package? Maybe it contained something Juanito could sell. She started to open the Ancient History box and then stopped. Whatever was in Jacob's package would be for her alone. A symbol of some sort. No, not just of any sort. She knew Jacob well enough to know that. It would be a symbol of hope. Well, she did feel hopeful. She had a chance for a new life. Away by the lake. No need to open Jacob's package. There must be something else for Juanito. She made a mental inventory of her house but couldn't think of a thing. And then she remembered the look the jaguar had given her when she had left the notes on the table. He could go to Juanito, and his coyote and baboon friends.

When she turned to close the laundry room door, she paused. The case with the trumpet inside caught her eye. Give it to Juanito? She moved toward it. And then she stopped herself. No, not the trumpet.

Before she put the key in the entry door, she checked off her mental to-do list. Notes and an extra house key for her mother on the table. Cash card, water bottle, and clothes in her backpack. The jaguar, coyote, and baboon lined up ready for Juanito. She considered retrieving the cell she had left with the notes. Just in case. And then decided, no. The philosopher did not have one, and neither would she. Besides, her mother could use it. She smiled. Everything was under control.

Her backpack on and all ready to go, she put her key in her entry door, turned to wave good-by to the animals, and then tried to turn the key. It would not move. She jiggled it. It still would not move. She tried leaning against the door while turning the key. No luck. Neither did it help to pull the door. The jaguar looked on. "Well," she said, "no reason to panic." She would take the key out and put it back in again. More carefully this time. Everything would be all right.

She pulled on the key. It would not come out.

She felt feverish with excitement. There must be a way to get out. And she would find it. She looked down into the garden. Of course. The avocado tree. The pile of rubble. She would be out in no time.

On the way down the stairs, she shivered, but thought nothing of it. The exertion of climbing the tree would warm her.

She stood for a moment under the tree. Droplets of water fell from the leaves. But the rain had stopped. She put on her windbreaker. She would be fine. She stood back to calculate her route. Juanito had shimmied right up the trunk one day. But she would need something to help her reach even the lowest limb. A patio chair would do. She carried it to the tree and shoved it against the backside of the trunk. She looked up to the guest room window. Even if her mother woke and looked out, she wouldn't notice her there behind the tree. And, besides, she was dressed head to toe in black.

She made sure her backpack was secure, patted the zipped side pocket to feel the key to the painted box, and then she stepped onto the chair. She studied the structure of the tree. The trunk divided in two about a foot above the back of the chair. Above the division, a thick limb went over the wall. All she had to do was pull herself up into the V of the tree limbs, and then she could stand and swing her right foot over the limb where she could settle down, as if she were riding a horse. From there she could scoot backwards along the limb to the wall and lower herself down to the pile of rubble.

Easy. She grabbed hold of a stub from a cut branch and steadied herself while stepping onto the back of the chair. She put an arm around the trunk rising from the left side of the split and stepped her left foot into the split.

When she drew her right leg up, she knocked the chair over. Oh, well. She wasn't planning to go back down anyway.

She felt a little dizzy and had goose bumps, but she wasn't worried. If Juanito could get to the limb that crossed the wall, why couldn't she? She held onto the trunk to swing her right leg over the branch. Her foot fell short a couple of times, and she got a hitch in her hip. She looked at the balcony of her mother's room. No giving up now. She took in a breath and swung her foot up on the outbreath. This time it made it across. In no time she was straddling the branch. Ride 'em, Cowgirl. She laughed. And then shivered again.

She looked up to the sky. Clouds were swarming around the crescent moon. It would rain again at any moment. She needed to get over that wall and down. Luckily, she was almost there.

As she scooted backward toward the wall, she felt a wave

of nausea. She paused to steady herself. Just a little way to go. You can make it.

But the nausea was stronger than her will. She leaned her head over the limb just in time to cough up the remains of the egg sandwich. She sucked the saliva remaining in her mouth and spit it out. She shivered again. It didn't feel like it was over. Maybe if she would just relax, she would make it. She rested her forehead on the limb and counted to ten. Another wave of nausea hit, and this time, she felt her bowels loosen as well. She tightened her sphincter. Not that. Oh, God, not that. But she could not stop it. Nor the vomiting, which went on until nothing came up but viscous fluid.

Too weak to move, she lay her face against the bark.

And then the rain started. At first in big soft drops that plopped on the leaves and trickled down her back. And then in torrents that soaked her clothes, diluting the diarrhea that came in wave after wave.

Wet, cold, and empty, she shivered and clung to the tree, more out of instinct than will, imagining herself floating in a secret river and praying the log would sink. But then a burst of lightning roused her. The rain. Gwendolyn. The photo. Locked in a box. Hidden. Ruined. It was all her fault, and there was nothing she could do. Nothing.

Forty-Five

THE PLACE CALLIE LAY FELT WARM AND SOFT. DRY and safe. She heard murmuring. The place before had been dark and cold. A man had come. Her father? He covered her with something, but she kept on shivering. She was still shivering, though now she was warm. And drowsy. She felt a hand on her forehead. It felt cool. And then a damp cloth. She roused and saw a figure leaning over her. "Go back to sleep." The voice sounded like aunt Ida's. Was she in Chicago? She turned on her side and drew her knees to her chest, cuddling herself. She liked Chicago. Warm, dry, and safe. She was happy there. Drowsy. Hearing the murmuring voices.

She roused again. Her right hip hurt. Why? And then she remembered the tree. Being sick. Grasping the limb. Sheets of rain. Someone on the limb near her feet. Trying to stretch out her legs to push him away. *"Está bien, Señora."* Then she heard Pamela's voice. "Ready." An arm on her shoulder. Armando's face by hers. "You can let go, Calecita. We have you." She had shaken her head. No. No. No. But he kept his arm around her. *"Suéltala, Calecita."* She had only held on tighter. But then, in the language of love, he had said, *"Lâche-la, Chou. Lâche-la."* She let go and slid like a big fish into a net.

It seemed like a dream. Being carried in the net. Someone telling her to breathe. Warm water flowing over her in the shower. Someone washing her. Then the towel against her skin. Someone buttoning her pajamas, walking her to bed. Lifting the smooth sheets. Someone putting a straw in her mouth. "Sip, Callie, sip." The sound of the curtains sliding shut. So, it had been light then, and now it was dark. How long had she been in bed?

There were candles all around. And voices. Subdued tones. As if at a wake. But she was not dead, just drowsy. She should let them know. But she was too exhausted to talk.

SHE heard the curtains open and then her mother's voice. "Can you sit up, Callie? I made you some tea." She opened her eyes. Light shone through the windows. "I had a dream, Mother. I was caught like a fish in a net."

"Not a net. Your hammock. That kind Jehovah's Witness suggested they use it to get you down. He's the one who found you."

"In the tree?" He had seen her like that? She started to sit up, and then she saw the box. Gwendolyn. Someone had found her, too.

"Would you like to take a shower? You have company," her mother said.

She took her eyes off the box. "Company?"

"A houseful, actually," a familiar voice behind her said.

She turned to see her aunt approach the bed. "So I wasn't dreaming your voice. What are you doing here?"

"Making breakfast at the moment. But I suppose you mean, why am I here. You can thank Armando for that. He called right after they found you 'white as a sheet and incoherent.' Your mother's dear John raced me to the airport."

Her mother put her hand on her shoulder. "Do you feel like eating?"

"I sliced some papaya," Aunt Ida said.

"Yes, then papaya. Thank you."

"And chamomile tea," her mother said.

"Will do," Aunt Ida said and left.

She turned to her mother. "A houseful?"

"Oh, not so many. Let's see. Armando, of course. And that other young friend of yours, Pamela. Pearl went to get vegetables for soup, but she will be back soon. And Aunt Ida. The others left."

"Others?"

"Juanito, Doña Petra, and that nice Jehovah's Witness, Señor González. After they got you down, Señor González tipped his hat and left, but he came by every hour or two to check on you. He's been by several times this morning, too."

Hoping for some vulnerability to exploit? She had thought that once, hadn't she.

"Armando wanted to take you to the hospital, but we convinced him to have a doctor come instead. The doctor said you were dehydrated and needed rest. He prescribed electrolytes and a sedative.

"Armando started yelling, then, in some mixture of French and Spanish I didn't understand. Pamela finally figured out he thought the doctor was out of his mind not sending you to the hospital. Pearl convinced him we should start with the electrolytes. Pamela planned to go to the pharmacy so he could stay by your side, but Señor González was at the door again when she opened it, so he went instead. Pamela stayed. And Pearl. All day and all evening. By then Aunt Ida had arrived, too. Armando took her to a hotel and came back with her early this morning. It was still dark, she said, when his driver Jorge knocked on her door." Callie's mother smiled. "I thought Armando never got up before noon, except for rehearsal."

He would have circles under his eyes. "Pamela and her mother, how did they know?"

"Armando called them. It was a good thing, too. You only had one ladder. Pamela brought another one. I was so worried. It seemed to take hours for them to get everything ready, but Pearl stood by me the whole time. She tried to reassure me. But still, when Armando finally convinced you to let go, I screamed." She covered her mouth with her hand. "It seems silly now. But then I was terrified you would fall."

"I suppose I was afraid, too." She looked beyond her mother to the box. Was that the key on top of it? She looked back to her mother. "How did they get me down?"

"Pamela climbed up a ladder on one side of the branch, and Armando climbed up on the other side. Señor González and Armando tied the two ends of the hammock to the branch on either side of you, so the hammock was just below the branch. Pamela pulled one side of the hammock out, and Armando the other, opening it wide. Then when you stopped gripping the branch—it took a while for Armando to convince you—he and Señor González gave you a little push, and you slid right into the hammock. Armando and Pamela let go of the sides they had pulled apart, and there you were wrapped in the hammock."

She sighed. Or caught like a fish in a net.

HER legs were trembling, but she managed to convince her mother she was strong enough to shower and dress herself. At the door, her mother turned to say that papaya would soon be on the way. She sounded as if it were a normal morning.

But there was nothing normal about it. She didn't normally have breakfast in her bedroom. Nor with a houseful of company.

And certainly not after having been found filthy and soaked, clutching the limb of an avocado tree.

And though neither her mother nor her aunt had asked any questions, they and the rest of them must be wondering what she was doing in that tree. Not picking avocados. They would have known that she'd been running away from the notes she left and from the broken lock. But they wouldn't have known why was she in such a rush that she would climb a tree. Or why she would flee during her mother's visit, and with no plan to return.

She stood before the box on her dresser. What had come over her to bury it? Had she thought that there in the dark earth Gwendolyn's photo would lose its power?

Her father's photo stood beside the box. That crooked smile, she realized for the first time, was Gwendolyn's. And so, if she were to be safe, she would have to bury that photo as well. For she could not look at it without wishing her father could have seen Gwendolyn's smile. So like his own. And what else? Jacob. She would have to bury him, too. His package, anyway. And anything else that reminded her of him. She opened her armoire. Her "uniforms." They would have to go.

She shut the armoire, sat down on her bed, and flopped back. When Jacob had run into her aunt and learned that they were leaving town, he had come by to see her. "There wasn't another man, was there?" he had said.

"No," she said. "Not another man."

"But there is something. Something you're not telling me."

"Yes."

"I can handle it. Whatever it is. I can handle it. So tell me or don't tell me. But stay."

She had known that was true. Jacob could handle knowing or not knowing. Jacob could handle anything. But she could not. She could not go back with him without telling him, and she could not tell him. Telling was her daughter's decision. And so, it followed, she could not be with him. A simple question of logic. She could not stay.

She sat up. But now, by that same logic, she was in a fix. Now she had to leave everyone. Her mother, her aunt, Armando, Pamela. For if she stayed, she would have to explain, or so she felt. Armando, Pamela, her mother had all been open with her. Didn't she owe them the same consideration? Especially now that they had read her notes, which seemed, she realized, crazily cool, which wasn't how she felt about any of them.

Her mother, of course, would know she was taking flight from talking about her baby. Not that her mother would tell the others. But still, she had already opened Pandora's box with that little fit of hers. She should have stayed calm. Reasoned with her mother. Why hadn't she? And then there was her admission to Armando. She had been weak from exhaustion, but still it seemed odd, after all these years, that she had not been more careful when he asked whether Pamela reminded her of someone. And as for Pamela, wouldn't she be pondering her admission that *she* was the woman in the black scarf who sat in the back of the auditorium? It would be easy enough to piece some kind of story together, if they all compared notes. And then, who knew what she had mumbled in her delirium. Had she called out Gwendolyn's name? She must have betrayed the location of the box. How else would it have appeared?

Her mother had asked if she had been afraid. If that's why she hadn't talked about her baby. Of course, she had been afraid. She could still feel the shiver of fear when Noah put his arm around her in the car, and she had asked "Is it all right? You and me. Is it all right?" A fear that turned to panic when she felt the stir of their child within her. If anyone suspected Noah, there would be nothing she could do to protect him. And so she kept silent. She had signed the papers. But all the while she had waited for a miracle. Noah would come. He would take them home to a house like the one with the stained-glass lily. Denial had been the only way she could manage her grief.

She walked to her dresser, picked up the key to the box, and turned it in the lock. She paused and then opened the lid. Not a drop of water. She started to cry. She stood there a while, her head bowed and her shoulders shaking, and then she took out the photo of Gwendolyn and held it next to the photo of her father.

Yes, they had that same crooked smile. Gwendolyn was undeniably his granddaughter. And her daughter. And beautiful. And happy. And kind. And that's how she would sound. She knew that somehow. She was sure of it. But there was something else. She saw that clearly, too. The woman in the photo wasn't her baby. She put her hands against the dresser to steady herself. And nothing would bring her baby back.

She walked back and sat on her bed. Was that what she couldn't face? That finality? That even if she became fast friends with Gwendolyn, she would never have her baby back? The only way she could keep her baby was to keep her memory alive. See her dimpled arms. Smell her head. Feel her mouth against her breast. And wouldn't those memories lose their immediacy if she were face to face with the woman her baby had become?

She could not talk about Gwendolyn. But what of those hints she had given? Those threats to her secret's safety? Had something been added to the equation? Something that threatened her resolve? Armando's voice came to her, "Lâche-la, Chou. Lâche-la." And she had let go. But it hadn't started then, had it? It had started years before when he had knocked on her door, wanting to improve his French "for love," and she had let him in.

All those years in Chicago, she had seen the beauty in all her students. Loved them all equally, but, in a way, distantly. But then when she learned where her daughter was, that she was safe, and loved, then she had opened her heart to Armando, and then to Pamela, who had taught her how to breathe. She picked up the postcard from the philosopher. The lake and mountains that had drawn her looked peaceful. A peace she had sought from the time she let her baby go. A peace she had never found. Not by organizing, not by working, and even not by breathing. None of them brought lasting peace. So why would a silent retreat? However long. Especially not now when retreating meant letting down her mother and Armando and Pamela. There would be no peace in that.

She began to shake again and wrapped her arms around herself. She felt like a sphere in Plato's Symposium. Cut in half. Unable to find comfort. Her mother must have felt that way. And now she had a chance at happiness. All she asked was to share her story with John. How could she deny her that?

WHEN her mother came down with the papaya and tea, Callie asked her to call the others.

With barely a toe in the room, Pamela blurted out, "Don't you want to be Granny?"

She stood, turned toward the door, and was in the middle of responding, "Yes, with all my heart," when Armando entered a step behind Pamela. "I need you here, Callie." He caught himself and put his arm around Pamela. "We need you here."

Tavelé ran to her and jumped up, putting his front paws on her chest as if to express his agreement.

She lowered his feet from her chest and then turned to Pamela and Armando. "I want to stay. But there are some things I need to tell you."

She went to the dresser and waited until her mother, her aunt, Pearl, and Juanito, who had turned up, too, entered the room.

Pearl, her hand on Juanito's shoulder, paused at the door, looking as if she weren't sure they should join the group of intimates.

Her hesitancy confirmed Callie's sense that she could rely on her. "Please." She reached out a welcoming hand. "Come in."

Pearl let go of Juanito and sat down on the end of the bed. Pamela joined her on one side and Armando on the other. Callie's mother and Aunt Ida sat together on the bench in front of the windows to the patio. Juanito sat cross-legged by Tavelé on the floor in front of them.

Juanito's eyes went to the painted box. "*Es la caja que encontré en tu jardín?*" He went to the bureau to look more closely.

"*Sí.*" Callie patted him on the head. It was the box he'd found in her garden. "*Gracias.*"

She turned toward the group, looking from one to the other as she spoke. "I am sorry for what I put you through. Not just my recent desperate flight." She paused and then went on. "But my years of silence." She held up the photo of Gwendolyn. "I thought I was protecting her." She turned toward her mother. "But I realized I was trying to protect myself." She looked at Pamela and then at Armando. "And that I risked hurting the ones I am closest to." She held the photo in front of her heart. "I knew this woman when she was a baby."

She turned toward Pamela and opened her mouth, but could not speak.

Pamela looked at her encouragingly, and when she did, her

words came to Callie. Sound is a gift of the breath. Callie let out her breath fully and then her lungs filled as easily as the crystal pitcher filled from the mountain stream. "You may already know her, Pamela. You went to the same high school."

Pamela looked up a moment and then whispered. "So *that* was it." She opened her mouth to say something else, but she stopped when Pearl put an arm around her. Pearl then nodded to Callie as if to say, it's all right. Go on.

She took a step toward Armando.

He looked as if he wanted her to continue but was afraid of what she would say.

She spoke to him quietly, sweetly, as if they were the only two in the room. "That night, in the Jardín, when Pamela played 'The Lost Child,' it was *she* I thought of." She looked at the photo. "Her name is Gwendolyn." She looked again at Armando, paused a moment, and then added even more quietly. "I am her mother."

Armando just sat there, as if waiting for the other shoe to drop.

She wanted to reassure him, but she had to finish first. She turned to her mother and her aunt. "I let you assume her father was Steve."

Her mother said, "Oh, Callie. How hard that must have been." She paused with tears coming to her eyes. "Not trusting us."

Everyone was quiet, and then Aunt Ida asked, "Will you tell us, Callie? Who he was?"

"Oh . . . I know," Armando stood up and approached Callie. His voice was soft. "His name was Noah, wasn't it, Chou? Noah."

She smiled and put her hands against his cheeks. "*Oui, mon cœur, c'était Noah.*"

Epilogue

ONE FINE SUNDAY THE FOLLOWING JUNE, ARMANDO stretched out the window, his cell by his ear. The busy signal again. He shook his head. Busy, busy, busy. Even on the *one* day of the week they were all to be together. Otherwise it seemed like he hardly ever saw her any more. Not with that baby around. And *she* wasn't even the best with the baby. *He* was the only one who could settle her down when she got into a fit. Everyone said so. Even Pamela. Not that Little Flea *had* many fits. She was sweet as pie, and looked just like him. So there. He waived the cell at Callie. "The spittin' image," Aunt Ida had said.

God knows who she's on the phone with this morning. Things just hadn't been the same since she opened that box she'd buried. And then there was the package she sent Juanito for. He'd wanted to go for it. But she'd said, "Let's let Juanito go, this once." *Once,* when Juanito had been the one to find the box in the garden? Oh, well. Juanito had brought the trumpet down, too. He wouldn't have done that, for sure. She'd started up practicing, practicing, practicing. As if she didn't have anything else to do. And now she was always on the phone with someone. Talk, talk, talk. Who in the world has called her this time? Can't be Aunt Ida. She knows Sundays are family day. Must be that philosopher calling about the retreat. Well, Chou could use a silent retreat now, that's for dang sure.

Still, after she has finished her gallivanting around the States and France this summer, she could be silent right here in her own garden instead of prancing off to Michoacán. He'd suggested that. Even said he wouldn't call her more than once a day. Scout's honor! But she had just smiled and said, "Oh, Armando," in that soft voice of hers. He glanced at the Virgin and then looked back out the window.

Well, she'd better get off the phone soon and get ready for their outing. Tavelé had been carrying his leash in his mouth all morning. And it was nearly noon.

And there she was on the phone. Busy. Busy. Busy. When he wanted to remind her to pack a jacket. It could be cool in the mountains. And, no, they weren't going to the mine shafts or in that death trap of Pamela's. He crossed himself. Jorge would be driving them. He'd seen to that. They would picnic in the forest meadow Jorge had told him about. With a stream on one side and a rocky outcropping rising on the other. It sounded perfect. *Perfecto. Parfait.*

He had already packed Tavelé's favorite cake. Callie would be bringing along her usual healthy meal. Veggies. Veggies. Veggies. There would be nothing but breast milk for Little Flea. He rolled his eyes. She would prefer cake, and he would make sure she got some—as soon as she was ready for solids. A little cake never hurt anyone. Look at him. He'd eaten cake all his life, and he was a fine specimen. He looked in the mirror and flexed his biceps. He smiled, and then he leaned in closer. Was that a gray hair he saw?

He frowned. It's a wonder he didn't have more of them, given what she'd put him through. He turned back to the window. Was that her green silk scarf on the line? He had said how pleased he was she was finally wearing it. And what did *she* say? "Little Flea's favorite place to burp." Thanks a lot.

He shook his head. She had no business up there with the phone under her chin and hanging those blooming sheets that she should be having someone else hang. He'd offered to find someone now that Doña Petra was so busy with Little Flea. But she just wouldn't listen to reason.

And as for her leaving for the summer. That was crazy. *Loco. Complètement fou.* She wasn't just leaving *him*, she was leaving Pamela, Ami Mai, and that innocent little baby. Didn't she ever think about anyone but herself? He had told her that, too, and all she had done was smile. He looked again at the Virgin. Yeah, he knew Mrs. Fischer was coming for the summer, but she spoke even less Spanish than Pamela or Ami Mai. Little Flea was fluent, of course, but at three months she could hardly be expected to translate!

The familiar swish of a rocket from the *Iglesia de Guadalupe* sounded, and he looked to see Callie jump and drop the phone. He laughed. Served her right.

He took a step back from the window. The poster of Claude was still there rolled up and leaning against his congas. He fingered the edge of it. Chou had been right about some things. He had to give her that. He leaned out the window again and blew her a kiss across the canyon.

-Fin-

Acknowledgments

I want to thank Patricia Damery, Jan Beaulyn, Jimalee Plank, Elizabeth Evans, and Elizabeth Herron. We wrote together in Sebastopol, CA, on Thursday nights and weekend retreats for decades. They kindly commented on the first draft of *The Trumpet Lesson*, which I wrote after moving to Mexico. I owe seeing myself as a potential novelist to Maria Luisa Puga, who encouraged me in her workshops for novelists in Erongarícauro, Michoacán. Writing coach Sarah Lovett's wise and wonderful advice got me through the first draft of my novel. She also offered delicate suggestions for fine-tuning the final draft. A. J. Buckingham, Ana Cervantes, Marc Smith, Anna Adams, Julie Allen, Dolores Miller, and Joyce Chong provided comments that helped me improve my manuscript. I also received encouragement and questions from authors and audience members at the monthly open mics here in Guanajuato. During the first five years of the novel, I had the good fortune of taking trumpet lessons weekly from Jason Pettit and occasionally from John Urness here in Guanajuato, from Daniel Norris in Rohnert Park, CA, and from Stanton Kessler in Kansas City, MO. Markus Stockhausen permitted me to sit in on his week-long master class in Guanajuato, and Anton Curé invited me to observe his classes at the Conservatoire National Supérieur de Musique et de Danse de Paris. When struggling with an embouchure tremor, I got advice from Laurie Frink and later from Charlie Porter. In the last few years of writing the novel and during more drafts than I can count, Erin Ferris and Mark Sander provided developmental editing and copyediting with wit and wisdom. At Brooke Warner's enlightened suggestion, I spent a month in Madrid cutting 10,000 words. Stephanie Elliot's eye for timeline mishaps led to additional fine-tuning. My sister Nancy Bentley gave me top-notch tips for book club discussion questions. Lirio Garduño-Buono and Jean Pierre Buono kindly pitched in at the last minute to review the Spanish and French. Everyone affiliated with She Writes Press was super: proofreaders Jennifer Caven and Chris Dumas, editorial project manager Samantha Strom, cover designer Julie Metz, book designer Stacey Aaronson, and publisher Brooke Warner. I'm grateful to all of them and to the community of mutually supportive She Writes Press sister authors who generously share their experiences. I am also grateful to my family, friends, and acquaintances who, on hearing a line or two about my novel responded, "I want to read that!" And, finally, I am thankful for my love, novelist Sterling Bennett, a model of playful creativity and dedication to craft.

For Book Clubs

Dianne Romain would be delighted to visit book clubs in person or via Skype. You can contact her and find additional discussion questions at dianneromain.com.

Discussion Questions:

1. With whom do you identify in this novel, and why? What character drives you crazy and why?

2. Of the following factors, which do you think most affected the characters' choices? Social attitudes about race, sex, and family; early childhood experiences; parenting styles; personality; family and friendship bonds. Explain. What would you add to the list? Explain.

3. Do you find parallels between Callie's situation and Armando's? How would you describe those parallels?

4. Pick a scene where you would have acted differently than a character did. What would you have done differently?

5. Do you feel differently about yourself and others after reading the novel? Explain.

6. What images did you have of Mexico and Mexicans before reading *The Trumpet Lesson*? Have any of your views changed?

7. How would you describe the different types of families found in the novel? Do any of these families remind you of families in your own life?

8. How might the stories of adoption in the novel change in a different time period or in a different culture?

9. How do you feel about the use of French, Spanish, and "Midwestern talk" in the novel? How do you feel about the use of "*flaco*," "*gordo*," "*moreno*," and "*guëro*" ("skinny," "fat," "dark," and "light") as nicknames?

10. Does the title *The Trumpet Lesson* suit the novel? Explain. Do you believe that people learn life lessons from music lessons? Explain. Would you propose a different title for the novel?

11. What was your emotional experience of reading the novel? How did you feel when you finished the novel?

12. Some questions are left unanswered in the novel. How would you answer them?

About the Author

DIANNE ROMAIN lives with novelist Sterling Bennett in Guanajuato, a colonial city in the central Mexican highlands. She grew up and went to college in Missouri before moving to Berkeley for graduate school. After completing her PhD in philosophy, she taught feminist ethics and philosophy of emotion at Sonoma State University and published *Thinking Things Through*, a critical thinking textbook. When writing *The Trumpet Lesson*, she took up the trumpet. Now she teaches Lindy Hop. Her current writing projects set in Guanajuato include short stories and another novel.

dianneromain.com

SELECTED TITLES FROM SHE WRITES PRESS

She Writes Press is an independent publishing company
founded to serve women writers everywhere.
Visit us at www.shewritespress.com.

American Family by Catherine Marshall-Smith. $16.95,
978-1631521638. Partners Richard and Michael, recovering
alcoholics, struggle to gain custody of Richard's biological daughter
from her grandparents after her mother's death only to discover they
—and she—are fundamentalist Christians.

A Cup of Redemption by Carole Bumpus. $16.95, 978-1-938314-90-2.
Three women, each with their own secrets and shames, seek to make
peace with their pasts and carve out new identities for themselves.

Anchor Out by Barbara Sapienza. $16.95, 978-1631521652. Quirky
Frances Pia was a feminist Catholic nun, artist, and beloved sister
and mother until she fell from grace—but now, done nursing her
aching mood swings offshore in a thirty-foot sailboat, she is ready to
paint her way toward forgiveness.

Shelter Us by Laura Diamond. $16.95, 978-1-63152-970-2. Lawyer-
turned-stay-at-home-mom Sarah Shaw is still struggling to find a
steady happiness after the death of her infant daughter when she
meets a young homeless mother and toddler she can't get out of her
mind—and becomes determined to rescue them.

Eden by Jeanne Blasberg. $16.95, 978-1-63152-188-1. As her children
and grandchildren assemble for Fourth of July weekend at Eden, the
Meister family's grand summer cottage on the Rhode Island shore,
Becca decides it's time to introduce the daughter she gave up for
adoption fifty years ago.

In a Silent Way by Mary Jo Hetzel. $16.95, 978-1-63152-135-5. When
Jeanna Kendall—a young white teacher at a progressive urban school
—becomes involved with a community activist group, she finds
herself grappling with issues of racism, sexism, and oppression of
various shades in both her professional and personal life.